Wild
Harvest

This Release
To
AMIE

Wild

Harvest

Eleanor Gustafson

Zondervan Books
Zondervan Publishing House
Grand Rapids, Michigan

A Note from the Author: Wild Harvest *is a work of fiction. In it I have used literary devices as part of the plot. While not intending to convey reality, these devices help portray a deeper artistic and spiritual truth.*

WILD HARVEST
Copyright © 1987 by Eleanor Gustafson

*Zondervan Books
are published by Zondervan Publishing House
1415 Lake Drive, S.E.
Grand Rapids, MI 49506*

Library of Congress Cataloging in Publication Data

Gustafson, Eleanor.
Wild harvest.

I. Title.
PS3557.U835W55 1987   813'.54   87-21614
ISBN 0-310-37391-3

Scripture references are taken from the King James Version of the Bible and from the New International Version (North American Edition), copyright © 1973, 1978, 1984, by the International Bible Society. Used by permission of Zondervan Bible Publishers.

Printed in the United States of America

87 88 89 90 91 92 / CH / 10 9 8 7 6 5 4 3 2 1

To my strong oak,
and to our saplings and their seedlings,
down to acorns as yet unsprouted.
The shared work and laughter
of tree farming has thrust our family roots
deep into the bedrock that is Christ Jesus.

Wild
Harvest

chapter 1

*P*ay attention, Hannah!"

At her father's voice, Hannah leaped from her reverie to the foaming pan threatening to boil over. She grabbed the spoon and began a frantic stirring while her other hand groped along the workbench for the tub of margarine. Her eyes probed the steam to read the maple-syrup thermometer.

Should she draw off and ask questions later, or was there time to check the syrup hydrometer? Her hand finally found the oleo. With a quick motion, she touched the spoon to it and again stirred. This time the foam fell back obediently, almost magically, and Hannah drew her finger down the fogged-up thermometer.

"It's up there—219 degrees. I think there's time, but good grief, I haven't even got a pail of sap ready to dump in after the draw! C'mon, Han, get it in gear! Forget that business in the woods, and tune up your brain!"

Again she reached back to the workbench, this time for a slender metal beaker holding a heavy-bottomed glass rod. Carefully opening the draw-off valve, she let a thin stream of golden liquid into the beaker until the glass floated free of the bottom, rising to a line that indicated the syrup was indeed ready.

She jerked up the draw-off valve on the finishing pan, opened another on the stack pan, leaned over to let through more sap on the far side of the evaporator, and with her skimmer began pushing the still-foaming syrup into the pail.

Then she remembered that she hadn't closed the draft to slow the fire. *Oh, well,* she thought, *I'll leave a little syrup so the pan won't scorch.* After closing valves one and two, she grabbed the number-two pail and dumped its contents into the finishing pan.

"Whew! That was close!" Hannah sagged against the work-bench for a moment before straining her yield through a felt pad into the settling tank. She was glad her father hadn't stayed around to watch her feverish performance. He had dumped his two pails of sap into the outdoor holding tank and gone off for more.

Even with snowshoes, the deep snow made navigating difficult, and the seventy-five taps that were level with or lower than the sugar house were a nuisance. The uphill taps drained by gravity through tubing, but the lower ones, hung with buckets, had to be serviced by tedious slogging.

Her brother Steve became tiresomely profane over the illogical location of the sugar house. "Only poodle-brains would set up shop in the *middle* of a sugar bush!"

Despite their complaining, both Steve and her father, Tom Valdegar, thrived on the work of sugaring. They enjoyed it as the first "spring thing" and as part of their overall tree-farm operation. They were tree farmers through and through: burly men who ate nickel-sized wood chips spewed from a well-sharpened chainsaw, drank tractor fuel, brushed their teeth with pine pitch, and were perfumed by a special blend of oil, sweat, and chainsaw exhaust.

Though their dedication to the enterprise was definitely vocation, unfortunately the income from it was still barely avocation. And so, for the present at least, Valdegar's Ski Shop remained their "part-time" occupation eight months of the year to pad out the family receipts. The store stayed open year round, but during the summer months, Hannah's brother Peter was left alone to peddle skis while the rest of the family went off to manage trees. In sugaring season, though, only Tom and Steve vacated the shop. Because Hannah was still in high school, her tour of sugaring duty was limited to school vacation and up to a week additional if the sap run warranted.

Hannah's mother adamantly refused to go sugaring with them. Jane Valdegar would as soon hunt alligators in a Louisiana bayou as spend the tail end of a Vermont winter in the woods. So she remained at home, helping occasionally with the huge end-of-season sales that daughter Ardyth and her husband, Mike Cramer, organized and promoted.

"Ardyth is pure genius in this business," Tom Valdegar often told his wife. "She didn't get it from me, and she sure didn't get it from you. Is she another one of your misbegotten kids like Peter?" he asked, with only half a smile.

Hannah's chief sugaring skill lay in tending the evaporator—stoking the fire every twenty minutes or so, checking the sap levels in the various pans, skimming foam, and drawing and straining finished syrup about every hour. There was a lot to pay attention to, but she was good at it—better, more reliable than her brother Steve. She had scorched a batch once, but Steve had let the front pan go dry and melted some of the solder. He heard plenty about that. But in general, as far as the tree farm went, he could do little wrong in his father's eyes.

For Mike, Hannah's brother-in-law, tree farming produced a lot more kick than the ski shop, but it was just a job and not a calling as for Steve. And though Tom Valdegar would never have admitted it, a fine distinction lay between a favorite son and a son-in-law.

Hannah went around the evaporator to check the incoming sap and the depth in the stack pan, closing the forgotten sap gate. How many miles did she walk around this thing in a day? "One of the first things I'll get when I come by a little cash," her father's familiar litany ran, "is a new rig like Bill Havener's. You'll love it, Hannah—bigger than this one, but a lot less work—automatic float valves that keep sap coming in at the same rate it boils down."

Well, Hannah wasn't so sure she'd love it. With this old one, she had developed a sort of rhythm, and it pleased her to be able to take care of so many things at once—even when she got to wool gathering, which happened very seldom. And she made good syrup, too, fetching a handsome price as a complementary product at the ski shop. But they never had enough to satisfy their appreciative customers, thus her father's yearning for bigger and better.

Good syrup. What kind of syrup would she make if they sugared the way she'd seen through the trees this morning? Steve had given her a break between syrup draws, and she went off on his snowshoes to get a little exercise. Just as she was about to turn around, she glimpsed the strange operation down on the lower hillside. She couldn't take time then to check it out and still get back for the syrup draw, but maybe the next day.

The next day, though, was even busier. The long spell of cold nights and warm days produced sap faster than they could process it, and by the time it let up on the weekend, Hannah was too exhausted to go anywhere.

It was a good tired, though. She loved sugaring as much as her father and brother. She loved the thick cloud billowing up through the open cupola, the sun slicing through cracks into slanted slabs of swirling steam, the gentle fragrance of boiling sap, the roaring fire that shot flame through the pan flutes to the chimney stack eight feet away. She loved to watch for the first tentative boil fifteen minutes after the fire got going, and then the glistening, creamy cascade of full boil in the deep-fluted stack pan. She loved to suck pure sweetness from the clean underside of the straining cloth when she changed it between draws. She loved the time to think and be alone while her father and Steve were off collecting sap or checking frozen lines. With little enough peace in her family, she gladly took her moments when she could get them.

You've come a long way from what the Indians had, she often thought. For one thing, had she been an Indian squaw, not only would she have had to tend the fires that heated stones for boiling, but she would have sewn her own birch bark buckets. Well, the group she saw sugaring on the hillside hadn't been quite that primitive, but they were using a team of oxen to collect sap in a large wooden barrel and boiling the sap in big kettles on an open fire.

She had mentioned all this to her father, but he told her she had moss on her brain. "That whole hillside you're talking about is our land, and there's hardly a sugar maple left after the logging they did back in the forties. All that sugar steam is softening your noodle, Han!"

Hannah had learned not to argue with her father. She preferred to wait until all the facts were in before making judgment on perplexing matters.

There wasn't anything there, but she had seen something. Hannah had seen several people making maple syrup in three kettles on a pole over a big open fire. Her brain might well have moss on it, but her eyes were pretty trustworthy—that much she knew.

chapter 2

*I*t was Hannah herself who sold the last of their fifty-three gallons of syrup the day before they were to leave for their summer encampment at the tree farm. The two remaining brown pint jugs went to, of all people, Olympic downhill silver-medalist Dorvie Helson, one of their more famous "connections."

He had wanted more. "Hey, I know syrup, and you folks make the best. You betcha." He winked at Hannah. "It's your special touch, I can tell!"

Yah, it's all that dirt and sludge. Hannah chuckled grimly to herself. *Valdegar's Vermont Maple Syrup, filtered through the finest blend of scum, aluminum paint chips, mouse dirt, and hemlock needles.* Nevertheless, she was pleased by the compliment. In this one small area of the family enterprise she had superior skill, to which she carefully and frequently pointed. "Glad you like it, Mr. Helson. Get here earlier next year!"

Then the family took off for the woods, leaving Peter to work the miracle of selling skis in summer.

Mike, Ardyth, and Hannah left first in the Cramer pickup, glad to escape the tumult that routinely accompanied the family's annual removal from Darbury to Gilly. They rode for miles, their silence overlain with the contorted groanings and patter of the truck radio.

"Hey, all you lovers out there, lookin' for something sexy in a sports car? Smoke on down to the hottest car deal in town . . ."

Looking out the window, Hannah studied the cool dark porticos of woodland sweeping by. *Funny how different the woods look when you're walking inside,* she thought. Here along the road, the edges were closed and grown over, the leaves light against dark. *You can hardly see the stone walls that stick out so plain at sugaring time. Who built those walls, anyway, right in the middle of the woods?*

". . . Here's your chance to win nine thousand big ones. Just pop your name on a postcard . . . You're listening to WCVT—four minutes in front of two o'clock . . ."

They passed what had once been a farm. The faded house and barn, plus a few tenacious apple trees, looked out across fields that sprouted evenly spaced rows of development houses where corn had once grown. That perfectly good farmland should come to such a degraded end seemed somehow obscene.

"Need a body job in a hurry? Shag on down to Fannie's Figure Factory . . ." *Someone plowed those fields once,* Hannah reflected, *and grew things, raised cows, maybe had a pony for the kids. Now it's all lost to a bunch of tacky little boxes—just like at home.*

Her thoughts returned to Peter, sentenced to live alone in their own treeless "hot box" with its half-hearted air conditioner. *Peter loves the woods more than the rest of us put together, yet he has to stay home and sell turtle-neck leg warmers.* Hannah wished she could have traded places with him. *He'd actually be better than me, at least for a while,* she thought. *Dad wasn't exactly hysterical when I told him the doctor said not to haul wood until my back healed. But he'd be even less hysterical watching Peter try to work. Why does Dad hate him so? Why can't he just accept Peter for what he is instead of being so crackled over his not being Paul Bunyan?*

"Yo, Poopsie, whatcha thinkin' about over there?"

[15]

Hannah grinned at Mike over the din.

"Ha! With the radio crankin' like that?" she shouted.

"Hey, you're gettin' to sound just like your old man."

"Yah, well, why don't you hand out chainsaw hearing protectors?"

"You like nice soft sweetie-pie music like Peter?"

Hannah turned on him. "Don't you go riding Peter, too!"

"Hey, I ain't ridin' him. He's doin' us all a favor. I'm just glad to be gettin' outta the joint for the whole summer. Hey, Pete baby is like bread 'n' jam!"

"Well, I just wish Dad thought so. After all, his own flesh and blood. But just because he's different—"

"He's different, all right! And it wouldn't take much to make Daddy-o spike the flesh and blood bit. You've heard—"

"Oh, come on, Mike. Cut it out! Peter's as much a Valdegar as I am; you know it and Dad knows it." She swore and kicked the door with the side of her foot. "It makes me so mad to—"

"Okay, okay. I'm sorry. Don't get so frosted. Let's just leave it that Pete Valdegar is a different cookie than Steve Valdegar."

Hannah winced when he said *Pete*. Tom Valdegar's sons, like respectable work horses, would of course have good solid men's names. Jane had had free rein with the girls, and hating her own plain label, she made sure her daughters wouldn't be lost in the bumper crop of Debbys, Cheryls, and Lynns. But when Peter decided he didn't like to be called Pete, his father had one more grievance against him.

Ardyth spoke up with total irrelevance. "Well, I'll be glad to go back home for a few days so I can get some new fall clothes before everything decent is gone."

Hannah brightened at the mention of clothes, glad for a way to turn the conversation away from Peter.

"We come up here at the wrong time," Ardyth complained. "Everybody still has summer things out, and there's no way to find out what the fashions will be—the local fashions, I mean, not the ones in magazines. What'll they be wearing in Darbury, Vermont, this year?"

"Oh, who cares? Baby, the less you wear, the better I like it."

"Mike, don't be vulgar."

"Hey, I saw the neatest dress in Jacobson's the other day—a Garachi," Hannah exclaimed, steering the conversation back on track. "I tried it on just for fun. Leslie was working that day—y' know, Leslie Strieken? And she brought over this fabulous Italian choker necklace with gold geometric designs and diamonds in separate panels along the bottom. Well, it was just right with that dress, really neat. You'd love it."

"How much?"

"How much what? The dress or the necklace?"

"The dress. I don't even want to hear about the necklace."

"A hundred seventy-five."

"Hm—not bad. You think if you haul enough wood this summer, Daddy'll let you get it?"

"Fat chance. Besides, Dr. Levin says I'm not to haul wood."

"Why not, for heaven's sake? Oh, because of that gym thing? When did he say that?"

"I called him yesterday."

Ardyth grinned. "Honey, you don't miss a pineapple seed. You plan well. I like that. Think Daddy'll swallow it?"

"Oh, he knows. He's not too happy, but I figure I've hauled as much wood as anybody around here, certainly a lot more than you. You always managed to get a splinter or bleed conveniently so you wouldn't have to dirty your pretty little hands."

"My pretty little hands! You think—"

Mike cut in to head off the approaching tempest. "Hey, c'mon—neither of you've lugged a tenth of what us guys do in a day. And besides, who wants football shoulders on a girl?"

They reached camp a good two hours before Tom, Jane, and Steve arrived in the van. For Hannah's mother, the whole summer loomed as such an ordeal that her preparations had become a slam-bang filibuster. But when she could stall no longer and Tom's patience ran out, she climbed into the van and began heaving things from one of the back seats in order to lie down for the relief of her emotional indigestion. This procedure brought a further angry salvo from both husband and son, who had meticulously organized and loaded three months' worth of needs and comforts.

When nightfall finally saw the Valdegars settled into the cabin and the Cramers in their tent, they were all exhausted from the internecine warfare that had spread rapidly from van occupants to those of the truck.

The cabin was a marvel of sorts to everyone who saw it. It had been built after an early experiment with two tents (one for parents, one for kids) proved both unworkable and expensive. Four rowdy children rapidly made shredded wheat out of their tent. Jane and Tom's fared better and was, in fact, in current use as Mike and Ardyth's shelter. Back in those early days, it quickly became apparent that a cabin was an absolute necessity.

Constructed from poles and rough-sawn lumber, the structure encompassed three tiny bedrooms, an all-purpose kitchen-living area, and a porch of sorts. One of their more tactful visitors had called the cabin rustic, but the consensus ran more along the lines of dump.

"Even the sugar house is put together better than this!" Jane grumbled ceaselessly. And it was. Tom and the boys had made their mistakes on the cabin, and by comparison, the sugar house had grace and elegance.

But they couldn't live in the sugar house. The cabin did have a few comforts, such as running water from an uphill spring, a gas water heater, and a two-burner stove—amenities Tom frequently pointed out to Jane. In her mind, however, these did little to make up for the outhouse. That this "convenience" was located directly upwind of the porch only served to aggravate a sore point. Nor were hot running water and a stove adequate compensation for the lack of cupboards and closets.

But with all its deficiencies, the cabin gave them shelter, a degree of privacy, and at least minimal warmth during the sugaring season with the little box stove that could be installed or removed as heating and space needs dictated.

Tom and Steve were up the next morning with the hermit and wood thrushes, though the flutelike tones were lost on the men. Peter could have told them what birds they were listening to, pointing out as well the wide-eyed warble of a rose-breasted grosbeak and the raspy melody of a scarlet tanager. Peter's observations, though, would not have been accepted graciously. Tom and Steve had work, not birds, on their minds, and at the breakfast table with a map of their property in hand, they lined out a rough plan for the summer.

"We need to open a new road into this section." Tom pointed. "There's a few sawlogs in there—mostly hemlock, but a lot of cordwood that needs to be gotten out."

"Who you got lined up for firewood customers?"

"Uh, let me think. I got 'em written in my book. There's five cords, six maybe, to Walsh up the road, a couple to Mrs. What's-her-name over in Fellsburg . . ."

Steve nodded.

"And there's that old beagle in Denton. He wants—"

"Yeah, he wants three cords of rounds—no split pieces, thank you, anywhere between five-and-a-half and five-and-five-eighths inches diameter, the ends sanded and varnished, neatly stacked flush in his garage, and the floor swept and scrubbed before we leave. Yeah, I know him!"

"You forgot they have to be exactly sixteen inches and not a splinter longer."

Steve glowered. "I'll slam-dunk 'em right down his chimney!"

They went on to discuss problems known and unknown with

their equipment. Bulldozer, tractor, three chainsaws, and a splitter all ranged in age from forty-odd years to three months in the case of the newest saw. "When I scrape some money together," went a variation on Tom's litany, "I'm going to get a decent skidder. Just keeping these bleedin' machines running eats up all our time, and even when they do work, they're slow and touchy for woods work. Dozers are made for construction, tractors for farm work; we need a skidder for hauling logs."

By the end of their second cup of coffee, they had sketched out their campaign: a new road down here, a skid loop off this road, work up and deliver fifty cords of firewood from the trees cut last year (provided extra customers could be found), knock down next year's wood, open up the sugar bush a bit more, prune that stand of young pine, and maybe, just maybe, they could find time for some serious logging in August.

"There's always those huge trees over yonder, handy to the road," Tom mused. "You could practically fell 'em right onto the log truck. But I know of at least two hundred others here and there that should be gotten out to free up young growth. We'll see, though, when August comes."

Jane and Ardyth had their work, too. Their major responsibility as far as their husbands were concerned lay in keeping board and bed adequately supplied. Given their temperament and conditions in the camp, however, both board and bed were largely a matter of caprice.

They did have to put up with a lot. Theirs was an ongoing battle with chipmunks, mice, spiders, bats, flies, ants, and mosquitoes—to say nothing of leaks in the roof, scanty storage and living space, and woods-dirt coming in through door and crevice.

Ardyth, young and malleable when first exposed to forest life, accepted her lot with less trauma than her mother. Then too, since Ardyth's marriage, she had happily graduated from woodpile to cabin. But neither she nor her mother enjoyed existence without blow-dryer, microwave oven, or proper plug-in television instead of their small portable that suffered frequent attacks of snow.

Hannah had certain set chores such as dishes and sweeping, bad back or no, but beyond that she was free to do as she wished. During her years of hauling wood, she had had little time to be bored, but if this back injury had come even two years earlier, she would have sighed and groaned and lamented her sorry lot, stuck off in the middle of nowhere with nothing to do.

Peter had changed all that. Now the bright and the dark beckoned her to explore, learn, and think. It was actually Peter who had discovered the glen. Not that its existence was unknown, but discovered in the sense of seeing and recognizing its apartness. Though Peter had identified its special qualities, it became peculiarly Hannah's, partly because of Peter, partly because of her own inner needs.

When they were younger, the four children had amused themselves predictably. Steve dogged his father's footsteps in hopes of just a few minutes at the wheel of the old jeep. Ardyth the Beautiful lay with her mother on the altar of the sun god.

Peter kept his mind off the suffering his flaccid body endured from hauling firewood by busying it with schemes of exploratory forays in off hours. Little sister in tow, he would live out the exciting parts of the books he had read. Whether mushing across frozen tundra, clambering over the desolate reaches of a dying planet, or making a desperate stand against Indians, fighting from tree to tree, the woods rang with his all-purpose rallying cry, "Vu-shon-dio!"

At age sixteen, however, Peter was immediately drafted to man the store, and the woods adventures ceased. Hannah's imagination suffered a decline at that point, but she had gained enough freedom to find refuge in the woods from the stresses of her early teen years.

When Peter came across the glen, he showed it to Hannah and gave it to her as a place that was big and solid and permanent, sensing that she had a need of all those things. It was not like the fire rings around home, those trysting areas in the woods littered with beer cans, contraceptives, and drug apparatus. No, the glen was pure, unsullied by baser passions.

They shared its delights, the two of them, Peter pointing, teaching, and discovering; but it belonged to Hannah, a holy standard against which she could measure and test herself. Was this virgin forest, these great tall pines and hemlocks, anchored in bedrock?

Hannah was still a virgin, but she didn't know exactly why. Certainly not because of any particular scruples, nor from lack of coaching by her friend Leslie. Here, though, under these magnificent trees she was glad. In other places she fantasized love affairs with football captain Drew Harney or practiced what she would say if she were propositioned by any one of several TV or rock stars. But not here: this was sacred ground.

"What a beautiful place," Peter would say. "Maybe Indians once worshiped on this spot. And we're the only two people in the world who care about it. It's sort of like a forest preserve where they charge $3.75 just to park your car, only on a smaller scale." It did have everything—trees, rocks, ferns, mosses thick and thin, even two modest waterfalls. A list of the furnishings, though, can't communicate the essence of a place. The seemingly endless chittering of the winter wren or the haunting, breathy spiral of the veery did that best.

Peter and Hannah often played a game. "I hear a bird that sounds just like Mrs. Slakey," Peter would say. And Hannah would pick up the call of a nuthatch that mimicked the math teacher's nasal twang.

In Hannah's mind, however, the veery especially would be inseparable from the glen, unrelated to any person—except perhaps Peter.

chapter 3

Hannah had not forgotten the strange sugaring scene of the previous March. Now that she had plenty of time, she made an attempt to locate the site. Everything looked different in summer, however, and she became confused. The hillside where she thought it should have been was as her father had said: an area with scarcely a decent tree of any sort. It had been heavily logged, and all she could find was a thick stand of saplings—quite different from her mental image of huge maples, kettles over the fire, and oxen. An ox wouldn't even fit between these little trees!

All right, if this wasn't the place, she would look elsewhere. No other location seemed right, but she couldn't just stand there and wait for little black birches to turn into big maples.

As she turned to go, she was startled by a man hiking toward her through the trees. Had it been hunting season, she wouldn't have given it a thought except to make sure he knew she wasn't a grouse or a deer. This was June, however, the off-season for woods wanderers.

The tall stranger, looking much like a bent tree, blended with the surrounding saplings. He had the slight stoop of those who spend their time considering tiny inward matters, rather than far-off galaxies. His glasses, dark framed and years out of date, reflected the style of his clothing. A small brown plastic notebook was kept busy journeying between his nervous hands and a baggy pocket.

"Uh, hello . . ." His myopic eyes adjusted slowly to the sudden intrusion of a human being into his solitude. "Are you . . . let me see . . ." He thumbed through his notebook. "You must be Mrs. Valdegar. I don't believe you're Mrs. Hilcox," he said, looking around as though to find name plates on the trees.

"I'm Hannah Valdegar. My father, Tom, owns this property. If you're looking for him—"

"Oh, no," he smiled, a trifle embarrassed at misjudging Hannah's age. "I'm not really looking for anyone. I've been doing research." Again he sought refuge in his notebook. "I'm trying to locate old cellar holes in order to plot the historical demographics of this whole area west of Gilly. As you may know, the dirt road over there—" He waved vaguely toward the ridge. "—was once the main road into town. Several farms prospered through here, but the homesteads are all gone now, along with the plowed fields and pasture land. All that's left is—"

"Gimme a break! Farms with fields—around here?" Hannah surveyed endless trees in every direction.

"Oh, yes. Just look at the stone walls. They marked the edges of the fields and were useful repositories of rock as the land was cleared and prepared for the plow.

"Why, at one time," he referred to his book, "your entire three hundred and twenty-five acres was mostly open land. This is all second-growth forest," he said, looking wryly at the slender saplings, "or possibly fifth or sixth growth. Most likely the forest has seen loggers every forty to sixty years in the past century or so.

"Yes," he went on, swaying slightly in the breeze, "back in the early days, trees and rocks were the enemies. Not enemies in the same sense as disease or hostile Indians. No, the settlers needed trees to build with and to make tools and—and to sell. Such trees, and what a market! Enormous white pines that made sturdy masts for the king's fleet. Great yellow birches, oaks, and ash trees that were shipped to wood-starved England. Magnificent forests in those early days before the settlers came in." His eyes sparkled, not as her father's would have at the thought of all those board feet and the money it would bring, but as an historian milking the glory of the past.

"But trees were enemies, just the same," he continued, "the wilderness versus the harvest." He shook his head sadly, adding quietly, "And the wilderness always wins."

He roused himself and pulled once again at his book. "Do you know of any existing cellar holes on your land? I've been told there is at least one, perhaps on the side of the next hill, but so far ..."

Hannah shook her head. "My father might know. He's been over every inch of our property. If you'd like to talk with him, just go down that road over there and follow the sound of chainsaws. They're working just beyond our camp. You can't miss 'em."

"Yes, perhaps I'll do that. Thank you very much." He smiled and moved as though to tip his hat, only he wasn't wearing one. As they parted, he called back, "Cross over the ridge and keep straight on past the ledges. And don't betray the harvest!"

With a frown Hannah tried to figure out what he meant, but as he continued toward the camp road, she shrugged and moved off to renew her quest for the other sugar bush.

Hannah went only a few steps, however, before stopping. She didn't really need her sweatshirt on such a warm, humid morning, yet she didn't want to just leave it on the path. So following in the footsteps of the willowy man, she tossed the extra garment inside the cabin. As she came out, she tucked in her short-sleeved blouse and noted with satisfaction that the researcher had arrived safely within sight of the men. "Anybody who says weird things like 'Cross over the ridge and don't betray the harvest' could get lost just cruising between his bedroom and kitchen!" she muttered.

As Hannah retraced her steps, she noticed her own distinctive sneaker print with its U-shaped heel and circled sole, but she could see no trace of the man's passage, though she had watched him walk that very piece of ground. A deer and raccoon had left their mark during the night, but hers were the only other footprints. She frowned and then shrugged again. "Maybe he's such an airhead his feet don't touch the ground!"

For want of a better plan, she decided to follow the stranger's directions. As she crossed a stone wall, she tried to picture the land as it once might have been. Had those early farmers just dumped rocks on the edge of their fields, or had they taken time to set them straight and smooth like the calf pound next to—

Of course! The calf pound! The small, high-walled enclosure near camp had always been called that, but Hannah had never made any connection between it and a farm. The label was just one of those nebulous phrases that never quite settled onto the surface of her brain.

The calf pound was a work of art, especially when measured against the outdoor fireplace her father and Steve had built in front of the cabin. Hannah had lugged stones for that project, but even with the bone-crunching labor that had gone into the effort, the end product was a sorry comparison with the work of that long-ago artisan. Muscle wasn't enough for stone work; skill and an eye for—

She stopped in her tracks, musings cut off by an unexpected bright area ahead, an opening in the woods. Where in the world was she? Had she somehow gotten turned around and wandered off the property? She couldn't hear the chainsaws, but then, she was over the ridge. Her head began to pound. Could she really get that confused? But seeing the rise behind her right where it ought to be, she shook her head and decided to take a closer look.

Staying carefully out of sight, she peered out onto a small clearing. A man and horse were hard at work, pulling tree stumps and hauling them to a stack of brush on the far side, up against the newly exposed line of woods. On the near edge lay a pile of stones, yellow dirt still clinging to them. A fresh supply of rock for this rudimentary wall rested on a wooden sledlike affair in the middle of the opening. The snorting of the horse and jingle of harness blended with the blows of the woodsman's ax to the stump roots.

Hannah grew increasingly angry as she watched. Who was this turkey, and what was he doing on their land? The trees he was taking down were some of their best timber! Even worse, he had girdled the biggest trees to kill them, ruining upwards of five-hundred board feet apiece. Those trees could still be salvaged, though, if the men got to them within a year.

Was this what the stringy bent-tree historian was talking about when he called back to her about betraying a harvest? Perhaps he'd seen it on his way by and wanted to warn her. But why didn't he just say, "I think your timber's being ripped off. You'd better check it out." Maybe he didn't know if it was their property.

But was it? She'd better be sure before she stormed out there. This indeed was a time to keep her mouth shut, eyes and ears open until all the facts were in.

Her return to camp was exactly as it should have been according to her original calculations. Could she be mistaken about the boundary line? Maybe her conversation with the woods historian made her invent the whole thing and see clearings in the sky. Perhaps she had even conjured up the historian. She smiled to herself. Peter would like that kind of imagination.

When the men came in for lunch, she spoke to her father about it, but his frame of mind precluded any discussion of boundaries.

He swore in exasperation. "Every tree I cut this morning got hung up on me, and I lost two wedges. *Two,* mind you. It's not easy to lose an orange wedge, and I managed to lose two. Jane, will you *please* quit your brickle-batting about the water heater and get some mustard over here? I'll get it fixed, but not this noon!"

Before Hannah started out the next morning, she studied the property map, the pride of her father's hand. He had drawn it meticulously from a topographic map and an aerial photograph. The map showed brooks, logging roads, and major skid trails, with contour lines indicating hills and steep slopes. It even included important stone walls, but the one Hannah was interested in didn't appear.

A thundershower during the night had cooled things down considerably, so Hannah needed not only her sweatshirt, but a windbreaker as well. With head held high, she stepped briskly through green fern banners waving bravely on the forest floor. Even without discussing the situation with her father, she felt a renewed confidence in the rightness of her case. She approached the opening, determined to defend the Valdegar honor to her dying breath.

The clearing appeared empty, which threw Hannah off balance. It hadn't occurred to her that there might not be anyone to confront. But then she spied him. Was it the same man or someone different? What did it matter? He was chopping down a tree on their property and must be stopped. *Chopping* a tree? Yes, he was, using a peculiar ax with a skill that would have brought even brother-in-law Mike to attention. Seeing the wedge already cut and aimed at the clearing, she remained at the stone pile until the tree fell.

She had plenty to observe while she waited. He was only a teenager perhaps her own age or a little older, but no more than twenty. His long brown hair was pulled back and tied with what looked like a bow. A long vest, his only concession to the biting wind, topped a rough shirt. His coarse light-colored pants met high boots just below the knee.

Hannah quickly shifted her attention from his dress to the graceful strength of his tree-felling demonstration. He was fast, he was accurate, and the flying chips soon brought the bushy top of the hemlock arcing to the ground with a crash.

"All right!" Hannah cried out despite her anger. He might be a thief, but he put on a good show, and she knew enough about tree cutting to recognize that he was no slouch with an ax.

The lad straightened with a look of alarm.

Good! thought Hannah. *At least he feels guilty.* She jumped from the rock pile and hopped over the feathery tree top, stiffening her face and resolve as she paced through the soft bicolored forest soil. As she approached, the boy's face lost its defensive alertness and took on a friendly warmth.

"Good day to you, sir!" he greeted her.

Even before the *sir* hit her ears, Hannah's rehearsed speech vaporized when she felt the impact of his electric blue eyes. The sky was cloudy, but that burst of blue colored the whole clearing. Even though damp and breathing hard from his exertion, his aliveness—a backdrop to those blue eyes—took her breath away. Her heart beat faster at the thought of doing business with such a boy as this.

"Uh . . . yes . . . I . . . ," she stuttered. This guy was definitely classy, and she wasn't prepared for that. How could she confront him about boundary lines and still keep on his good side? But on the other hand, was she to go down in ignominy without firing a shot just because of a pair of blue eyes? Steady, girl. *Vushondio!* as Peter would say. "Hello, I'm Hannah Valdegar, Tom Valdegar's *daughter.*"

Now it was his turn to look surprised. When the hoped-for recognition didn't come, she went on. "I checked the map of our property very carefully, and I believe you're way off. You're trespassing on our land. I mean, we're talkin' a wicked bunch of acres here!" She laughed self-consciously. "Those are our trees you're cutting, y' know."

The boy raised his eyebrows, then frowned. "Wicked? *Sinful* acres?"

"Oh, you know. A whole pile, a lot. You're on our land, and these are our trees."

The boy smiled again, and the bright rays of sunshine stabbed at

Hannah's armor. "You seem very certain, Miss, but I can assure you that I know the bounds of my father's land very well, since I have worked on it these many years. It has been in the family nigh four decades, Grandfather having received his land grant before the war."

Hannah frowned back at him, trying to process the information quickly without appearing stupid. *War? Which war? Vietnam? World War II? Would forty years be before World War II? And what does he mean by land grants?* "Well, my father bought this land ten years ago," she argued. "He walked all the boundaries with the former owner and made a map that clearly shows this is our property. Do you have a map with your boundaries?" *He certainly doesn't look like your average land thief. I'm going to feel awfully dumb if he's right and I'm wrong.*

"Ours is a large tract, extending from the north watercourse," he said, waving vaguely in that direction, "to a number of boundary pins and witness trees arrayed along the edge of Henry Bartholomew's homestead, and then down here along the road to town." His gestures completed the circle.

What was he talking about? For the sake of those eyes, she was trying desperately to understand, but nothing he said made sense. Henry Bartholomew? Road to town? She knew of a trail down in that direction. Was that the main road her treelike historian had talked about? Maybe so, but no vehicle, not even a jeep, could get over it now.

"Look," she said, "I don't know what you're referring to, but my father might know. Why don't you go over the hill, or drive around if you'd rather, to our camp and talk to him. I think this whole thing needs to be straightened out before you do any more cutting."

Again he looked puzzled. "Camp? Where is the site of this camp?"

"There's this ridge back here, right? And you go up over it and bear right till you come to a log yard. From there a logging road takes you on into camp."

His eyes had followed the lateral movement of her gestures. "You must mean the scattering of fine pine just before the mire. I know it well. Father and I plan to remove the pine next year. There are a fair number of young maples in the understory. 'Twill make a tolerable syruping place one day."

Hannah rolled her eyes. *This guy is really off the wall. Is he some granola type just claiming turf? What am I getting into?* "The place I'm talking about *is* a sugar bush, or least near it, but there are no big pines, at least not till you get to the glen. You go talk to Dad. Or maybe I can get him to come here."

The young man's eyes crinkled in friendly laughter. "Perhaps your father will come with the Green Mountain Boys and their Beech Seals to convince me of your just claim."

"Beech Seals?"

"Yes, rods of supple beech to repel holders of questionable land grants. Surely you have heard of them, or at least of Ethan Allen."

"Him I've heard of, but please don't confuse me any further. I'll talk to my dad, and we'll get back to you." She turned away, leaving him looking as puzzled as she felt, then walked back through trees and over a gray stone wall.

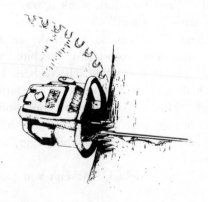

chapter 4

When Hannah arrived back at camp, she found a small crisis in progress, with Jane in a state of frothing ruin. A snake had fallen from one of the pole rafters onto the floor beside her. She and Ardyth were shrieking convulsively outdoors. The men, who had just come in for lunch, were heaving things in all directions in an attempt to find the creature.

"Wild panthers couldn't drive me back into that cabin!" Jane yelled at her husband. "You know I can't stand snakes and mice and spiders and . . . and bats. Last week it was bats, all over the place, a whole army of them!"

"Two bats, Jane. Two bats do not make an army."

"It doesn't matter how many. Just one bite can kill you!"

"Name all the people you know who've been killed by a bat lately," Steve challenged with a wink at his father.

Mike grinned. "They don't kill you, Jane, honey. They just hook their claws in your scalp and snarl up your hair for a nest so when the little batlings hatch out of their eggs, they have some ready blood to—"

"Mike, stop it!" she shrieked. "Haven't you found that snake yet?"

"If you'd come in here and help instead of jiggling up and down out there ..."

"It's all your fault, Tom Valdegar! If you had built a decent house in the first place, instead of this ... this *migrant* lean-to that harbors all kinds of vermin and dangerous—"

"'Seems to me I've heard that song before,'" Mike crooned.

"Michael Cramer, you shut up!" Ardyth shrieked furiously from the doorway. "You don't like this cabin any better than Mom. In fact, you give thanks every night that you don't have to sleep in it! As much as you hate the tent, you know you wouldn't swap it for the cabin!"

"Hey!" Steve cried, "I saw him. Between those boxes!"

"You're not the one who has to bury garbage and have it all dug up again. It's like living in the jungle!"

"Pull those boxes out. Get on the other side in case he comes out there."

"What have you got to grab him with?"

"All these years I've wanted a decent car, and we have to put up with a crummy van."

"My hands, stupid. Man, I hate snakes! If I get my mitts on him he won't last long!"

Mike brightened. "When I was a kid, we used to go out snake hunting. Our biggest day's total was sixty-three. All kinds of 'em—grass snakes, milk snakes, water snakes. Now water snakes, they were fun! They'd fight like blazes! Killed 'em all—every one."

Hannah shuddered at Mike's recitation. She didn't like snakes, notwithstanding Peter's pacifism toward all living creatures.

When the men finally pulled out the frightened reptile, heaping anathemas on its head for the insult to Mike's hand and a bite to Tom's, they held it up for all to see and scorn.

"A rattlesnake!" Jane screamed. "Tom, you got bit by a rattlesnake!"

"Rattlesnake!" Mike scoffed. "It's just a little ol' milk snake.

Here, take a closer look." He made a move as though to throw it at the women, even though Tom still held it.

Hannah ran as fast as the others, but partly because she didn't want to watch the execution.

A pitched battle ensued among all six of them. Triggered by the snake, it shot back to the cabin, catapulted easily from there to the deficiencies of the house back home, gathered ammunition from Jane's longings for a swimming pool and Ardyth's hardship with proper body maintenance here in the wilderness, and exploded with the subject of Peter and whether he should contribute some of his summer earnings to goods and chattel that could be enjoyed by the whole family. Hannah argued hotly that Peter needed money for his night classes. "He shouldn't be penalized for being the only one in the family with brains or gumption enough to go on to college." Whereupon her father muttered with a touch of wonder, "What a fine daisy of a thing he turned out to be!"

Hannah's fury stopped her tongue. She stormed into her bedroom and slammed the door with all the strength she possessed, then turned up her radio to the full power of its weak batteries. The noise of the door sent the women into a nervous wail, and they cowered with hands on heads in anticipation of another bombardment of snakes.

The tempest continued among them over the lack of food on the table. It didn't abate until the men fixed their own lunch and left the household in sullen silence.

After all had quieted down, Hannah snapped off the rock station, still angry. She was sick of noise, sick of all the fighting, the clang of machinery and snarl of chainsaws, the roar of Mike's motorbike up and down the logging roads when he had nothing better to do.

Her thoughts returned to the little clearing. It had been quiet there. An ax makes far less noise than a chainsaw, and in that boy's hands, it wasn't a whole lot slower. The strength in those arms . . . How would they feel around her? Would he even look at her? She wasn't beautiful like Ardyth. Hannah's nose was strong like her father's. But she wasn't as funny looking as Peter, just somewhere in between.

What was it that made Peter look like the weirdo everyone took him to be? When you analyzed his face piece by piece, nothing seemed really wrong with any single part, but when you put them all together, it came out skewed or off balance or something.

Then too, he could never quite succeed in things others did easily. When they were younger, Steve was forever swinging birches, pulling the slender top into a graceful arch and riding gently to the ground. When Peter tried it, the tree simply thunked over, coming up by the roots.

Add to that his marshmallowy body. Peter wasn't fat, just soft, cushiony. Mike actually had a bigger pot, but the rest of him was solid and masculine. With the additional enhancement of his dark beard, he was, in Hannah's eyes, the standard by which all other men were measured.

This boy out in the woods wasn't soft, nor did he have a beer belly. He was all muscle, every lean inch of him in shape. Hannah gazed at the underside of the top bunk in her room, seeing again those electric blue eyes, the kindness in his face. Yes, that was it—kindness—more than mere friendliness, more than the usual reaction when a girl appears on the scene. In fact, he had mistaken her for a boy. How come? She'd have to look in the mirror to see what was wrong.

Well, it would be a while before she could talk to her father about the situation in the clearing. *What a family!* Peter was the only sane one in the bunch. What would he have done if he'd been there? He wouldn't have killed the snake, that was for sure. But then, it wasn't likely he'd have had any say in the matter with her father and Mike and Steve in on it. He would just walk away and not get sucked into the mess. *But what good are snakes, anyway?* she wondered.

"Plenty good," Peter told her later when they talked about it.

[35]

"Milk snakes especially. It was probably on mouse patrol when it fell off the rafter. Those poles are smooth. Snakes need a rough surface to move along, so it just slid off. That snake was really doing everybody a favor by getting rid of the mice Mom hates so much, but it got itself killed for its pains." He was silent a moment, then added quietly, "I know how it feels."

Hannah lay on her bed a long time, thinking about her family, about her encounter with the strange woodsman and what might come of it all. She'd have to wait, though, till her father was in the right mood. There was also the possibility of just keeping quiet and getting what she could out of a potentially promising relationship. Men like that didn't come along every day! Then too, with her knowledge of trees and woods work, she'd have quite an advantage over other girls. She could handle an ax respectably herself, having helped in the early tree-thinning process.

But the more she thought about it, especially considering the size of the trees he was cutting and girdling, the more she saw dollar signs going unchecked into somebody else's pocket. She could use a few of the things that particular bit of money would buy.

Along with the rest of the family, she had her private shopping list. She badly wanted that dress by Garachi, for instance, and even though the Italian necklace was out of the question, Italian boots and a ruana cape were quite possible, given a little luck and proper timing of her request.

She needed all the help she could get in the cutthroat jockeying for social leverage, and if she could only wear that blue-eyed hunk on her arm at, say, the Senior Prom . . . Money would never buy him, she felt sure. There were other means, though, even if her father did chase him off. She could at least find out where he lived and invent an excuse to go there sometime.

When Hannah finally did get her father's ear, he was indeed interested. She laid the map before him. "I've gone over this thing at least twelve times, and I know I'm right. The place I'm talking about is over here on the far side of the ridge. You know those nice mossy ledges down there?" They were another of Peter's discoveries and the setting of some lurid dramatics. "Well, it's just a little beyond that. That guy hasn't chopped down much yet—a quarter acre, maybe—but at the rate he cuts, he'll have it cleaned out in no time."

Tom Valdegar rubbed his chin and frowned. "I don't remember any particularly big trees out there, but we'd better go have a look."

They drove down the logging road to the yarding area, then continued on foot. "What's this fellow's name?" her father inquired.

"I forgot to ask. But he mentioned a Henry Bartholomew. Is that anybody you've heard of?"

Her father shook his head. "He didn't mention Hilcox, did he? Or Matthis?"

"No, I would've recognized them. Maybe he's a Hilcox. Doesn't his land meet ours sort of on top of the next big hill? By the way, did you talk to that skinny geek the other day about cellar holes?"

"What skinny geek?"

"You know, the tall guy with a notebook?"

Her father shook his head. "I don't know who you're talking about."

"Oh, come on! He was right there. I saw him walking toward you. You must've seen him!"

"Nobody has come along all summer that I know of. Maybe Steve or Mike talked to him."

"No, he was headed directly toward you, less than a hundred yards away. I saw him!"

"Well, I didn't. What about cellar holes?"

"He was looking for some. Said there used to be farms all over this area, and he was checking out the historical ... uh ...

something-or-other. You're sure he didn't show up and you just forgot?"

"Nope. But there is a hole up on the slope where we're headed, as a matter of fact."

"That's what he said! Why in the world didn't he just go look for it? He seemed to want to talk to you first, but I can't understand . . ." She frowned a moment and then giggled. "He called me Mrs. Valdegar because he didn't think I was Mrs. Hilcox. He was a funny bird—a stork, maybe. Do the Hilcoxes have a son, like nineteen or twenty?"

"I think Val Hilcox is a bachelor, but that doesn't necessarily rule out a son." He grinned slyly.

Hannah sighed and then peered ahead for a glimpse of the clearing. The farther they went, the more nervous she became. Where was it? They should have reached it, but it wasn't there.

Her father frowned. "This the area you're talking about?"

"I know it's here somewhere, maybe farther downhill in the valley. No, it couldn't be. Uphill, maybe. Oh, I don't know, but it's got to be here somewhere!" She was almost crying.

Tom began to cloud up like a summer thunderstorm. They circled around several times, going as far as the boundary atop the hill. Partway down, he showed her the cellar hole dug into a flat shelf and long enough abandoned to have large birches growing out of it. But they found no trace of a clearing.

Hannah and her father walked back in silence.

chapter 5

*H*annah stayed close to camp all week, afraid to go back over the ridge. Her mind waffled between fears over her mental competency and resentment toward the clearing that wasn't there and toward her father as though he were somehow to blame. Tom did nothing to ease her distress, either; his kindest words were jokes about "pillow-brained excursions."

Toward the middle of the week, though, she began retesting her map-reading ability with forays in other directions and was encouraged by reaching her destinations without a single mistake. She even walked the spine of the ridge, along one of many ancient trails that laced the hillsides and rocky slopes.

These well-defined pathways, worn by countless generations of deer, were helped here and there by Peter's judiciously placed orange flagging. He had to be careful with markers. Tom had little use for trails, preferring to range more freely. And because it was Peter who made the trails, Tom ripped off every marker he came across.

This particular trail was one of Hannah's favorites, winding through tall spruces and pines, a carpet of needles and multicolored mosses deadening all sound except for the wind that whispered high above. An occasional quartz outcrop gleamed white in the shifting shadows.

She stood there now amidst bracken fern on this cool Sunday afternoon, staring down from the trail toward where the clearing should be. Sighing, she shifted indecisively, looking first up the trail, then back toward the log yard. Finally, with a big breath and a whispered "Vushondio," she stepped off toward the riddle that lay ahead.

The clearing stood empty and silent—and real—in the late afternoon sun. Hannah, teetering uncertainly on the rock pile, wasn't sure whether to be glad or sorry. It was enough that she hadn't been dreaming.

Not much had changed since—when was it, Friday? She had come with her father on Saturday, so over a week had passed since she last saw it. A few additional trees had been cut, but the stumps remained. More stones had been transferred to the pile; it seemed less a heap now and more the beginnings of a wall.

Figuring that the boy must get himself and his horse to the clearing by some route other than her entrance, she struck off to the right where skid marks seemed to lead through the soft duff on the forest floor. A narrow track meandered through the trees to what looked to be a second clearing, a very large one.

She stopped to marvel at another stone wall. Though not freshly made, it was new enough to be whole and solid, straight and true, a masterpiece of craftsmanship.

The track ran through a break and followed another wall perpendicular to the first. Now the trees became shorter, as on overgrown pasture land. These soon gave way to a wide-open area that left Hannah thunderstruck. She stopped short and stared.

Directly ahead on the right was a log dwelling and assorted outbuildings, plus a ramshackle barn hardly more than a three-sided shelter. These all were set among large pines that looked out across planted fields below.

"Well, you just wouldn't *believe!*" she exclaimed out loud. "This is awesome! Where'd it all come from?"

Across the way on the uphill side of the road, she could now see another cabin, also with sheltering trees—hemlocks, a maple, and a beautifully shaped ash. This house seemed better cared for than the other. The closer one, she decided with a giggle, was as bad as their own shack—even worse with garbage and trash dumped helter-skelter.

The more distant house had a barn, too, and while it was in better condition than the other, its logs waved and curled, leaving huge cracks. Hannah shook her head at such construction. The cabin was considerably tighter, though, with a log-and-stone chimney at one end. A shed arrangement at the back may have been for firewood, she guessed; a chopping block and ax stood nearby.

A short distance uphill, a moss-backed springhouse hunkered close to the ground, protecting the source of the stream that flowed down a wooden trough toward the back of the house, then under the road to a small pond.

Behind the barn, another rough, soot-blackened structure held assorted barrels and empty hooks. A smokehouse, maybe? On beyond that, just before the orchard, a well-worn path directed her eyes to what was most likely an outhouse.

Up along the hillside to the left, behind the second cabin, she could see open pastures. A number of sheep grazed the rocky upper slopes, while below them straggled a few small cows with ferocious-looking horns. Conspicuous among them were two great oxen, safe and docile among the "ladies." Assorted barnyard birds roamed freely, pecking around newly piled logs. The geese in particular made a ruckus as Hannah drew closer.

There wasn't a soul anywhere around, and except for the geese and chickens, an intense stillness lay over the whole scene.

"Check it out!" Hannah turned all the way around and jumped up and down to make sure she wasn't asleep. Was this the commune of some back-to-nature types? The boy certainly fit in. She had heard they sometimes had strange ways of speaking. But where in the world was all of this last Saturday? She knew they had walked this very area with no sign of open land anywhere.

The appearance of the boy himself on the road below interrupted her thoughts. He stopped for a moment when he saw her, then with a wave, he jogged on up the hill. Though warm from his climb, he seemed hardly out of breath. His clothing was different this time but had the same rough texture. He greeted her with sincere friendliness. "Welcome, Miss Valdegar! Have you come with your father?"

Though innocently spoken, this vexing reminder of her fruitless expedition drew a frown from Hannah, but he went on. "I regret not being at home when you arrived, but I have just now come from church meeting. My family wished to remain some longer, so I agreed to walk back to tend the stock."

"Church? Up here?"

"In town."

"In town? What town?"

"Why, Gilly, of course."

"You walked back from Gilly?"

He smiled. "'Tis only a matter of two miles."

"Not the way we go, it isn't. But two miles, all uphill?" Yet what was two miles, even straight up, to someone who could chop down a tree in less than ten minutes? "Your whole family walked to church?"

"We drove down this morning, the four of us, but I left the wagon and team—"

"You've been in church since morning? Whatever for?" *There's got to be a girl in this somehow,* she muttered to herself. *He must have dozens hanging all over him!*

He raised his eyebrows. "You are not a church attender?" His scrutiny was unsettling. "I see that again you wear a man's clothing, or perhaps your younger brother's. I thought on the

[42]

previous day that perhaps you were doing a particular sort of work that required such attire. But on the Lord's Day ..." He shook his head. "It is incumbent on us who love our Lord to gather with His people for worship."

Hannah felt her face turn red, and she looked down at the designer jeans she had felt so good about while standing on the ridge. One of the deciding factors for choosing to come had been her satisfaction with how she looked in these best and tightest of jeans. *Younger brother's? Gimme a break!*

But he had spoken kindly, and that was the problem. Had he rebuked her with refrigerated disdain, she could easily have answered in kind. But what could she add now to her silly stammering? She decided to change the subject.

"Where were you last Saturday—a week ago?"

"I was undoubtedly here, engaged in my usual labors. I am hardly ever elsewhere, excepting Sundays."

Hannah chewed her upper lip. "Oh!" she exclaimed. "I forgot to ask your name the other day."

"I am Ephraim Ward."

Ephraim? What an odd name! In all her musings, she hadn't considered that possibility. "Are you the owner of this—no," she interrupted herself, "you said your father owned it."

"Yes, my father owns the land above the road, and my Uncle Latham all that lies below."

"Is that his cabin up in the trees?"

"Yes. My grandfather obtained the original land grant from the colonial governor of New Hampshire, and when Grandfather died, the land was divided between his stepson—my uncle—and my father. But Grandfather cleared, planted, built the first necessary shelters, fought Indians, laid—"

"Indians?"

"Oh, yes. Back then they were most troublesome, but not since the War, though many still remain in the vicinity. One does hear of an occasional isolated attack. That is why I may have appeared uneasy when you came into view Friday last."

One word had clicked in Hannah's mind. "Which war is it you're talking about?"

"The War of Independence, of course."

"You're putting me on!"

"Pardon me?"

"You're not really serious. You're joking, aren't you? The Revolutionary War—1776—or whenever it was?"

He stiffened, his eyes glittering icicles. "The War of Independence was no mean struggle. It altered the destiny of—"

"No, wait. I don't mean the war wasn't important. It's just that—" *Wrong move, Hannah. Go back three spaces and pick another card.* How could she get him to smile again? "It's just that things are different where I come from, and we've had other wars, like World War I, World War II, even Vietnam. Have you heard of— no, I guess you haven't. Well, let's see. How about things like cars, TV—television, I mean—movies and VCRs—"

"I am sorry, but you speak of things of which I know nothing. Will you please explain your reference to cars, TV, VC . . . ? I regret I cannot even—"

"All right, cars." She swelled with the momentousness of enlightening the ignorant. But how do you explain to someone who has never seen or heard of one? "A car is a motorized vehicle—wait—self-propelled vehicle that goes along hard, wide roads, like maybe ten times wider than this. And they go sixty miles an hour, even faster. Some racing cars go like three hundred miles an hour."

Her eyes flashed as she drew on Mike's love for his motorbike, trying to think of something that would soften the boy's frown. "And television is a box thing that shows sports and rock groups and soaps—well, you probably wouldn't like them—but cop shows, comedy . . ."

Ephraim frowned even more and shook his head.

Hannah looked closely at him. Was he just stringing her along? She despised gullibility and was wary of being victimized. *I gotta watch my step here!* She decided to humor him.

"Okay, let's give television one more try. It runs on electricity—don't ask me to explain that—I only know you plug it in, and it lights up and a picture comes on the screen. Anyway, you can watch sports, y' know, games like baseball or football; or shows—plays, y' know, where some classy woman is held hostage and the good guys shoot their way through and drive off with her, screeching around corners, jumping over—"

He put up his hand to stop her. "These are matters of trifling uplift, and I do not wish to hear of them. You come here on the Lord's Day, dressed as a man, albeit in fine apparel, your face painted in a way unbecoming a virtuous woman, in all probability not a church attender, speaking light of our recent political conquest, and manifesting interest in debauched theatricals and things occult. I perceive you to be an emissary of Satan and will bid you good day."

She immediately backed off, her face burning. "I'm sorry, Ephraim. I'm sorry! Maybe I shouldn't even call you by your first name. You see, I don't know these things, and I need to be told what's all right for me to say. Please don't hate me and think I'm Satan!" She tried smiling but was too close to tears. "I just want you to be a friend."

Is that wrong, too? Evidently not, for his eyes softened just a bit. She continued. "Please, may I come back to learn more about your ways? I promise I won't talk about my world unless you want me to."

He answered gently. "There is only one world worth talking about, and that is the kingdom of our Lord."

"Then we'll talk about that," Hannah declared firmly.

chapter 6

*H*annah went straight to her bedroom when she got home, guarding her treasure close within. Mike hollered after her, "Hey, Sweetie, don'tcha even want a donut?"

She opened her door. "Toss me a couple." But from then on she was quiet—sifting, puzzling, trembling over the prospects. She focused most of her energy on matters that could be handled or at least understood, putting the major ambiguities on hold. How could she possibly analyze such a staggering turn of events? She could easily enough write Ephraim off as a cracked teakettle, but not so the open land where trees ought to be. The fields and cabins and barns had not been there a week earlier when she and her father had walked the area. But they showed up today. And the "recent war" Ephraim spoke of, the Revolutionary War, 1776 to 1781 . . .

The implications made her stomach and feet tingle.

Ephraim was a real live person, though. The damp smell of his warm body, those electric eyes, and the contours of his face made a fresh assault on her emotions. He was real, all right. Could it be that she alone had access to him—she, Hannah Valdegar, the social rebel when it came to boys. Had Ephraim been some uninspiring clod, she'd probably stay as far as possible from that stone wall. But Ephraim Ward was no clod, and she had plans. Everything else could sit on the back burner while she concentrated on what to wear, what to say, and how to win his friendship.

His objection to makeup was no problem. She just wouldn't wear any even if it wasn't cool. Clothes, however, were a problem. She didn't even have a dress with her, and he would undoubtedly view any kind of slacks as men's clothing. She hoped to get by, for a while at least, with passing them off as work clothes. He'd get used to seeing her, and with the right clothing she should have no problem using her body to good effect in furthering the relationship.

Hannah had a special sense where dress was concerned; even Ardyth consulted her judgment. Hannah wore clothes well and gloated over this small balancing of accounts in the distribution of beauty among the family members. She had many of the same features that made her parents remarkable: her mother's straight, even teeth and perfectly sculpted cheekbones; her father's subtly dimpled chin and broad, strong forehead, his copper hair.

She also had Tom's nose, however. On him it looked good, but somehow it didn't fit Hannah's face. At least she didn't think so. She worked hard at her deficiencies with cosmetics. But with all her efforts, she still saw her ratings down next to Peter's in the family charts. Even her brother Steve was better looking than she. He combined Jane's classic elegance with Tom's handsome ruggedness and was set apart from them both by his thatch of bronze chest hair that crawled up through open-necked shirts.

Hannah's figure was nearly as perfect as Ardyth's, and she knew just what to do with it. Yes, clothes might be an immediate problem, but in the end they would be her ally.

The next day the clearing again stood silent and empty, which added to her nervousness. What, or who, would she find down the lane this time?

Suddenly she heard what she least expected: the sound of children laughing and playing. When she rounded the bend near the first house, two little girls nearly ran into her.

"Whoa, there—traffic on the road today. Better rein in your horses!" She smiled.

The children stopped dead and stared, taking in not only the strange face but the iniquitous clothing as well.

"Hi! My name is Hannah. What's yours?"

The two continued to study her solemnly, grubby fingers at mouths. About six and eight years old, they wore long skirts with dirty aprons and blouses and light capes against the cloudy dampness. When they turned and ran toward the cabin, their bare feet appeared accustomed to rough ground.

By the time Hannah approached the weathered and dilapidated house, a larger audience had lined up to observe her passage. A sharp-featured woman stood with six girls ranging in age from mid teens to a babe in arms. The older two, along with their mother, wore identical gray dresses, but there the similarity stopped. The eldest girl's bright, clean cap and front-fastened shawl stood out against the slovenliness of the other two. The only mark of disarray about the eldest was a wet, wrinkled apron on which she had evidently just dried her hands. *This one must be the family washer woman,* Hannah reflected. On approaching the house, she had noticed a steaming laundry tub standing just outside the back door and next to it a bundle of what looked like old rags, badly soiled and stained.

The girl's long, golden hair hung in a cloud, unlike the thin, greasy knot of the mother and the moldy-looking strings of the other children. She had a pretty, though furtive face and studied Hannah with eyes that seemed magnetized by the ground.

The second in the lineup had more assurance than her sister and glared at Hannah with her mother's sharpness. But she had none of the older girl's physical attractiveness. *Wow!* thought Hannah, *I thought my nose was bad! She's almost as ugly as what's-her-name in my homeroom—Thecla Turner! How can two sisters look so different?*

The younger girls, with rather nondescript faces, wore somewhat shorter skirts, and their costume included neither cap nor shawl. The next-to-youngest, however, just barely toddling, had some sort of soft cloth rope around her head.

"Hello, I'm looking for Ephraim—Mr. Ephraim Ward," Hannah amended carefully.

Oh, I hope that's not Ephraim's mother. She looks acid enough to curdle ice cream!

When the thin line that was the woman's mouth broke open at last, such a volume of directions, complaints, criticisms, and pious ejaculations poured out in a high skittery voice that Hannah would later tell Peter, "I met a winter wren in a person!"

Hannah gleaned from the squawkings that the woman's husband was sick—a distemper, she called it—that Ephraim was working but not at the right things, that Hannah was dressed in a disgraceful manner, and that the woman's children would soon be thrown on the mercy of God if more care were not devoted to their daily needs.

As soon as she could tactfully break away, Hannah thanked her. But when she turned to go down the lane, the sounds of lusty singing and jingling harness heralded Ephraim's approach:

> "God moves in a mysterious way
> His wonders to perform;
> He plants His footsteps in the sea,
> And rides upon the storm."

Again her nervousness rose in a lump, but Ephraim smiled warmly in greeting, sending her spirits soaring.

As they made their way back to the clearing together, Hannah told of her encounter at the cabin. "Is that lady your aunt? I didn't ask her name. You said yesterday that your Uncle Latham—"

"Yes, that would have been Aunt Latham."

That's how it works: Latham is the last name. "And the children? Especially the little ones who nearly ran me down. What are they called? They were cute."

He smiled. "That no doubt would have been Felicity and Honora. The babe's name is Constance, and the next little one is Mercy."

"She must be the one with the rope thing around her head. What's that for?"

"Ay, the pudding. That is to keep her from harm should she fall. Have you never seen one before?"

Hannah shook her head. "No. Sounds like a good idea, though. Let's see—Constance, Mercy, Felicity, and Honora. Such funny names! What are the other two called?"

"Chastity and Patience."

"Chastity and Patience, hm?" *I bet that second one has about as much patience as a pig on a diet,* Hannah thought, but aloud she said, "All girls!"

"There were boys, four of them, but the Lord took each in turn. It is singularly difficult for a family with no sons, and Uncle has a great many physical infirmities to bear. We, Father and I, do our utmost to carry his portion of the labor, but there is much to do to keep the wilderness at bay. For example, this wood through which we have just come," he said, waving at Uncle Latham's property, "was all cleared in Grandfather's time, but wilderness has been allowed to encroach at the cost of much-needed pasture. My purpose here is to gain back some of what has been lost and to add to it that level portion on which I now labor. Much, too, has vanished along the upper reaches of the pastures above our cabin, but better forage will grow here than on the rocky slope."

Hannah nodded thoughtfully, trying to follow his strange way of speaking. "So you're starting here and working back out?"

"Yes, 'tis easier to haul stones over cleared land than through trees. And there are many stones," he added ruefully.

"Yeah, Vermont's best crop," Hannah muttered wryly. She was bemused when he slapped his leg at the old joke.

"I gather from what your aunt said that she doesn't exactly appreciate your working at this, rather than in the fields."

His face darkened, and Hannah's nerves jumped with each shadow of change.

Ephraim nodded wearily. "There is always more than can be done, but the land as a whole must be given consideration, as well as the structures that require repairing or rebuilding. The corn crib, for one, shows much rot and must be emended or replaced. The barn constructed by my Grandfather was meant to be temporary, and it is my hope and desire to build a new one next year after the logs I am now cutting have cured."

"How come you girdle the biggest trees? There's an awful lot of board footage for your barn in those babies."

He snorted. "It would require two span of oxen to move such logs, and 'tis far less labor to await their death and then burn them. Smaller logs will do well for any structure we shall want."

"You wouldn't build another log barn, though, would you? You should see some of our barns, big and red, some of them a couple hundred feet long. And even if you use logs, you should put splines in between to tighten them up. Splines are thin pieces of wood," she explained in response to Ephraim's blank look, "that fit in slots, y' see, where the logs come together." She demonstrated with her hands. "My father sells a lot of spruce to a log-cabin outfit, and splines make 'em really snug. That old barn of your grandfather's has cracks wide enough to throw a cat through."

He smiled tolerantly. "Such design was purposeful, for it allows air to circulate freely throughout the structure to better cure hay and grain."

Hannah winced inwardly.

Ephraim returned to an earlier thought. "Aunt does speak sharply ofttimes, but she is a virtuous woman and labors hard at the exacting task of six daughters. Uncle is a man of God, and though he suffers much from sundry distempers, he attends to Scripture to raise his spirits, and he seeks heartily to bear with patience whatever the Lord lays upon him."

He looked at her squarely and seriously. "Is it your habit to read Scripture?"

She shook her head, a new wave of embarrassment gathering strength. "I'm ... afraid not. You see, my family—"

"Do you know the Catechism?"

"The what?"

His frown grew. "You are not acquainted with the Catechism? The first question is, 'What is the chief end of man?' Surely you are sensible of the answer. Even a child can make reply to question one!"

She shook her head, the lump in her stomach growing rapidly.

He looked at her narrowly. "Your ways are strange to me. Even godless men who do not attend meeting—drunkards and blasphemers—even these could with ease recite that much of the Catechism."

"I'm sorry, I just never ... I really would like to learn, though. Will you teach me?"

It was becoming increasingly clear that her body, clothing, and manner of walk—the usual weapons of male conquest—would not dent Ephraim's moral armor. If gaining ground required a little mental exercise, so be it. She had always been quick at memorizing, and her school grades reflected more brain power than her vague career plans implied. So while the part about wanting to learn was a lie, it would be effort well invested if the Catechism became a ticket to his arms.

After an alarming pause, Ephraim nodded thoughtfully. "Yes, I will teach you. 'Twill be good review for me, as well. But I must work now, and you must depart. Before the morrow, however, you shall endeavor to say in reply to question one, 'Man's chief end is to glorify God and to enjoy Him forever.'"

She repeated it several times and promised to say it all the way home.

The ensuing days fell into a routine, a litany of work and questions.

"How can you do so much—milk, cultivate, harvest, thresh— all those hard jobs, with no time to relax?"

"Are you now able to give adequate explanation to the phrase 'fell from the estate wherein they were created, by sinning against God'?"

"Do you ever go to parties?"

"What is 'justification'?"

"What is heaven like?"

" 'What are the outward and ordinary means whereby Christ communicateth to us the benefits of redemption?' "

"Do you ever wish you could fly? I was in a plane once, y' know ..."

From planes, they moved to a discussion of transportation in general. Hannah wanted to know if Ephraim ever rode one or the other of the horses, or if they were just for driving.

"Indeed, in his day, Captain had few rivals as to speed or bearing. He still remains a fine trotter, better than Major, and age has rendered him more placid. He protests not, even if I leap on him from the ground—thus." Ephraim backed off for a running start and vaulted onto the animal. He misgauged his momentum, however, and landed in an ignominious heap on the far side of the horse.

Hannah gasped, but before she had time to worry about his being hurt, he jumped to his feet, brushed his clothing in dignified silence, and prepared for a second assault, this one successful. Hannah hid her laughter.

She made a serious blunder herself in one of her early visits, a blunder that nearly brought the whole campaign to an abrupt end. Ephraim had been tolerating her "men's clothing" reasonably well, so on a particularly blistering day, she thought nothing of her usual hot-weather attire: shorts and a "nippy" halter top, as Mike called it.

Hannah's mind was occupied with a good-will gesture in the form of root beer to add to her lunch. She had it all ready—two cans in an ice-packed insulated bag, along with a sandwich for herself—when the appalling thought struck that he would more than likely object to anything with the word *beer* on the can. She quickly substituted two Pepsis and went happily along over the ridge, glad that her brain had been in gear.

Despite the heat, Ephraim was hard at work, this time with the oxen. Sweat poured from both man and beast. Seeing her cheery wave, he stopped. Then with a look of shock, he ran to her in alarm. "What befell your clothing? Were you attacked?"

At the word *clothing,* she realized her mistake immediately and tried to douse the impending explosion with a tidal wave of words. "Oh, it's such a hot day, I thought I'd wear something cool. Aren't you terribly warm? It's a wonder you're still working. Look at the oxen. Their tongues are actually hanging out! Is that where the expression comes from? My father says that when it gets over eighty-five degrees, it's too hot to work, so they take the rest of the day off. But I brought something to cool you down." She fumbled in her bag for what she hoped would defuse the bomb.

"You *chose* to be naked? To expose yourself in this way? No woman of honor walks about thus unattired. Surely you have taken leave of your senses. If not, then you are but a common hussy with base carnal designs, insensible to virtue, and I cannot look upon you again!" He turned his back, but not with the self-righteous vindictiveness Hannah expected. A sad finality weighed down his shoulders.

"Ephraim, please. I'm sorry. I didn't know . . . didn't think. You're right. I shouldn't be dressed this way. I promise not to do it again. Oh, Ephraim . . ." She sobbed miserably, feeling as though her secret inner self, as well as her body, was open for all to view.

Only vireos sing in the heat of the day—a slow, ploddingly persistent warble that lends a custom backdrop to any circumstance. Now the sound seemed to pick up Hannah's woe and plead her cause.

Ephraim turned, grief and just a touch of yearning in his eyes. "It is unthinkable that you should come here so clothed. But Scripture says, 'The grace of our Lord was exceeding abundant toward me. I obtained mercy, that in me Jesus Christ might show forth all longsuffering, for a pattern to them which should hereafter believe on him to life everlasting.' We are also instructed: 'Be kind one to another, tenderhearted, forgiving one another, even as God for Christ's sake hath forgiven us.' Go now, and return on the morrow." He didn't even add, "—properly clothed."

Relief shone in Hannah's face, but still she risked a momentary delay to make her offering. "Ephraim, I did so want to bring you this cold drink. It's not alcoholic or anything. I think you'll like it. Will you please take it as my thanks for your kindness, please?"

Again a long look, one that held surprise, perplexity, even longing. Slowly, he reached out to receive Hannah's gift; in so doing, he gave an even greater one to her.

She was able to breathe again. "You just pull this tab here. It comes off easy. And I'll see you tomorrow!"

In her haste, she almost ran into a tree between her and the wall, but it was not until much later that the anomaly sank in: Ephraim had cut all the trees close to the wall.

All the way home, words from the Catechism kept running through her mind:

Question: Did God leave all mankind to perish in the estate of sin and misery?

Answer: God ... did enter into a covenant of grace, to deliver them out of the estate of sin and misery, and to bring them into an estate of salvation by a Redeemer.

chapter 7

Within four hours of her return, Hannah had driven into Gilly and purchased an ankle-length skirt and a plain long-sleeved blouse. The skirt had more of a print than she wanted, but except for bright yellow or red, no solids were available. She worried that wrinkle-resistant fabric might stand out against the rumpled Wards and Lathams, but it was necessary to her plan.

The second part of the plan proved more difficult. She drove an extra fifteen miles before locating a fast-food restaurant that would sell her a five-gallon plastic tub with a tight lid. Her father used pails like that to haul sap, but she was afraid he wouldn't have the right-sized lid.

Though not exactly a Garachi, the new outfit pleased her, lending an air of demure modesty, yet detracting nothing from her "agreeable" figure, as Ephraim might have called it, had he been inclined to talk along those lines. And, she fervently hoped, perhaps he soon would.

With the clothing carefully packed in the pail, she drove home and on down the logging road, hoping the men and their disconcerting questions were elsewhere. Leaving the car, she hiked over the ridge to the mossy ledges and deposited her pail in a sheltered crevasse, piling leaves in front to hide it. Satisfied, she brushed her hands and skipped back to the car.

The enterprise succeeded beyond her hopes. As Hannah stepped over the wall in her costume the next day, Ephraim practically leaped in her direction. Evidently, he had been struggling with apprehensions of his own, and relief washed over his face at sight of her clothing.

He walked around her with approval and perhaps just a smidgeon of admiration. "You have indeed made fitting amends to your attire. I feared you might affect the gaudy dress of fashion, but you have proven yourself amiable and worthy. Forgive me for thus seeming harsh yesterday."

His obvious concern over his ultimatum sent Hannah's heart soaring. She was in for a warm summer under all that cloth, but this whole embarrassing incident might actually serve to heat up their relationship.

Ephraim seemed more willing now, eager even, to take her beyond the clearing. On the way back, with a twitch of firewood chained behind Captain, they met Ephraim's father just coming out of the Latham house. Before this, Hannah had seen him only from a distance. Now he nodded and smiled and extended a warm greeting.

She was particularly glad for his friendliness. Daniel Ward, a tall, rugged, pleasant man, differed from his older stepbrother both in looks and manner. In talking with him, Hannah felt sheltered, protected in his solidness. Any man who could split rails for fencing, shear a sheep, and scythe a swath of hay with ease and grace offered security even from wolves or Indians. That sense of safeness extended within as well, bringing new meaning to *green pastures* and *still waters,* words familiar even to Hannah.

The Latham clan also came forth. Mrs. Latham and Patience curtsied in grudging endorsement of the new attire, whereas Mr. Latham, who had read some pointed Scripture to her at an earlier meeting, now smiled, bobbing his head and rubbing his hands together in approval. But for good measure, he read to her from his ever-present Bible:

> "Mortify therefore your members which are upon the earth; fornication, uncleanness, inordinate affection, evil concupiscence, and covetousness, which is idolatry: For which things' sake the wrath of God cometh on the children of disobedience. . . . Put on therefore, as the elect of God, holy and beloved, bowels of mercies, kindness, humbleness of mind, meekness, longsuffering.

"Thou art indeed recommending thyself to our Lord by thine amendments, my child," he told her. "I cherish the hope that thou wilt remain sensible to the prudence of a virtuous course." Again he smiled and bobbed and went back indoors, most likely to pray for the salvation of her soul.

The following day when Hannah arrived at the clearing, she found Ephraim hunting game for supper at his mother's request. He had already brought down four birds, and they were arranged in a row under the tree where Hannah usually sat to watch him work.

After examining the strange long rifle ("Flintlocks are a substantial advancement over muskets," Ephraim informed her), she bent down to inspect the birds. "What in the world are they? They look like mourning doves, but they're huge!"

"They are but wild pigeons. We have them in abundance all through the forest." His eyes twinkled. "On days when the squirrel has longer and cooler legs than I, we eat pigeon for supper."

Hannah's eyes narrowed. "Wild pigeons? These wouldn't be passenger pigeons, by any chance?"

"Yes, they are called so ofttimes."

Hannah sank down beside the birds, her head reeling from the revelation. "Oh, wow! What would Peter say if I told him I'd seen passenger pigeons, gone now for what, a hundred years?"

"I beg your pardon?"

"No, I mean ... they're beautiful, aren't they?" Almost reverently, she touched the long, steely-blue feathers of a wing and rubbed her forefinger over the soft buff-colored breast. "They must be a good sixteen inches or more."

"There is a tolerable amount of fine sweet meat on each bird, and in truth, my mother will prepare a veritable feast with these."

Hannah had not yet met Ephraim's mother. "What's she like? No, let me guess. She's tall and slender with brown hair and bright blue eyes like yours." Seeing him glance away uneasily, she quickly amended her course to Mrs. Ward's being a diligent worker, good cook, and—"What else does she do?"

Ephraim laughed. "What does she not do? Principally, she cares for my brother."

"Your brother? I didn't know you had a brother. Where has he been?"

"He is not right in the limbs and cannot walk, thus requiring much additional care." His face, sad and reflective for a moment, quickly brightened. "But we are much blessed by God as a family, for the lad is cheerful beyond understanding, despite continuous pain, and he is a delight to us all."

"How old is he? What's his name?"

"Jonah is eight years of age. My mother had other children, but they lie buried in the family plot."

"Oh, I'm sorry. How old were ... is it all right to talk about them?"

He smiled reassuringly. "Two girls both died before reaching a year, and my brother Nathaniel was killed two years past at age twelve when he pitched from a neighbor's runaway wagon."

"How terrible! And even more than losing a member of the family, there's all the work ..." She bit her lip.

Ephraim gazed off thoughtfully and sighed. "Yes, the work. But," he said, smiling, "God has granted Father and me strong bodies as well as a good, kind, and loving wife and mother to care for our needs."

Turning back to Hannah, he said, "You inquired about the duties of my mother. In addition to the care and education of Jonah, she grows and prepares food and sees to the root cellar and smoking of meat. She cleans, cards, and spins all her wool and flax, and most of our clothing is of her own manufacture. During the war, she did much weaving as well with the women of the town, but now, aside from work on the small loom, she consents to having Mr. Kittredge perform this task. Mother prepares tapers and lamps for our lighting and makes quilts for coverlets and bedding from the finest goose feathers. She grows weary, as do we all, but one seldom sees her ill-tempered."

Hannah tried to take in the enormity of all that work, yet Ephraim's half smile suggested another dimension that she could only guess at until she had met Abigail Ward. "You love your mother very much, don't you, and she loves you?" She spoke softly as though not to shatter a rare and fragile spell.

"Yes. I wish only that I had greater opportunity to give assistance in return for the many hours of labor and tutoring she has lent me."

"She taught you, too? Didn't you go to school anywhere?"

"Oh, yes, but my mother endeavored to overcome the deficiencies of the Gilly school by additional instruction. Her father was a clergyman who shortly before the time of her marriage became a professor at the new college of Dartmouth. He provided a thorough education for her, and she has faithfully given her sons the benefit of that training."

Hannah was quiet, measuring this woman against her own mother. "Is your mother afraid of snakes?"

He snorted. "Afraid of snakes? Why should she be? It is neither fashionable nor safe for country settlers to fear unwonted intruders."

After a moment of reflection he went on. "My father oft tells the tale of when first they wed. Certain scoundrels, their tempers heated over issues of war, went from cabin to cabin seeking to sway opinion by force, if necessary. My uncle had suffered persuasion at an earlier time; thus, my father saw their approach this day and sought to hide both himself and my mother. She, however, would have none of it and marched forth, the fire of indignation in her eyes. She delivered such a discourse as to plant the fear of God and the dread of woman in the visiting partisans.

"From that time," he finished, his eyes twinkling, "there have none of us dared defy her in matters of virtue or moral rectitude. Fear snakes?" he laughed. "My mother fears only God!"

As Ephraim spoke on about his world, Hannah found that his days were strictly regulated by work. Up before daybreak, he milked the cows and turned them out with the three calves that had been separated from their mothers overnight. He cleaned the barn and released the chickens and geese to forage, and then went in for breakfast. The hours right afterward were taken up with work in the fields, depending on what needed doing.

Midday he spent in the cooler woods, though Hannah in no way could see that chopping trees was any cooler. On his return, he worked up a good pile of firewood and carried a day's worth of cooking wood to his mother. Hunting, if needed, was squeezed in where convenient. In late afternoon he hoed a bit in the garden or did assorted chores for his aunt, depending on the vagaries of Uncle Latham's health.

After an early supper, he separated the calves, herded the fowl away from foxes and raccoons, and saw to the well-being of the other animals. In the evening he either read to his brother or strapped him on his back for a walk, pointing out birds, an occasional deer, all the glories of God's created order.

"Isn't there time just to relax?" Hannah asked.

"The Lord's Day, of course. And is not the ramble with Jonah a time of rest? Also, we sit each even and discuss the events of the day, how God has blessed and helped us. Father reads from Scripture and leads us in prayers, giving special thanks for the good life we enjoy and the bounteous provision He has made for us all. We sometimes sing. Mother is well versed in psalms and hymns and spiritual songs, and Father ofttimes lines out hymns in meeting."

Hannah was silent a long time after this lengthy recital of responsibility, knowing enough about work to realize that far more was involved than the telling would indicate. A kind of superior anger rose within her.

"You're killing yourself here! Life shouldn't be that hard. Hey, in my world, nobody does that much. Even workaholics fly off to the Bahamas once in a while. There must be a way to get better tools, more machines. A tractor alone would save countless hours—plowing, cutting hay, hauling logs. You need time just to sit around and listen to the radio or watch television; you need a little fun."

Ephraim cast a pitying eye on her as though she were a trifle feeble-minded. "These things you speak of, do they excite love for God? I think not. There is no lack of profligate idlers or men of wealth whose sole aim is to be at ease. They fall into divers temptations which serve only to harden their hearts against God. Did Ethan Allen die a blissful man? Strength, talents, riches, fame—all were his; however, he loved not God, and earthly gain is as nothing in the end."

That's the trouble right there, Hannah grumbled to herself. *This religion jazz has cut him off from reality. It's like he doesn't even know or care that my world exists! He never asks about it. I'm interested in his world. Why doesn't he care about mine? I bet there are people here who'd be glad to know about electric stoves and refrigerators and chainsaws, to say nothing of listening to Steve's stereo. Man, wouldn't that singe their eyebrows at "meeting"!*

While her thoughts busily accumulated annoyance, a sideways glance brought reality of a different sort crashing down upon her. The major ambiguities she had earlier placed on the back burner of her consciousness suddenly slid to the fore. The row of pigeons beside her were not just dead; the specie no longer existed. Yet she could pick them up, examine their feathers, and presumably eat them.

Ephraim was real and alive, but he too was "extinct," a boy of two centuries ago. His time had somehow slipped into hers, or was it the other way around? Hers into his? Yes, most likely that was it.

Ephraim didn't seem to feel the fracturing effect of the two worlds. He fretted about her ways but apparently wasn't wrestling over problems with the two times. But then, up until now she herself hadn't given much thought beyond her access to a gorgeous boy and how to keep the door from slamming in her face.

Going backward in time to where there were no cars or tractors, where work was hard and endless but the people didn't seem to care all that much . . . Was it possible? As she sat in the dappled shade at the edge of the clearing, watching Ephraim and hearing nothing but the variegated concert in the canopy overhead, the quiet of this place did lure her. No noise from jets overhead or trucks on a distant highway. Sometimes at home she got sick of the package of noise she lived in—though she wasn't willing to give up the things that noise provided. But here it was nice to sit for a few hours each day in this funny little time bubble of stillness . . . even if it meant sitting next to a bunch of dead, extinct pigeons.

chapter 8

Now, that's dumb! Hannah berated herself. *Why should I be surprised that the Wards and Lathams will celebrate the Fourth of July? Where'd I think the holiday came from—Vietnam?*

This mental lashing took place while Hannah waited near the Latham cabin for Ephraim. He had not been at the clearing when she arrived, so she walked down the lane to find him. When the slow, muted clanking of chains told her he was using the oxen today, she stopped to chat with Felicity and Honora who had exploded out of the house, followed more sedately by Chastity, wiping her hands as always. They, too, had heard Ephraim and were fairly popping with excitement.

"He's coming! He's coming!" Felicity jumped up and down. "Ephraim," she called, "Father says we may go early Monday next!"

The two younger girls danced down the lane toward the slow-moving animals. Chastity, however, remained.

"Well," Hannah remarked companionably, "they're all wound up! What set them off?"

The other girl stood silent, staring off toward Ephraim.

Well, be a space cadet, then!

Hannah's annoyance was short-lived as Honora came flying back.

"Chastity, Ephraim says we may go early with him, but we must carry boards and barrels to make tables, we must erect a tall platform from which the Reverend Mr. Allen will speak, and we must build the bonfire five score and twenty-nine feet, but he says we may not dance with any army lieutenants."

Chastity did not smile at Ephraim's playful exaggerations, though a soft glow stirred her eyes.

Hannah laughed, though, and grabbed one of the leaping sprites, making her stand still. "Now, just what is this great thing on Monday you're willing to do such work for? Here it's only Thursday, and already you're roaring for Monday!"

Felicity's eyes widened at such ignorance. "Why, Monday will mark a full score years of inpendence for our country, and—"

"Independence, Felicity," Ephraim corrected.

"Independence, yes. July four, seventeen seventy-six to July four, seventeen—what it is now, Ephraim?"

"Seventeen ninety-six."

"Seventeen ninety-six, yes, and we shall ring cow bells and bang anvils and—and—"

"—And pray for two hours and attend to an equally lengthy sermon," Chastity cut in, "along with the Reverend Mr. Allen's address that will commence after noon-meal when everyone can scarce stay awake."

Ephraim ignored the edge in her voice. "Yes, the Reverend Thomas Allen—a great man, Hannah. You have heard of him, surely? When word came from Bennington of the impending battle, he urged his people to go forth and smite the Philistines. He led a band of parishioners from Pittsfield to where the armies gathered, and then he went directly to rouse General Stark from sleep. 'My people have often been called out before,' the Reverend Mr. Allen shouted, 'but we have never been permitted to fight. If we are not led to battle this time, we shall never come out again!'

Whereupon, General Stark cast his eye upon the unceasing rain. 'If the Lord should once more give us sunshine,' he returned, 'and I do not give you fighting enough, I will never ask you to come again.' "

"And the Lord sent forth the sun!" shouted the little girls. "And they conquered!"

"Ephraim," Felicity prompted, pulling at his arm, "tell Hannah about the first shot. Tell her about jumping on the tree. Tell her—"

"Now, hold. Be still! I will tell her, but you must stand in dignified silence as rehearsal for Monday's address. Right over there. Array yourselves next to Chastity—yes." He lined up the girls in mock seriousness.

"Now then. After the Reverend Mr. Allen entreated the Lord to teach their hands to war and their fingers to fight, General Stark's band of three hundred marched back and forth before the little hill where stood the Tories in readiness. Reverend Thomas Allen, however, felt compelled to address his fellow countrymen. He leapt upon the trunk of a fallen tree and exhorted the loyalists to desert their common enemy. His answer, however, came in a fusillade of bullets. Whereupon, he turned to his brother: 'Now, give me a musket. You load and I'll fire.' And thus the battle began."

"But he wasn't to shoot, was he, Ephraim?"

The storyteller held up his hand. "Stay! Hush! You are every bit as disobedient as Mr. Allen! Yes, he did fire against the general's orders, but have not Yankees always kept their own minds?" His eyes twinkled.

"Was this man related to Ethan Allen?" Hannah asked. "Now, *there* would be a Fourth of July speaker!"

But Ephraim frowned and shook his head. "No, I think not— not to commemorate the War for Independence, even if he were yet alive. Ira and many of the others still live, I believe, and engage in their speculative pursuits, but the Allen brothers, by and large, are a greedy, blasphemous, anti-trinitarian lot, and they would not be welcome in godly company. Their cousin Thomas, though, has much to recommend him as a discourser on such an occasion."

Ephraim sighed and was silent, staring off through the glories of the recent war. "But *such* a man was Ethan—some say he could pick up two strong men and butt their heads together. And the diverse ways he found to make sport of the enemy . . . Though Father says," Ephraim went on, rousing himself, "that if the New Hampshire grants had not funneled money into his pockets, he would have been quick to sell the entire cause of independence to the British. Such a man was Ethan Allen."

Honora, the older of the two little girls, looked solemnly up at Ephraim. "Will Aunt Ward weep at the reading of names as she did last year?"

Ephraim smiled. "Perhaps she will, little one. The loss of life, as well as hardship suffered, touched many to whom she was very close. Her own dear brother was slain in the conflict at Crown Point, and she may very well weep. Will you carry your best handkerchief to lend her?"

During this interchange, Chastity had drifted closer to Ephraim, and her whole demeanor quickly changed from dull to coy, setting Hannah on her heels.

Whoa! This girl is one smart little fox! Hannah thought. But even as she absorbed what was going on and began her own move, Chastity faded back to gray apathy and glided off toward the cabin with only a sideways look at Hannah.

Hannah stared after her, dumbfounded. Ephraim dismissed the little girls, and when he started the oxen moving once again with "Gee up, Buck. Bright, gee up!" she jumped, not wanting to miss a step of the torpid procession to the clearing. But until a turn of the lane obscured the cabin, she kept a sharp eye on the shadowy figure near the door.

Hannah had settled for a sort of coexistence with the time issue, accepting but not understanding the anomaly. So while she continued to chew through the philosophical implications of an impossible time reversal, her practical goals in relation to Ephraim changed very little. In order of priority, they were: first, to talk alone with Ephraim for as long as possible—that usually meant a three-quarter-hour lunch break—and thus gradually move physically closer to him; second, to help him in whatever small ways she could without being a hindrance or nuisance; and third, to continue learning from him—Catechism, lifestyle, whatever—as a means of identifying with and entering into his long-ago world. She had been faithful in her memorization, writing the Catechism questions and answers in a small notebook. Despite herself, she began to probe for deeper understanding of the precepts. Her mind could not content itself with simply parroting words, and she kept after Ephraim to explain the antique, convoluted phraseology.

That same day, indirectly through her second-priority efforts to be helpful, Hannah had her first meeting with Abigail. Hannah found that by offering to haul brush for Ephraim, she could usually double her time with him. Having been indentured to her father for so many years, she knew all about logging slash. So without a thought for her bad back, she dragged limbs as Ephraim chopped, piling them for later torching. An unfortunate move while her arms were full, however, made a large three-corner tear in her windbreaker.

"Oh, beep. I caught it on that prickly spruce over there. Well, this old thing is history anyway. I've been wanting to get one that would match my . . . that would . . . uh . . . that was a different color," she stammered.

Ephraim studied it. "I believe my mother could emend that."

"Oh, it's all right. I can buy another. She's got enough to do without making up for a klutz."

He looked shocked. "Another one? You would discard a

garment with so much fine fabric remaining? I will finish pulling this stump, and then we shall take the cloak to her." Silencing her protests with a wave of his hand, he chopped the last two roots holding the stump and hauled it to the stack. Then with a long pole he levered two sizable logs onto the pile. After securing the remaining firewood sticks, he hooked the chain behind the oxen. "Come along now. We shall see how clever a mother I have. Gee up, Buck, Bright!"

Hannah had been a little afraid to meet this supermother. But when the stout plank door opened to them, the girl was completely disarmed by the warm welcome and acceptance offered by the small, somewhat dumpy woman wearing, of all things, short sleeves. Abigail Ward was indeed owner of the blue eyes handed down to her son, as well as the wavy hair. Otherwise, she was in no way attractive except for a beauty of spirit that had been clarified in the furnace of hard work and sorrow.

A large stone fireplace dominated one end of the cabin, its cooking pots and utensils completely undoing Hannah's fuzzy notion of black woodstove and oven for cooking and baking. With only flint, steel, and tinder for matches, the fire had to be kept alive twenty-four hours a day, even on the hottest days of summer. *And my mother complains about not having a microwave up here!* Hannah reflected.

Pegs over the fireplace held the flintlock, and on the mantel itself were assorted utensils, a candle box, and an old clock.

A kitchen arrangement on the back wall included a soapstone sink adjoining a work table, a butter churn, and open shelves for dishes and food containers. Next to these, a door led to the woodshed and a multi-purpose workroom. A continuous trickle of spring water flowed to a small barrel near the door and down through a sunken stone-lined pit that supplemented the spring-house for keeping food cool. From there, another trough led it away from the house, past the garden, and under the road to the little pond where Abigail soaked her flax for making linen.

A narrow trestle table with benches took up the middle of the kitchen area. In the remaining living space were two rough beds, several slat-backed chairs, a large and a small spinning wheel for wool and flax, a small loom, and assorted work projects. A corner cupboard held their small store of unmatched dishware, and a bookshelf along the front wall boasted a scant thirty volumes.

Over the sleeping area hung a loft. *Probably where Ephraim sleeps,* Hannah decided. A vertical row of pegs behind the door served as an access ladder, and clothing hung from another row of pegs up near the ceiling. Rugs, both rag and braided, gave warmth to the smooth-hewn puncheon floor. In addition, fresh flowers and pictures on the walls reflected yet another kind of beauty within this unusual woman.

Several things surprised Hannah about the cabin. She knew it was small from the outside, but it appeared even more cramped inside. How could they all live in such limited space? The Valdegar cabin seemed a mansion by comparison. And how did the Lathams—eight of them—manage in their little shanty?

Then, too, Hannah wasn't used to such casual acceptance of dirt as a way of life. Abigail's clothing wasn't as dingy as that of the Latham women (excepting Chastity), but even with a few touches of elegance adorning the cabin interior (an old clock on the mantel and a highly polished chest near the larger bed), a good amount of squalor still remained.

Off in a corner on a heap of blankets sat a small boy—much too small for eight—arms and legs twisted and seemingly useless except for very clumsy, awkward manipulation. At sight of Ephraim, he began yipping and chirping and scrabbling about until the older lad swooped down on him, lifting him high above his head.

"Ah, little grasshopper!" Ephraim teased. "You think I have brought you wild strawberries or perhaps a leaf of the wintergreen to chew upon, but today I have brought you nothing—nothing at all!"

"Yes, you have! Yes, you have!" He squealed all the more as his excitement grew.

"I fear if I neglected to bring you something, you would abandon your love for me! You care not for me, only the trinkets I bring."

"Yes, that is so." The boy pretended to pout. "And since you in turn have brought me nothing, we shall both suffer privation." But he could restrain his laughter no longer and hugged Ephraim tightly as they whirled around the room.

"If you choke me to death, I shall in no wise be able to fetch your present." Ephraim set the boy back on the blankets and drew out of his pocket a flat silvery rock with reddish lumps like chicken pox.

"Garnets!" Jonah shouted. "You found some garnets! Large ones, too!"

"Yes, and I expect that by tomorrow you will have them all disengaged. I shall fetch a mallet and chisel for your use."

The boy gave Ephraim a pleading look.

"No," Ephraim responded. "You may need to forego sleep all this night, but you can accomplish the task on this occasion without my assistance. Then we shall lay them away with the others and your accumulation of arrowheads. But now, Grasshopper, I have business with your mother and mine, and I pray to be excused."

While all this was going on, Abigail had drawn Hannah to the high-backed settle near the fire and poured for her a steaming cup, an herbal brew of unfamiliar flavor. But it tasted good on a cool day, and she sipped it appreciatively.

"Mother, Mistress Hannah has torn her coat whilst helping me in the wood. I told her you were only indifferently clever and could scarce mend anything, but she refused to believe me and insisted that I plead her cause anyway. And so she has dragged me here, all unwilling, to test my words."

Hannah felt her face go red and could hardly believe what she was hearing. These were lies like her brother Steve might fabricate, but not Ephraim. She had never heard him speak this way.

But were they lies? He had given Jonah the same sort of line, and Jonah had dished it right back with obvious love exchanged between the two. Could this be a way of showing affection to his mother, or even to her? If so, it was unlike anything Hannah had seen in her own family.

Abigail looked at the tear, admiring (without the least touch of envy) the fabric as a thing of beauty—fabric so different from the homespun worn by the two families. "Yes, I can indeed mend it, but will you not feel the chill on your way home?"

"No, I'll run home quick. I won't notice it at all. Are you sure it won't be too much work? I appreciate your willingness, and I thank you, but I don't want to be a bother."

"What bother is one more tear, child? It will be as a fly brushed away without notice."

The mending was finished the next day, and Abigail had somehow managed to pull everything together so that it lay flat and even, with just two thin lines showing. But they did show. On the way home Hannah decided to use it only as a work jacket. "Me? Wear a mended windbreaker to school? Not this kid!"

When she reached camp, Mike's parents and grandmother had arrived to spend the Fourth of July weekend with them. At first Hannah gloomily expected to be cast out of her room in favor of the company, but Ardyth pointed out the visitors' camping trailer. "Can you imagine taking an old lady like that—at least a hundred and ninety—*camping*? I'd want to have a heart-lung machine along!"

Grandmother Cramer sat on the porch in a chair padded with pillows, a tiny pink ball of fluff that seemed much closer to the other world than to this. Hannah made one or two attempts to be polite but got little more than blank mumbles.

While she was standing near the chair talking with Mike,

though, she felt the old lady's spidery hands examining her mended jacket. "Not for years and years have I seen such work — not for years and years! In the old days, women knew how t' mend things, but not today. Ain't nobody'll lift a finger t' darn a sock. Such fine work. I never thought I'd see such fine work again!"

A few days later, Ephraim handed Hannah the Pepsi can, still unopened. "Thank you for your kindness in bringing me this refreshment. 'Tis not the sort of drink for our kind of life, however. I fear it lacks the chill it had when first you brought it, but I have kept it with the milk lest it spoil."

Hannah's face fell. "I'd hoped you might try at least a little of it. I think you'd like it. It's not alcoholic or anything."

Ephraim shook his head. "No, again I thank you. I did reflect for several days on drinking it, but accepting such from you is not allowed. I doubt not that it is a most agreeable beverage, but in truth, I would as soon have a strong mug of beer."

chapter 9

*P*eter came for the long Fourth of July weekend, and he and Hannah roamed for hours, enjoying the woods and each other's company. Hannah did not relate her unaccountable experiences, but some striking similarities between her brother and Ephraim began to come clear to her. Not in looks, certainly, but in other more important ways.

That thought surprised Hannah. Up till now, she could not have conceived of anything more important than what a person looked like. At school, the girls talked about only one thing: appearance and its equivalent purchasing power. The amount of glitter on the wrapper determined one's total worth.

Peter had counterbalanced that outlook by simply being himself, a person of obvious worth in her eyes, despite his looks. As a matter of fact, she quite likely owed her virginity to this sense of loyalty; the particular boys who came knocking at her door were ones who made a game of Peter, and Hannah would have none of them.

No, Ephraim and Peter neither looked alike, nor were they equal in physical condition. But along with sharing the same age, they both had a deep respect for the natural order, both were gentle and kind, and both thought beyond the superficial to the important issues of life. Yes, she saw it now. Peter had been doing that all along, separating out the essence of life, but it had taken her acquaintance with Ephraim to bring it into focus.

Perhaps, though, this business with Ephraim wasn't real after all, just some out-of-the-belfry attempt of her mind to deal with her inner struggles.

"Peter, have I lost my marbles, do you think? Is my brain out to lunch?"

"What are you talking about?"

"Y' know, like crazy?"

He peered at her quizzically. "Why do you ask that?"

"Oh, I don't know. . . . I just wonder sometimes. But you haven't noticed anything . . . oh, forget it. The whole world's crazy, and maybe we're the only ones who are sane." She paused a moment. "Peter, do you believe in God?"

His eyebrows shot up in surprise, not sure if she was joking or not. Seeing her earnestness, he responded in kind. "Yes, I do." He waited.

"Do you believe that Jesus Christ is 'the eternal Son of God who offered Himself as a sacrifice to satisfy divine justice and reconcile us to God'?"

He looked at her narrowly. "That's quite a mouthful. Where—"

"Never mind where I got it. Do you believe it?" It wasn't likely she could hallucinate the Catechism into existence. Having never read it, she knew it had to have come from somewhere. She had even looked it up in the Gilly library to make sure it was real.

Peter leaned back, considering her question. Finally he sighed. "I don't know. I guess I've just never given much thought beyond the fact that God is. That's a pretty universal core belief, but everything going out from there splits in a thousand directions, and who knows who's right? Why don't you tell me what you believe, since you seem to be pretty conversant with something or other." He smiled.

Hannah shook her head, frowning. "I don't know . . . for sure . . . any more than you do. It's all so complicated . . . confusing. Yet in a way, it's simple and plain and almost too easy. If God does exist, and if there's such a thing as sin—and you'd better believe our family makes the charts on that one, everything from adultery to . . . what starts with Z? Zapping snakes and business competitors? Do you remember what happened to that little old lady when Daddy pulled off his big deal?"

Peter nodded grimly.

"She lost her shirt, and I guess there's been even worse. And if Jesus got rid of sin . . . Peter, it really works, too. I mean, it does make families different so they love each other. They help each other instead of fighting all the time."

Tears welled in her eyes as she recalled yesterday's scene over the unopened Pepsi. While Ephraim was getting it from the springhouse, Daniel came in with a few light words to Hannah and went over and kissed his wife. As Ephraim reentered, presumably drawing her attention away from the older couple, she saw Daniel whisper something in Abigail's ear that made her smile like a teenager, and she pushed him playfully, a secret closeness bringing sparkling joy to their toilsome lives. A little gesture, a brief moment of play, but it was light-years away from what Hannah knew, in spite of all the conveniences her family enjoyed. If believing the Catechism could do that . . . "Oh Peter, I just don't know!"

She debated about taking Peter to the clearing. Chances were it wouldn't show up, but then, Peter was not like their father. Maybe that would make a difference. But how would Peter react, and would it affect their relationship? Or Ephraim's relationship with her? She leaned first one way and then the other, unable to make up her mind. Finally, when they happened to be on the ridge, she suggested they wander toward the old cellar hole. Her heart beat fast as they neared the wall, especially since she couldn't put on her skirt without stirring up a swarm of questions.

But nothing happened. Hannah didn't know whether to be sorry or glad, but at least she knew a little more of the situation. She alone had access to Ephraim's time; yet once there, she could interact freely with others in addition to Ephraim. In reverse, though, Ephraim had access only to her. What would happen if he tried to enter her world? So far, he hadn't seemed a bit interested.

Peter noticed her uneasiness. "What's wrong? You look like you're about to give a speech in front of the President. What's up?"

She laughed nervously. "I'm sorry, Peter. It's nothing, nothing at all." She found herself relieved to be able to say it.

Other visitors stopped by during the weekend, people of influence, people who mattered in Valdegar circles. But instead of enjoying the company, Hannah resented the intrusion. Had these visits overlapped, they might have served some useful purpose in empire building. Who, though, other than Mike's grandmother, was around for the notables to impress?

First to come was Carleton Buford, publisher of *Ski Down,* the monthly bible of area skiers. He was a thundering bore, but his interest in the Valdegar store held more in the balance than just social status. His endorsement, or lack of it, could make or break them.

Not long after he left, Ziggy Baretski breezed in. Ziggy was the opposite of Buford in every way—bouncy, ebullient, a good mixer with people. He lacked the publisher's intellectual capacity, but as the owner-operator of the exciting new Buzzard Valley Ski Resort, he had put together a very successful package that more than compensated for its small size and relative remoteness. By emphasizing creative trails, the very latest in snowmaking equipment, and the ultimate in luxury accommodations, he catered to a select clientele that had become almost fanatically loyal.

He got along well with all the Valdegars and teased Hannah mercilessly, to her enormous delight. These ski greats, however, missed each other by less than an hour, and disappointment cast its pall over the entire family.

Leslie Strieken came on Monday to see Hannah, but even her visit was less than satisfying. The two girls had been close friends since sixth grade, and Hannah lived and moved in Leslie's shadow. Leslie was not a leader in any elected sense but was prime mover of all the currents and waves within the social stream of school.

She had arrived looking like an exotic specimen out of a giant's bug collection. Her latest fashion assemblage conformed to the strict code that all Darbury teens knew intuitively. Indeed, Leslie had helped shape that code. And to nourish the cause, she brought along a bagful of clothing items for Hannah to try on and drool over.

In turn, Hannah gave her an elaborate description of Ephraim, leaving out all reference to the circumstances. "He's definitely an older man, not some dumb high-school nerd. And you just wouldn't believe how strong he is! I timed him once. He can cut down a tree in less than two minutes. And those eyes . . . Leslie, you should just see his eyes!"

As Hannah's catechizer in matters of sex, Leslie responded predictably. "Have you been to bed with him?"

When Hannah tried to explain the situation without really saying anything, Leslie became annoyed. "Hannah, you're just not trying. You have to plot your moves, be totally in control. Why don't you take me to meet him, and I'll show you how to pull this off."

Leslie was about the last person Hannah wanted Ephraim to meet. She worried enough about Chastity. But it wasn't easy to explain the situation without offending her friend. "Well, I really wish I could, but he's not available right now. He's . . . uh . . . busy with his father and uncle, and how far would we get in that company?" She affected a knowing smirk, but without much enthusiasm.

"Well, if he's really as inspiring as you say, you'd find some way to parade the goods. Not available? Hah! He's probably a real dog!"

By the time Leslie left, Hannah had a headache and was glad to have the remaining hours of the weekend to spend with Peter.

After he left, she was really grouchy. At a time when she was coming to appreciate him more and more, she resented his having to go back to work, consigned to hell, as it were, away from the blessings and benefits of family life. Well, maybe his was the heaven, hers the hell. But they were apart, and Hannah was down.

Mike tried to cheer her. "Hey, Handsome Hanner, why the big pout? You still got the rest of us. Don't we make up for just one lil' ol' Peter? And didn't he say he'd be back in two or three weeks? Come on, Babes, get a little gas in your tank!" He swung her around in a crazy dance that made her laugh in spite of herself. "That's better. Just keep that smile, and Prince Michael will take you to a ball someday. C'mon, jump in the truck, and we'll buzz on downtown, full-tilt boogie, to pick up some lottery tickets. When you win the big bucks, we'll get you some clothes that'll make ol' Leslie look like a washer woman. I'll do ya one at the video arcade, too, while we're out makin' the town."

She liked Mike, his breezy humor, macho swagger, dark beard. She often wished that Ephraim would grow a beard, but he had told her that no man of gentility wore one.

Mike didn't have Jane and Ardyth's sophistication, though, and this was a major source of conflict among the three. His ability to charm and manipulate women, plus his contacts with the right people, had opened the gates of marriage, but the real Mike soon revealed just what they had let in. In the family business enterprises, he lacked Steve's sense of responsibility, and his whimseys often brought Tom's wrath upon his head. Still, he was cheery and affable, traits appreciated by Hannah in the war-torn family context.

When she wasn't with Ephraim, Hannah searched out the glen—lying on mossy slopes beneath soaring ledges, dangling her legs over waterfalls, or splashing in tiered pools. Here she sorted through her thoughts, trying to make sense out of the two worlds. As the glen was different from her life back in Darbury, so Ephraim's world was different from her own.

All that labor in his world rankled. Being a teenager, Hannah enjoyed her comforts, resisting any latent impulses toward work. Indeed, Ardyth and Steve (with parental support) were always on her for daydreaming. She was a good worker, though, when there was no choice or if it was her idea, but when she measured her output against the herculean tasks that Daniel, Abigail, and Ephraim faced every day, she seemed a lazy slouch. From morning to night: food, clothing, shelter, land, transportation, education, religion.

Then she thought of some things they didn't have to do, such as continual repair of machinery. Just that day the men had spent the entire morning replacing plugs and points in the dozer and fixing an oil leak. And last week Steve had driven seventy-five miles trying to locate an exhaust manifold for the old tractor. Even chainsaws required twenty minutes of sharpening every day, plus machine grinding every week. An ax might be slower, but it had no moving parts, and only a few minutes' honing put it in top working order. And even though horses and oxen required care, they were steady and dependable, not apt to burn up or tip over.

In addition, she compared the effort and money needed to maintain their respective lifestyles. The Valdegars owned a house and ski shop in Darbury, a tree farm and cabin in Gilly, a van, two small cars for Steve and Peter, Mike's pickup and motorbike, a tractor, bulldozer, and jeep at the farm, plus assorted lawnmowers, household appliances, and recreational equipment—all of which required service and maintenance.

Then there was clothing. Closets full and still not enough. Hannah had once totaled up the cost of just the clothes she was wearing—over three hundred dollars. Just how high was the price tag for the easy life?

By contrast, the Wards had a cabin, farm buildings and animals, a team and wagon, a span of oxen, assorted tools, and their hands and skill. Almost totally self-sufficient, they lived in enough comfort to feel contented and fulfilled. Sure, they probably wouldn't turn away extra hands to help with the work, or even a few conveniences like central heating, but their happiness did not depend on having them.

In comparison, the Valdegars lived in the gray murk of dissatisfaction, helpless as babes, dependent on others for everything from food to entertainment. Was an attack by Indians really worse than what happened in city subways and parks at night? Even here in the woods, the Valdegars had to secure their cabin and vehicles. The Wards probably didn't even own a lock.

What was important to each? Money and the things it could buy had always been the great god for Hannah and her family, although she had to admit that her father held some love for the outdoors or he would have chosen an easier way than tree farming to make money. The Wards sought only to "glorify God and enjoy Him forever."

True, they had a sharp eye out for anything sinful or carnal. Even as Ephraim waged a never-ending battle with the encroaching wilderness, so they were sternly united against the weeds of pride and self-indulgence. If Hannah had not wanted to be with Ephraim so badly, she would never have put up with such zealous moral vigilance.

Something else helped her put the two worlds in better perspective: she could see a marked difference between the state of Uncle Latham's property and that of the Wards, between the

Lathams' dour version of Christianity and the warm love shared by the Wards. The Wards were engaged with a wilderness of a different sort in their own little community; even the beautiful Chastity seemed a rank weed.

To complicate it further, wilderness itself meant something different in each world. For Ephraim it was a thing to be fought at all costs. For Hannah it had become a treasure to enjoy and appreciate: the glen versus a jungle of bulldozers and condominiums.

But how did God fit into the picture? "The redemption purchased by Christ" sounded so right and good when she was in Ephraim's world. But she didn't live there. She was a child of the twentieth century with its space exploration, science laboratories, and moral revolution that seemed to have punched irreparable holes in religion. Nevertheless, that same religion, holes and all, was punching its own leaks in her world system. Perhaps real life would boil down to the Catechism after all.

chapter 10

Abigail Ward, for all her warmth and hospitality, made Hannah nervous the first few times they were together. For one thing, her eyes—the same eyes that had once stared down a band of political goons—never missed a thing. Under their gaze Hannah felt utterly known and exposed. Whereas Ephraim seemed to accept Hannah's presence in his world with surprisingly little ado, Abigail inquired more closely into her family and ways—though only from a mother's concern. Even she did not seem to grasp the import of the two worlds. This particularized questioning put Hannah on her best behavior whenever she was at the cabin. It would not do to rouse suspicion inadvertently or to provoke Abigail. With one word she could bring the whole enterprise to an abrupt end. That Hannah could not adequately explain how or why she was there was quite bad enough.

Gradually, though, Abigail's genuineness put the girl at ease, and Hannah came to appreciate the critical role this remarkable woman played in holding the family together. Beyond just feeding and clothing everyone, she served as a living demonstration of the spiritual lessons that Daniel continually drummed into his sons. She was the virtue, the unifying factor that made it all work.

And that love and concern was reciprocated. Jonah adored her, Daniel found his peace and strength in her presence, and Ephraim often went out of his way to bring some special token of his affection to her.

One day Ephraim rode back from town on his horse Major with a large bundle perched behind the saddle.

"Mother!" he shouted as he dismounted. "Come view what I have brought you from Mrs. Amiel's garden! You have long desired to—" He stopped mid sentence as Abigail and Hannah came out the door. "Ah, Hannah! I did not expect that you would have arrived so soon! But in truth, the sun is nigh the noon hour. I am all contrition!" he said, grinning at the prospect of an immediate lunch break.

"Hannah, hold Major, if you would, whilst I unfasten my surprise."

She took the reins gingerly, then backed off to arm's length as the horse snorted vigorously, spraying her with green foam.

Ephraim gathered the sack and slid it to the ground with a yelp. He sucked his finger and straightened. "Now, Mother, I know you will say that it is not a propitious time to plant such as this, but I have taken great care in its removal, and with a hearty drink seventeen times a day, it should flourish despite its momentary vexation. And besides, Mrs. Amiel's son-in-law cares not for her flowers, and now that she is gone, will have them plowed under before the week is out. I'll wager this plant will suffer less from my hand than from his! Come now, Mother, and open the sack."

But as Abigail bent to the task, the boy put up a hand. "Stay one instant longer. The little one shall not be excluded from such an agreeable surprise. I shall go fetch him." Before Hannah could volunteer to get Jonah for him, Ephraim bounded into the cabin and returned with his gleeful brother.

"Now we are in readiness. You may commence again."

They stood in eager silence as Abigail worked the cloth from the mysterious plant, she too pricking a finger more than once.

"Such a rough welcome can betoken nothing other than a rose," she murmured with delight. The material finally came loose, revealing a number of flattened, bedraggled yellow blossoms on thorny canes that had been carefully curled for transport.

She straightened and clasped her hands in admiration. "Oh, son, you could not have purchased a happier token of your affection than this! Oft have I esteemed Mrs. Amiel's fine rose that bears flowers into July, yet I never thought to have it one day as my own! And you have done well in protecting the roots. She felt about with practiced hand. "Perhaps the plant shall require only sixteen drinks a day!"

They all laughed, feeling the warmth of shared love.

Jonah, confined to his corner most of the time, was content with his mother's company. But he had outside friends, as well, Hannah found out indirectly.

One warm, cloudy morning, Ephraim met Hannah at the clearing with no work equipment. Daniel and Abigail had been called to town, he told her, to care for a woman seriously ill. Dysentery was making the rounds, and this victim, having gone through a difficult childbirth, was weak to begin with. Jonah had a touch of it, too. His parents, not wanting to take him, had arranged for Ephraim to keep an eye on him while they were away. Ephraim, in turn, suggested that Hannah stay on, despite the cancellation of woods work. Perhaps she would watch Jonah while Ephraim repaired the fencing.

The staying on part suited Hannah fine, but she was not at all sure that she wanted to handle that kind of babysitting.

"What is dysentery, anyway?" she asked, immediately regretting her question.

Ephraim turned red and stammered a lot of nothing.

Hannah waved her hand. "Yah, yah, I know. It's just that we don't call it that, so I didn't understand what you meant." She laughed in embarrassment.

Ephraim became suddenly serious. "Such things are no cause for laughter. Many a babe lies buried—"

"I'm sorry," she interposed hastily. "I didn't mean it that way. Jonah's dysentery isn't too bad, is it?"

She watched anxiously until he smiled again.

"No, he is not direly ill, but it is time we saw to the lad. You will come help me, then?"

As the two walked to the cabin, Hannah felt more than a little apprehensive. She allowed Ephraim to lead the way indoors and timidly peeked around him at the sick child. Jonah lay on his little trundle bed, but aside from being abnormally passive, he seemed as cheerful and talkative as usual.

Jonah did not need to use the tin chamber pot at the moment, but Hannah noted that it had already seen service. When Ephraim left to work, she immediately looked around for something to cover it but could find nothing better than a towel, an arrangement that helped aesthetically but didn't mask the odor.

She hadn't thought to ask Ephraim about toilet paper. She wouldn't even know how to phrase the question. And what if Jonah had to throw up, too? While she paced nervously, pondering these weighty matters, the sound of shouting drew her to the door.

A queer waddly little man came scampering up the hill as though chased by a thousand monsters.

"Jonah! Jonah! I come t' play wit' 'ee! I come t' play! Jo-nah!" His crackled voice echoed the terror in his face.

Ephraim dropped the fencing rail he had been struggling to maneuver into place and bounded through the orchard and around the garden. So intent was the fellow on reaching the cabin that he didn't see Ephraim until he practically ran into him.

Petrified, the little man screamed and threw himself on the ground, his hands on his head. "Mercy! Mercy!" he cried, groveling in the dusty roadway.

"Stand up, Tobias!" Ephraim said sternly. "With such an apron of grime, you shall be as a stranger to Jonah!"

"Oh, Marster Ephraim, Marster Ephraim!" He quaked. "I be come t' play wit' Jonah!" He scrambled up and clung to Ephraim.

Ephraim disengaged Tobias' arms gently and set about brushing the dirt from his red face and clothing, much as a mother would her child. "Hush now, friend Tobias. Hush your roaring and tell me why you have made such haste to be with Jonah. You are quite out of breath, nearly as much as when you conquered me in the footrace on Independence Day. Do you remember your great victory, Tobias?" Even though Ephraim spoke soothingly, his eyes darted up and down the roadway and across the surrounding fields.

"Oh yes, I beat you, Marster Ephraim. I beat you! And you run faster 'n Caleb Thomas, you do!" Happiness rounded his lumpy face.

Hannah, standing at the cabin door, alternated between alarm and reassurance. Ephraim's manner was glacially calm, but his whole body communicated something quite different.

Suddenly, she stiffened. "Ephraim! Look down the road. No, way down, to the left. Men on horses!"

With no more than a glance in the direction she pointed, Ephraim put his arm around the little man and drew him toward the cabin. "Come now, 'tis time you turned your smile upon Jonah. He suffers today from a distemper, you know, and shall want some cheering. Mistress Hannah shall lead you to his bed."

After shepherding his charge through the door, he slipped quickly behind them and snatched the gun from over the mantel. With a hurried admonition to Hannah, "Keep all out of view!" he stepped outside and planted himself on the roadway, legs apart, gun barrel in his right hand and stock on the ground.

When the three riders saw him, they drew rein sharply and wheeled their lathered animals back and forth uncertainly.

It had all happened so fast that Hannah stood in shock at the window. But Tobias, oblivious to the unfolding drama, trotted over to Jonah's bed and greeted the boy with a moist kiss. "Me frien', me frien'. How you be, me frien'?" He patted the delighted boy and arranged the bed clothes, clucking happily.

Outside, Ephraim nodded in greeting but maintained his forbidding stance. The men, too, kept a sullen silence. It seemed to Hannah like a scene from a cheap western, except that even the bad guys would not have had such scruffy, moth-eaten horses. Nor had she ever seen an anti-hero quite so dirty and verminous. Each man held a stout rod, which, from the appearance of the wild-eyed mounts, had already seen service in speeding the assault on the hill.

Finally one of the men spoke. "Master Ephraim, we be lookin' fer Tobias the simpleton. He be here, ain't so?" The man eyed the gun nervously.

Before Ephraim had time to reply, another bawled the charge. "He set our barn ablaze, he did, an' we be come t' warm 'is hide!" He brandished his rod and added, "'Tis only just that you bring 'im out so's we shan't be needin' t' go in after 'im."

Ephraim remained motionless and flinty-eyed but nodded thoughtfully. "Ay, 'tis a serious matter to set fire to a barn. And if Tobias were a considerate man, as you or I, 'twould indeed be a matter for harsh censure. But Tobias considers naught but the agreeable picture made by flames and wots not the unlawfulness of his deed. However, when I do see him again, I shall acquaint him of his error and impress upon him the hazards of fire."

This was not what the men wanted to hear, and they scowled restlessly.

Ephraim continued undaunted as though chatting peaceably, neighbor to neighbor. "And when shall you be raising a new barn? Father and I shall attend, of course, and I believe we may find no less than twelve stout men of the church to assist us. Should you require logs, I have a supply already cut and want only another span or two of oxen to haul them to your land."

The end of the confrontation seemed anticlimactic. The opponents stared at each other, the men silently weighing their chances against the boy and gun and pondering his conciliatory gesture. Then, without another word, they swung their mounts around and beat them into a bone-jarring gallop back the way they had come.

When Hannah breathed again, the cheerful sounds of Tobias and Jonah began once more to filter into her consciousness. At the same time, an overpowering odor assaulted her nose, and she closed her eyes both, in dread of what lay behind her and in numb relief that Ephraim was still in one piece.

Reluctantly, she turned from the window to find that Tobias, without a break in his jovial nonstop commentary, had already serviced Jonah and was cleaning him up. After lifting the boy once again to his bed, the little man inspected the contents of the near-overflowing vessel and trotted out the back door to empty it in "the necessary."

Ephraim had followed the riders a short distance to see that they were indeed gone. Reassured, he returned to the cabin with a roguish grin and looked around for Tobias. "And where is our miscreant? Has he too taken flight in fear of my empty gun?" He replaced the weapon on its pegs, and Hannah's face lost another layer of tan.

"Empty?" Her voice faltered.

"Indeed. You saw that I had not time to prime it, but base designs are oft turned aside with naught but fraud and faith." He frowned and shook his head. "In truth, had any other than Tobias the simpleton burnt their tottering barn, the fellows would have considered themselves well served and thanked him fervently.

Tobias stumped through the back door.

"Ah, there you are!" Ephraim exclaimed. "Come now and stand before me to receive your just scolding. But first, return the chamber to Jonah, that he not be deprived of the weapons of his warfare."

While Ephraim delivered his stern but gentle reprimand, Hannah tried to assess the events of the last twenty minutes. On top of her being asked to deal with an unpleasant illness, a retarded person had exploded onto the scene and taken over her job with a competency and compassion she knew nothing of. And armed with little more than grit, Ephraim had endangered himself to protect such a one. This was the ultimate "Vushondio!" Such behavior was new to her. There were people who did these things, she knew, but for all the contact she had ever had with them, they might as well have been on another planet. The face-off outside was still producing aftershocks in her stomach, but in retrospect, it didn't hurt Ephraim's image one little bit. He had stood his ground magnificently in defense of a nobody. What might he be willing to do on her behalf?

chapter 11

How would Leslie handle Chastity? Hannah wondered one day. Then she laughed out loud at the play on words. Chastity, be it person or virtue, simply was not a matter of concern to Leslie, just as Tobias would be a nonperson to her.

Leslie's real concern, it seemed, was Hannah's virginity—a problem of principle. Leslie often expressed her incredulity that a girl blessed with the right looks and attitude could arrive at the ripe old age of seventeen and still be untouched by male hands.

How would Leslie handle Chastity? She would be straightforward and effective, albeit indirect, Hannah decided. Within fifteen minutes, Leslie would have analyzed Chastity and formulated a plan, all the while being sociable and cozy, to all appearances Chastity's best friend.

Behind the girl's back, though, Leslie would skillfully scrape and pare Chastity's reputation by mockery, mimicry, and malice. To other girls Chastity would be portrayed as an unscrupulous, double-dealing man chaser. To boys, Chastity would be painted as a dud, a waste of time, someone they'd never get past the front door with. Little by little, the girl would be isolated and ostracized, quarantined from spreading her nasty, self-serving germs to the rest of the social empire. She would be relegated to that shadowy purgatory reserved for outcasts, and for wimps and uglies like Thecla Turner, who happened to be both.

Yes, at school Leslie would dispatch Chastity easily and effectively.

Hannah, however, was up against unusual obstacles. For one thing, there were no other girls to use as a foil in the campaign. And Ephraim, the only boy, would not easily be influenced against a person so close, so familiar. Then, too, they were cousins or some mixed-up version of it. Although Ephraim obviously had eyes for Chastity's beauty, he didn't seem affected by either her advances or her designs.

Hannah would need to walk carefully indeed. Although she had not tested it, she felt sure that Ephraim would quickly come down on her if she showed hostility toward the girl. Hannah's position was precarious enough without making matters worse. Under the circumstances, the best she could do was appear friendly when she needed to, protect her self-interest when the three of them were together, and jab at Chastity when she could.

The girl presented a challenge in anyone's view. She came frequently to the clearing with a message or request from Aunt Latham and was alternately grouchy and moody, dazzling in her pure, unvarnished beauty, or distant, remote, strange. Occasionally she would cozy up to Ephraim for that effective split second that was her special aptitude; more often than not, however, she simply trudged up with her communication and, robotlike, trudged back again.

All the while, Hannah kept Leslie's system in mind, watching for some way to diminish Chastity in Ephraim's eyes. She thought she had it after one strange episode.

Chastity had been dispatched to the clearing at Aunt's behest, and this time, Ephraim felt he needed to respond right away. Uncle was in town, and one of the animals had somehow gotten caught in a fence. None of the women seemed to know what to do about it. The three went together down the lane toward the Latham cabin, Hannah keeping close to Ephraim and engaging his attention, while Chastity stayed off to the side, head down, feet dragging.

When they reached the house, Chastity sought Hannah's help with a project in the back yard. Hannah was surprised and thrown off balance.

"Well, I ... uh ... was going to give Ephraim a hand."

"No need," Ephraim interjected. "'Twill take only a moment's labor to release the cow." He jogged off toward the lower pasture, leaving Hannah in the midst of inner and outer disarray.

Evidently it was bed renewal time in the Latham household. Three rough wooden bedsteads had been hauled outdoors and disassembled. Pieces of canvaslike material lay soaking in what appeared to be one of the sugaring kettles. Chastity was emptying the mattress sacks of their powdery contents, and she handed one to Hannah.

"Shake it heartily, Mistress Hannah, and then we shall wash it. Honora and Felicity will later fill it with fresh straw."

Hannah took the linen sack gingerly, eyeing the color and wondering if it had started life with that shade of putrid brown or had arrived there after a whole year—more, perhaps—away from water. She kept it downwind and well away from her clothing as she shook, hoping that whatever was alive and at home in the contents would drift away from her on the breezes. She added it to the murky waters of the sugaring pot, and Chastity poked and stirred vigorously as though energy itself would purify the contents.

It was with rope tying, though, that Chastity needed help. "The cords must be taut, drawn with the strength of two. And then sometimes they part, or the knot gives way. And then I give way to tears."

She said it so matter-of-factly that Hannah, studying the tangle of rope that served as bedspring, almost missed the significance of the words. She looked up sharply, but the girl went on.

"We must needs replace several lengths, perhaps entwining two or more weak fibers to make a strong one. 'A threefold cord is not quickly broken.' These portions here," she said, pointing, "were added when Felicity leapt on the bed with too much spirit and fell through."

This new challenge of restringing a rope bed with homemade cordage kept Hannah at the task even after Ephraim returned from his cow rescue. The two girls grunted and laughed and tried not to be "overly vexed" when a knot wouldn't hold.

Working so close to Chastity, Hannah could not help but notice the other girl's red and rough hands. *Mine sometimes look like that in the winter, but this is July!* Chastity's fingers, though, were quick and agile with the twisted strands of fine spruce roots and the inner bark of what she called linden.

As the girls chatted, Chastity told Hannah about all the white things she owned—scarves, a ruffled chemise that her father didn't know about, several handkerchiefs. But she had a possession even more prized and heavily guarded, and when she spoke of it, she looked around, leaned toward Hannah, and dropped her voice.

"I have two white linen tableclothes," she whispered melodramatically. "But tell no one." Her eyes sparkled with conspiratorial triumph.

Hannah looked at her. "Big deal. Who wants tablecloths?"

Chastity's eyes widened and lost their spark. She stared at Hannah as though trying to fathom her slowness. She said nothing, though, and with another lightning shift began pumping Hannah with questions about her world—the design and manufacture of clothing and other things. "I remarked most particularly your fine shoes," she said, looking at her own bare feet, "and the gay flowers that bedeck your skirt." Hannah was flattered and perversely glad to find at least one person here who showed interest in something other than work and the Catechism. Perhaps this could be useful somehow down the line.

Like everyone else who had shown any curiosity at all, however, Chastity's questions revealed a narrow focus. Her inquiries centered mostly around transportation. What kind of conveyances had Hannah ridden in? How far could she travel in a day? How many coins were needed for the fare? She seemed uninterested in jetliners or trains and kept coming back to the kinds of travel she could understand.

"I once rode in a coach," Chastity said dreamily, hands still and eyes far away. Then her face clouded. She became flustered, quickly ripping broken strands from the last bed. "No, I . . . did not . . . ride a coach. I . . . desired . . . and perhaps someday . . ." She turned from the rope to attack the kettle and its contents with up-to-the-elbows vigor.

"I shall build a fire in a bit and scrub these with our strongest soap and then wash them again." Ordinary words, but said with such sudden, focused intensity that Hannah felt her scalp prickle.

The last bed remained bare and unstrung. Hannah stood a moment watching Chastity wrestle grimly with the heavy waterlogged bedding. Then for lack of anything better to do, she threaded new cordage into place as she had learned on the first two beds. "Okay, I think I have this ready to tie now," she said. "Do you want to give me a hand with it, and then I'll help you with the fire and hauling more water?"

Chastity neither replied nor looked up from her compulsive stirring.

Hannah shrugged. "Well, I can't do it alone, and I need to get back to the clearing. It's now or never, honey."

Again no reply.

Normally, such treatment would have upset Hannah, but as she walked back to rejoin Ephraim, she was more disturbed and puzzled than angry. Chastity had clearly been glad for Hannah's help and company. Twice she had expressed appreciation with

Scripture: "Two are better than one; because they have a good reward for their labour. For if they fall, the one will lift up his fellow: but woe to him that is alone when he falleth; for he hath not another to help him up."

But something was wrong with the girl, as though a spell rested upon her.

With that idea, Hannah thought she had hit on the perfect means of turning Ephraim against Chastity: the girl was a witch, complete with kettle and brew. With Ephraim's religious fervor and the historical witch-hunting context, Hannah had some excellent ammunition in her arsenal.

Before she even reached the clearing, however, she knew it wouldn't work. The Salem business, she was pretty sure, had happened a lot earlier, and public opinion had shifted away from knocking off witches. Still, the idea might be worth tucking into the back of her mind.

chapter 12

*F*or half of July, Tom, Steve, and Mike concentrated mostly on firewood, working up trees they had cut the previous year. This small army sallied forth each day, armed with a full panoply of hard hats and hearing protectors, steel-toed boots and coveralls, fortified against drought with an array of soft drinks and beer.

After assuaging the thirst of their assorted mechanical steeds and dispatching Ardyth to town for five-gallon refills, they roared off in stately procession to the current theater of war.

They aimed their initial chainsaw assault at tops and limbs of previously felled trees. Once those were subdued, the tanks came in to drag the stripped logs over rough skid trails to a yarding area on the logging road. There the ground troops took over, carving the sticks into sixteen- to twenty-inch pieces, the artillery deciding which ones needed further offensive action with the hydraulic wood splitter.

In the several pockets of resistance where for one reason or another the logs could not be hauled out, the three-man mop-up regiment sliced the wood on the spot and hauled it by hand either to the road or to the closest point a trailer could be positioned. In earlier days, this back-breaking work had been the lot of Buck

Privates Hannah, Peter, and Ardyth. They grew up and turned to other things, but Mike's arrival on the scene helped compensate for this loss of slave labor. His cheery refrain of "He ain't heavy, he's my blo-ockhead bro-oth-er!" eased the drudgery of heaving chunks of wood weighing up to a hundred pounds.

Although all three men handled the big machines with ease, Hannah's brother Steve was best at skidding sawlogs. Unlike firewood, the "pockets of resistance" in this case could not be dealt with by cutting and hauling by hand. Somehow those big eight- to sixteen-foot logs had to be pulled from where they had been cut to an open yarding area. Steve would maneuver either the tractor or dozer as close as possible, run out the winch cable to hook onto the choker chains of one, two, or three separate logs, and slowly winch his twitch around trees and stumps, drawing them off the ground at the rear of the skidding machine. Then with his special touch, he would begin the pull over rough and steep terrain to the safety of the log road.

Hannah had once watched with hands over her eyes as he skidded a huge yellow birch butt log up an incline, the tractor rearing and bucking the whole way. "Only Steve could've done that," her father boasted.

Shortly after that, however, they bought their dozer. It was safer on smooth ground but still not what they needed for rocky or stumpy areas.

Toward the end of the summer, they would begin knocking down trees for the following year, leaving them where they fell to dry over winter. All three enjoyed that part of the operation except when trees refused to come down. In theory, a good-sized notch on the fall side of the tree and an angled cut above it on the back side created just enough hinge to swing the tree in the desired direction. A few incantations on the part of the chopper would then bring the tree down with a mighty crash.

Or perhaps it wouldn't. Sometimes the tree remained tall and steadfast even when cut as far through as was safe without the butt doing something unpredictable. A wedge driven in the back cut or a jab with a long-handled, sharp-pointed log peavey sometimes helped tip it over, but the situation could get tense, especially if the tree fell backwards or if the chainsaw blade got jammed in the cut. If the tree started to fall but became hung up among neighboring tree branches, the men had to cut the trunk—four feet at a time—all the way down.

Hard hats were a must in such instances. The shrinking tree not only rapped their heads with branches, but its unpredictable line of fall often brought the top down upon them in arboreal blessing. Then there were dead branches, called "widow makers," loosened by saw vibrations, or what was even worse, the whole top breaking from a dead or partly rotted tree—all of which make insurance agents who underwrite the lives of loggers subject to heart palpitations.

Mike's accident came not from a dead limb or a tree poorly felled, but from a moment of carelessness. A chainsaw with its whirling circle of razor teeth just inches from the operator's hand has a way of inspiring respect in a first-time user. But months or years of familiarity lead to dangerous ruffles and flourishes—until that first nick of an arm or leg.

Hannah was preparing to visit Ephraim when Steven careened into the yard. "Where's Mom and Ardyth?" he shouted.

"They've gone into town. You told Ardyth you needed—"

"Yeah, I know. Grab towels and come with the van. Mike's cut himself."

"Oh, no! How bad!" But he was already back in the jeep. "Hey, wait!" she yelled after him. "Where is he?"

"Near the . . ." The rest of his sentence was lost to the unmuffled vehicle.

"Where?" Hannah repeatedly frantically.

"Just go down the south road, dingo," he yelled, "and holler if you can't find us. But hurry!"

Her trembling hands gathered all the towels on the shelf. What about bandage stuff? And shouldn't the towels be white? All they had were red, brown, and a few purples. Sheets maybe? *Oh, there isn't time! He may be bleeding to death!* She clutched the towels and ran to the car.

Steve waited at the end of the skidroad. "Better not try to drive up. Get in the jeep."

"What happened? Is he hurt bad?"

"I don't know. Hard to tell with all the blood. He was cutting up a big beech and got tangled in branches or had his foot in the wrong place—something. Anyway, the saw came down at a crazy angle and bounced off his leg in three or four places."

"Gross!"

Tom was kneeling beside Mike's leg when they drove up. Hannah, who was ready to hand the towels to her father, instead found herself mopping blood according to his instruction. *What a mess!* She shuddered. It was one thing to take a first-aid course and practice on people who don't bleed, but it was something else to handle the real thing! What if it wouldn't stop bleeding? *Jesus.* Where were the pressure points, and how long should you leave a tourniquet on? *Jesus, help me. You must know all about pressure points, and if you can make people in families love each other, you can sure stop a little bleeding!*

The actual hemorrhaging had slowed considerably, and once she got the wounds cleaned off, they could see the extent of his injury. The chainsaw had made five deep gashes on the inside of his leg, the lowest right through his boot. A final slice down by his foot had chewed the leather but only scratched his skin.

"Not too bad, Mike. Could be worse," Tom pronounced. "Doesn't seem to have hit bone anywhere, but they'll be able to tell at the hospital. Hannah, where's the van—down on the road? Go turn it around. We'll get Mike down there, and you can drive him over to the hospital. He'll be all right. Just keep an eye on his leg in case it starts bleeding again."

So Hannah found herself playing ambulance driver.

Two hours and nearly a hundred stitches later, they started back, making one stop at the drugstore to pick up pain pills. But a line at the prescription counter left Hannah reviewing corn pads, athlete's-foot remedies, and corrective arches.

In the same aisle a short dumpy woman also waited, preoccupied with the contents of assorted bags and purses. Despite the warm weather, she wore a soiled and sagging coat that rounded off her sloping shoulders, giving her the appearance of a toadstool just beginning to decay. She hummed a tuneless dirge and began muttering toward Hannah, all the while rummaging through her voluminous carryalls.

"So much you'll need. Pills jus' trouble a body, y' know."

Hannah started humming her own little tune and moved off to breath fresheners and dental floss. But the toadstool humped along behind her, and when one of the bags dropped and scattered its miscellany a distance of six tiles, Hannah could no longer ignore the nuisance. With a sigh, she waved off the old woman's disconcerted efforts and began helping her.

"What a clumsy fool I am! And you, busy waitin' for pills like me. You got worryments, or is one o' yer people sick?"

"My brother-in-law got cut by a chainsaw, and I'm getting some pain pills for him."

"Oh, a pity! Them chainsaws . . . ," she said, clucking. "You'll be needin' some things. Pills jus' trouble a body, y' know." She dug around in her other bags for something to solve this problem of inadequacy.

Hannah set the errant bag at the woman's feet.

"Thank you, dearie," she said. "Now you'll be needin' this . . . an' this . . ." Ignoring the girl's protests, she thrust into Hannah's hands a number of small items: assorted gauze bandages (wrapped and unwrapped), a tiny vial of antiseptic soap, and a slender, mother-of-pearl penknife. "Y' never know when you'll be needin' some o' these things. Jus' stick 'em in yer pocket. There's a good girl."

"Michael Cramer?"

Summoned at last by the prescription counter, Hannah stuffed her pockets with the woman's gifts, grateful for the chance to break away. She added the bottle of capsules to the collection and did an end run around the still-muttering toadstool.

"So much you'll be needin. Pills jus' trouble a body, y' know. . . ."

Despite the time she had already wasted, Hannah went next door and bought Mike an ice cream cone: his favorite flavor, pistachio.

chapter 13

*H*annah ran a good part of the way to the ledges and stopped just long enough to slip the skirt over her jeans, not bothering with the blouse. The jersey she wore was sleeveless, but it would have to do today.

"Oh, shoot!" she muttered, kicking the ledge in exasperation. "I've still got all that junk in my pocket, and Mike's pills!" Well, he could take aspirin till she got back. The delay had cost a good three hours. Ephraim might already have left the clearing, or he might not be there at all if he had gone with his folks and the Lathams to "attend to affairs of trade." Ephraim had told Hannah that he intended to stay home to work, but if they needed him, he would surely go, especially if Uncle was indisposed.

Hannah thought that unlikely with the prospect of a pleasurable outing before him. Uncle Latham's distempers and "scrofulous humors" seemed curiously geared to the heat of the day or the unpleasantness of the job at hand. They never seemed to interfere with going to town for church or business.

The truth of the matter—that Uncle was just plain lazy— never came out in so many words, but Hannah saw a marked difference between his property and the Wards', between his parasitical approach to work and the ceaseless labor of Daniel, Abigail, and Ephraim. Uncle cared little for long-range land productivity, and in a relatively short period of time, the wilderness had glided silently across the landscape, penetrating the very cracks of his cabin.

Hannah's haste, however, centered not so much on catching Ephraim as on a sort of inner exhilaration. First, she felt heartily glad that Ephraim did not have a chainsaw. A three-inch scar on her father's knee, to say nothing of horror stories passed around by assorted loggers, had long dramatized their danger for Hannah, but today's close look at Mike's gaping flesh drove home a lesson she would not soon forget.

Something else had happened, though, that she wanted to share with Ephraim. While waiting in the hospital for Mike to be sewn up, her mind replayed the whole scene, and she suddenly realized the momentousness of her panicky supplication. She had in those few seconds gone from using *Jesus,* the swear, to *Jesus,* the prayer.

At the realization, a soaring, overwhelming love had wrapped around her, melting all her pockets of resistance. A great adrenaline-like surge of joy poured through her now, giving wings to her feet. As she ran, the dappled sun-flecked leaves on the forest floor enveloped her in a kind of visual music.

But when she crossed the wall, a bolt of black lightning struck. Her mind had been so busy anticipating the joy on Ephraim's face and reveling in the new sense of moral superiority over her family, that for a moment she could not grasp the reality of what she saw before her. The horse Captain dozed in the shade, but Ephraim lay on the ground, helplessly pinned under the pile of logs. Hannah's heart stopped beating.

"Ephraim! *Ephraim!*"

He turned his head at the sound of her voice. At least he was alive and conscious. His eyes, dulled with pain, locked on her face with a kind of tortured relief.

"You did come. I feared—"

"Oh, Ephraim. I'm so sorry I'm late. My brother-in-law had an accident this morning, and I . . . oh, that doesn't matter. I've got to help you. Where's your father? Are they back yet?"

He shook his head. "I think not. I believe . . . only the girls . . ."

Only the girls. Could they give any aid? Or more to the point, would she get enough real help from them to warrant leaving Ephraim for ten minutes to run to the cabin and back? Chastity might be useful, provided she were not feeling strange. But Patience would only scold and pour out a torrent of conflicting advice. No, Hannah would be better served by her own wits.

Seeing his agony, she desperately wanted to hold his hand and wipe the dirt and perspiration from his face, but this was no time to take liberties.

Ephraim could hardly talk through his pain. "Please," he croaked, "some water."

Hannah ran to the cool hollow where he kept his small canteen-sized wooden keg and supported his head for the drink.

This can't be happening—not twice in one day! Was it some horrid, weird trick her mind was playing, doubling everything like this? Or was Mike's accident somehow to prepare her for this one?

Ephraim's right leg was pinned under the pile. Hannah tried lifting one of the logs, but they were terribly heavy. She might use his pole to lever them off, but what if they fell back or shifted the whole pile? Most ominous of all, one of the three logs directly on his leg was intertwined with the others in such a fashion that if anything shifted the wrong way, the butt end would roll down onto his head. Oh, for just one of her father's peaveys, that marvelous tool for moving logs! With it she could at least anchor one end of the log to keep it from rolling. But without it . . .

Ephraim licked his parched lips. "The horse, perhaps—"

Of course—Captain! Why hadn't she thought of that? But what did she know about horses? She had watched Ephraim, but not with a mind toward having to handle one herself. At least she had only one horse to deal with and not the team or the oxen.

"Ephraim, let me study it to see if it'll work."

"'Tis the only way. You must drag them off, no matter what."

"Yes, but I need to see how the pile is arranged. Can you bear it just a minute?" She squatted at the end of the pile, desperately trying to remember all the physics she had gossiped through in school. "Well, if I take out these, I think the ones on top will fall backwards, but—oh, Ephraim, it's so scary! I wish someone were here to help me!"

Maybe Hannah had been wrong not to go for the girls. She wanted to just sit and cry, but there was no time for that. She looked at the pile, then at the somnolent horse, then back at the pile again. "Well," she said, drawing a big breath, "I've got to try."

She had no trouble finding the choker chain to fasten around the first log, but her hands trembled so, she could hardly get the hook to grab. Now for the horse. He stood where he had been left, happy, with only deerflies to occupy his thoughts through this long interval.

"Whoa, Captain. Easy, boy!" Her panicky voice alone was enough to provoke a heart attack in the animal. Had he ever been talked to by such a scaredy cat? "Easy, boy!" She stood as close to the horse as she dared and picked up the reins.

The horse lifted his head and automatically gathered himself for whatever was next. His vacation was over.

Hannah, expecting headlong flight, pulled back sharply on the stiff reins. The horse tossed his head uncertainly. "Whoa! Easy, whoa! Oh, Ephraim, I'm terrible at this!"

"*Gee* is right, *haw* is left," he managed.

"Okay, let's try again. Gidd'ap, Captain!" She gingerly slapped the reins as she'd seen Ephraim do. She was surprised when the horse moved ahead normally. After a bit of maneuvering and circling, they managed to get properly positioned for the backing movement. Heart pounding and hands shaking, Hannah leaned down for the hook on the whiffletree bar at the end of the harness traces and straightened with a frightened-sounding "Back!"

The old horse had endured much over his lifetime, so he obeyed even these extraordinary proceedings, enabling Hannah to fasten the hook onto the chain. Captain gave her no further time, though, to worry or make a last check. Following the habit etched in his dull horse mind, he simply walked off with the log, nearly knocking Hannah off her feet.

So far, so good. After a couple more pulls, she gained confidence, shaken only when one of the logs on top of Ephraim was struck and he cried out. She continued on, heart in her mouth as each stick came from the pile. But then she could go no further without endangering his head.

What should she do next?

Again, she wished desperately for a peavey. It would be relatively simple to engage its large hinged hook underneath the log and roll it off. But she had only the ironwood pole— leverwood, Ephraim called it. It was better than nothing, but what if one of the logs slipped? *You thought Mike's leg looked bad,* Hannah told herself; *what would Ephraim's head look like?*

Her heart pounded. The remaining logs were heavy, and she had no way of knowing how they would react when moved. In this giant game of pick-up-sticks, the stakes were high, very high. There was no choice. She had to keep pulling them off.

"Pay attention, Hannah!"

She jumped and looked around, half expecting to see her father glaring at her. But there was only the horse drowsing, lower lip slack, tail swishing mechanically.

Pay attention? To what? What have I missed? Her eyes reviewed the tangle, but she'd have to know weights and fulcrums and— forget it. Her eyes flew to Ephraim. Was something going wrong there? His face looked gray, but otherwise he seemed okay. She gave him another drink.

As she knelt by him, flask in hand, it suddenly came to her. If his head were between two large logs, mightn't he be protected, even if the butt did come down? His leg, too. Getting something under the pile would be more difficult, but at least his leg wouldn't be crushed. But what could she use? All the short pieces of wood lying around were too small; the only things large enough were the logs she and Captain had dragged off.

Once again the horse, sighing in humble resignation, responded to her strange commands. And after a time of even trickier jockeying, Hannah put the finishing touches on a thick log stanchion along the sides of his head and splayed out as far along his body as she could move them.

"Now!" Again her heart pounded, and she checked everything through one last time. She heaved against the pole with all her might, and the first log lifted off beautifully. Standing a moment to catch her breath, she sent up quick thanks and started on log number two. But it slipped, bringing the butt crashing down over Ephraim's chest. Hannah screamed and Ephraim groaned. As she flew to him, he whispered, "I am all right. Please, my leg . . ."

The stanchion had done its protective job, but the shifting log had added more weight to his leg. She moved it off quickly and started on the last.

That one, for actual damage proved worst of all. Heavier than the others, it lifted part way and then slid sideways, the rough nub of a cut limb grinding into Ephraim's leg. He held his arm to his mouth, trying to stifle his cry, but his whole body vibrated in agony.

Yet Hannah could not stop now. With tears streaming down her face, she heaved with all her might and fell sobbing in exhaustion as the last log rolled safely out of the way.

She scrambled up quickly and knelt beside Ephraim. "I'm sorry I hurt you. I tried so hard not to!" She leaned over and cradled his head, not caring how forward he thought her to be. *Oh, please make the pain stop!*

His hand gripped hers convulsively, and for several minutes he alternately held his breath and released it until the searing pain began to subside.

[109]

"'Tis all right," he finally whispered. "'Twill be easier in a bit. Thank you. You performed . . . God gave you clarity of thought."

"Yes." She thought about that.

"Ephraim, I've got to get you to a hospital."

"Hospital?"

"Well, a doctor anyway."

He shook his head wanly. "No physicians hereabouts. My mother . . . one of the best healers in these parts . . . if I can get home. I'll try to—"

"No. Just lie still." She bit her lip, afraid to look at his leg. How else, though, could she decide what to do? It was twisted sideways, but just as she became convinced it was broken, he straightened it with another arm-stifled groan. On his upper thigh, blood had soaked through the cloth of his breeches, and a large tear near his knee showed lurid dirt-caked abrasions. To see his lower leg, however, she would need to get his boot off. How, though, without hurting him?

The penknife! Hannah remembered the toadstool lady in the drugstore with all her junk. "So much you'll be needin'. You'll see!" she had said. Right now that penknife was worth its weight in gold to her.

"Ephraim, I'll have to cut your boot to get it off. Is that all right?"

He nodded, and she moved out of his line of vision to scrabble under her skirt for the knife. Along with the knife, Hannah found Mike's pain pills.

"*Fantastic!* Oh, thank you, *thank you!*" As she drew a red-and-white cylinder out of the bottle, however, she was surprised by its weight—almost like that theoretical spoonful of an imploded star that would be heavier than the entire earth. She reached again for the water and tried to put the capsule in his mouth.

He turned away. "No, I must not. It is not allowed."

"What do you mean, not allowed? Of course it's allowed! It'll take the pain away. Now, just swallow it with water, but hurry up. It's breaking my arm."

He continued to shake his head. "Our Lord refused the vinegar and gall."

Hannah sat back impatiently. "What do vinegar and gall have to do with it? Is this like Pepsi and beards that aren't allowed? And just who won't allow it? Your parents or God? What do they know about Pepsi and pain pills, anyway?"

Ephraim licked his lips. "My mother will have an infusion of Simpler's Joy or some such."

"But she's not here, and you hurt now."

Ephraim lay silent, his eyes closed. "It will ease soon, I feel certain."

The weight driving Hannah's hand into the soft dirt compounded her irritation. "Ephraim, you're being just plain silly! I never saw such a baby in all my life. You'd think I was going to cut your leg off or something! Now quit making such a fuss, and take this." Again she heaved the capsule to his mouth and held the canteen ready.

Ephraim, stung by her attack on his courage, looked squarely at her, a mixture of doubt and pride challenging her exasperation. "It is not allowed," he repeated softly. Yet with all deliberateness, he took the pill and swallowed it, his eyes still locked into hers.

Hannah moved back in relief and shook the numbness from her hand. "Good. You wait. In just a few minutes you'll feel it begin to work, and then we can decide what to do with you."

As she operated on his boot, Hannah noticed for the first time that the sole had an unusual shape to it as though there were no right or left shoe. The contours of his foot had formed it into a right boot, but she felt sure it had started out as neutral.

Once split, the boot came off easily, and though the flesh beneath was angry and swollen, his leg didn't appear mangled. Dirt and woodchips had been ground into the abrasions, however, and her first-aid training gave her a clear idea of the scrubbing she would have to do, again with her pocket drug supply. First, though, she had to get him home. But how?

After fifteen minutes when his body had begun to relax, he again started talking about getting up. Hannah looked doubtful, but the only alternative was to wait until somebody came.

Her eye gleamed as it fell once again on the nearly catatonic Captain. It just might work. She helped Ephraim up, and he hopped to a large stone from which he struggled to the horse's back. In such manner they proceeded down the lane in a kind of ragtag triumph.

When they reached the Latham cabin, Felicity and Honora burst out of the cabin as usual, and when they saw Ephraim's leg, they set up a fearful screeching. This brought the two older girls to the door, and they joined the din with weeping, prayers, admonishments, and predictions of doom for them all. Hannah, with new-found authority, sent them all back indoors and felt supremely vindicated about not seeking their help earlier.

Daniel and Abigail did not arrive home until nearly five o'clock. By that time Hannah had scrubbed Ephraim's leg, wrapped it in clean cloths, and settled him comfortably on his parent's bed. As a final ministration, she left six more of the heavy capsules with instructions for their use, deciding that Mike would never miss them. This time Ephraim made no objection.

On the way home, Hannah was too tired to run, but she felt the same deep joy and peace as when she had come. She had called forth the best that was within her. It had not been enough, but what she offered had been accepted and augmented, and she achieved the impossible. Was this the meaning of grace?

Question 36: What are the benefits which in this life do accompany or flow from justification, adoption, and sanctification?

Answer: The benefits which in this life do accompany or flow from justification, adoption, and sanctification, are, assurance of God's love, peace of conscience, joy in the Holy Ghost, increase of grace, and perseverance therein to the end.

The late afternoon sun shone through the trees in broad, striated streamers. She spread her arms wide to embrace them, conscious only of the light, not seeing the slender dark threads mingled in.

chapter 14

Of the two, Mike was the better patient. He could not work, of course, and had to keep off his leg, so he spent the first couple of days indoors on a lounge chair, being a nuisance.

After that, the women rebelled. "Get him out of here!" Jane shrilled in exasperation. "I don't care where you dump him, just as long as it's *out!* If we had a decent house, it wouldn't be so bad, but with only one room to sit, and cook, and clean, and eat in . . . And he won't sit outside. Too hot, too cold, too many mosquitoes, too many deerflies . . . Oh, I'm sick to death of everything around here!"

So the men agreed to assume the burden, putting Mike to work sharpening and refueling saws. He felt fine and had used hardly any of the pain pills. To him, the whole incident was a big joke, an unexpected vacation that gave him opportunity to do a little "needlework" on the fabric of communal patience.

On the other plane, Ephraim took the enforced rest very hard. He worried about the extra burden on his father and regretted being unable to do things for his mother. Abigail tried to relieve that sore point by giving him bits of her work that could be done sitting down, but his dignity was offended, and he preferred to fret about the firewood that still "wanted cutting" in time to dry before winter, the new stock shed he had hoped to build, the cutting of brush around the buildings, and on and on.

After assessing the situation, Hannah came armed with an ax from home, one that was seldom used. Ephraim's was too awkward and unwieldy, and she wanted to help by getting in the daily stove wood for Abigail. She also hauled and stacked firewood Ephraim had already cut, gathered eggs, cleaned the chicken coop, and worked in the garden.

She rather liked weeding. It gave her a sense of actively joining the battle against the enemy of cultivation: the single-minded, fanatical hatred that nature directs toward a garden. The usual array of field-type weeds intruded, along with tree seedlings from the surrounding forest. In her mind, each one she pulled was the equivalent of chopping a tree at the pasture's edge.

All this work, however, brought on twinges of guilt about her bad back. Here she was toiling like a mule for virtual strangers and not lifting a finger at home other than doing a few dishes or running an occasional errand. But, she told herself, her efforts were more needed and appreciated here than there. If she started hauling wood for the men, she'd be locked into the job with no escape.

Ephraim had been mightily impressed by the "effective remedy for his pains" she had administered. Hannah was pleased, especially in view of his earlier rejection of it as not being allowed. This was the first thing she had successfully introduced from her world. She frowned, though, remembering the extraordinary weight of the capsule.

"Ephraim, did that first pill strike you as unusually heavy?"

"Ay, in truth it did!" He nodded vigorously. "It seemed as a rock in my belly. I considered it contrived so, however, as I reflected on the ease it offered."

"Were the others heavy, too?"

He shook his head, smiling. "No, indeed. They were but air. Do

your physicians ofttimes scruple honest weight with their remedies? The effectiveness was not trifling, though. I could all but
trace the gate of heaven after taking them!"

Humph! thought Hannah. *That's not what they felt like to me!
Maybe the old toadstool was right: pills—some, anyway—do trouble
a body.*

Ephraim was also quite taken with her ax—lighter, better steel,
the handle shaped for comfort and balance. She decided to leave it,
at least for a while, until he had a chance to try it himself.

In and around her work they had time to talk about her
"spiritual event."

"You have entered into a hope most glorious and animating!"
he exclaimed when she told him. "And Christ has procured not
only your salvation but mine as well—at least, that of my leg!"
His smile faded, though, in reflection. "While we continue as frail
creatures, we are liable to such hazards as these," he said, rubbing
his bandaged thigh, "and we can only recommend ourselves to the
God of mercy who alone can deliver us."

"Ephraim, I've been thinking a lot about what's happened. I
don't know if I can say it right, but I feel like God poured a big
bucket of love over me. But that's all. I can't wrap my mind
around the stuff I should believe. I know the Catechism pretty
well, but it just shows me how dumb I am. I don't even really
understand it. I know you've explained it a hundred times, but
right now it sort of all runs together into one thing: I love God
and He loves me. I don't even do what I should, like go to church.
I didn't know where to go. There's more than one church in town,
y' know. And I felt funny about what I'd say to my family. Am I
bad, Ephraim? Am I doing things all wrong?"

He smiled and shook his head, but he thought a moment before
speaking. "Attendance at services to worship, sing praises, and be
instructed is essential; but you hold the necessary perception of
what is truly important, namely, love for God. We must indeed
hold to right doctrine. No end of mischief can ensue if we do

otherwise. Many jarring opinions currently prevail, schemes which weaken the tempers and spirits of unstable souls. And we must likewise strive to live obediently, pursuing good works."

"Is it possible to do those things without the other? I mean, can you believe all the right things and go to church and do good deeds and still not love God very much?"

Ephraim looked sad, thoughtful. Then his eyes twinkled. "Question 42: 'What is the sum of the ten commandments?'"

Hannah laughed. "'The sum of the ten commandments is, to love the Lord our God, with all our heart, with all our soul, with all our strength, and with all our mind; and our neighbor as ourselves.' Yes, but—"

"You have a tolerable grasp of the central truth, that God is to be loved heartily and all else issues therefrom. Yes, one can live a life of outward compliance to all just requirements and still invite the disapprobation of God who knoweth the heart. I greatly fear that the love professed by some is but vanity, empty and insensible to the deeper aspects of the nature of God. You do well to love as you do."

Uncle Latham came frequently to perform his duty by Ephraim, reading prayers and sermons by respected divines. One discourse, however, he had marked out especially for Hannah, and he handed her the volume to read.

"Virtue has a great deal of *peculiar* happinefs . . . It is, for inftance, more *permanent* than any other happinefs."

"Wa-ait a minute! What's going on here? Are these f's or s's?"

"The pleafures of the vicious are *tranfient;* but virtue is a fpring of *conftant* pleafure and fatiffaction. The pleafures which attend the gratification of our appetites foon pall. They are gone for ever after the moment of gratification; and, when carried to excefs, they turn to pain and difguft."

Ephraim was trying unsuccessfully not to laugh. Uncle glowered at them both, launching into a lengthy lecture on the "ill deserts of heathenish levity, exciting disgust and inviting censure." He finished up with his usual exhortation for Ephraim to rest and take his time about getting back to work. "Almost," Hannah giggled when he left, "as if work is in the same category of sin as heathenish levity!"

Before Ephraim was up and about again, Hannah brought him a log peavey to help with his work. She expected him to reject it as an "idle toy" as he had everything else "not allowed" from her world, but her concern over his safety demanded that she at least offer it to him.

To her surprise, he showed great interest and listened closely while she extolled its virtues. In fact, his hands fairly shook in his desire to test it out, as well as the ax.

She also had come across one of Mike's crazy hats, and at a whim she brought that as well, visualizing how cute he'd look in it with his loose, wavy ponytail. In her mind's eye, the effect was "smashing," especially if he would consent to a beard.

Ephraim would have none of it, however, and tossed the hat aside to more closely examine the peavey.

Jonah, however, picked up the hat, and with the help of the murky little hand mirror he kept in his corner, set about exploiting its entertainment potential.

"I am Mr. Worldly Wiseman," he intoned in as deep a voice as he could make out of his squeaks, "of Carnal Policy, a very great town. There is not a more dangerous and troublesome way than that into which Evangelist hath directed thee. I see the dirt of the Slough of Despond is upon thee; but that slough is the beginning of sorrows that do attend those that go in that way." His imagination led from there to assorted residents of Vanity Fair, on to an eloquent portrayal of casting his world-tattered hat before the King and receiving the crown of life.

"Bravo!" Hannah and Ephraim clapped, and Jonah looked up in utter astonishment at having an audience.

"The little Grasshopper doth make a fine Pilgrim!" As soon as he said it, though, Ephraim bit his lip at the sudden distress in Jonah's face. Ephraim immediately set about fixing things. "What think you, Mistress Hannah, of such a child who has been loved as a Grasshopper for well beyond eight years, but who then reads a line in a book which turns him on his head?"

"What was that?" Hannah inquired.

"At the end of *Second Part of the Pilgrim,* Mr. Despondency was given a sign to cheer him, taken from Ecclesiastes chapter twelve, verse five: 'And the grasshopper shall be a burden.' But our little Grasshopper," he laughed, rolling off his parents' bed and swooping down on the boy, "doesn't know that he is far too featherish to be a burden. Love gives us the strength of lions!"

Ephraim growled and bit at the laughing, squealing child. "I see the dirt of the Slough of Despond upon thee, but it looks very much like a smear of thy mother's dye that thou hast been into. Go back to thy pageant, little Grasshopper." He shoved the hat back on the boy's head and pulled it down over his eyes.

Hannah sometimes ranged around the homestead just to find some little thing for Jonah, now that Ephraim was not able. She enjoyed looking at the familiar with an eye for what might please a youngster. A hermit thrush nest emptied by a skunk or a raccoon, a slice of mica, the banded feather of a hawk. She even came across a perfect porcupine quill that sent the boy into ecstasies.

"'Tis better by far than any Ephraim has brought me!" he crowed. "And the quills you discovered alongside demonstrate that it is indeed a hedgehog—or porcupine—as you say it."

She also enjoyed just wandering around and looking at scenery that was quite different from what she could see on her father's land. The hill above the upper pasture was the highest of any around, but because the very top was beyond the Valdegar boundary, Hannah had been up there only once before.

She puffed up the steep slope now, hoping for a glimpse of the town of Gilly. The hill lay in a series of nearly level plateaus, with rocky patches in between. Hannah halted at each to catch her breath, trying to remember what Peter had called the little pink flowers tucked among the rocks. *Herb something-or-other . . . Herb-Alpert? No, he's the trumpet player. Herb Rob-something . . . Robin? No, Robert—that's it—Herb-Robert.*

She was so caught up in flower naming that she might have missed something unusual, had not a restless porcupine decided to break up his long day's sleep and stretch his legs. When Hannah appeared, he forsook his hiding place among the rocks and hustled up the nearest tree.

"Just be glad Steve isn't here, Mr. Porcupine, or are you a hedgehog? Whatever you are, if Steve or Mike were here, or even Dad, you'd be dead! And if you know what's good for you, you'll stay out of our maple trees. If they catch you chomping on the bark, you'll find yourself headed full-tilt boogie toward hedgehog heaven!"

When she climbed toward the rock cave just vacated by the animal, she almost stepped on a wooden sap bucket, covered and turned on its side against the elements. Hannah looked around to see if the slope might be part of the Ward-Latham sugar bush, but the hilltop was mostly oak and hemlock.

"What's this doing way up here?" She kicked at the oddly shaped pail and then set it upright to examine it more closely.

Its classic trapezoidal design—wide bottom, narrow top, plus one long stave with a hole for carrying or hanging on the tree—made Hannah wonder for a moment if it had come straight out of the local tourist-trap gift shop. But no stain or lacquer brightened the staves that had weathered and shrunk in the summer heat. It was smaller than she expected, too, and would hold no more than a couple of gallons. "Wow! With only that much capacity, they must really have to hustle when the sap runs fast!"

An even bigger surprise awaited her under the round pluglike cover. Inside she found a piece of rough homespun wrapped protectively around a long garment of fine white linen.

Hannah held the mysterious dress at arm's length and then inspected it more closely. "This is weird!" Two pieces of fabric had been artfully joined by tiny, meticulous stitches into a loose, flowing robe, the design of which would have made even Leslie look twice.

Again Hannah glanced around for a clue to what it meant or who might have hidden it among the rocks. Not even the porcupine, though, remained on the scene to break the loneliness of the hilltop.

"Ephraim's mother sews like this, but why would she be hiding something up here? A Christmas present, maybe?" She shook her head. Abigail had far too much work on her hands for making such things, especially when she didn't have any daughters.

Daughters . . . ah, there was a clue! One of the Latham girls, perhaps. Patience, no, but Chastity . . . Yes, quite likely! In fact, Chastity had even told Hannah in dark, mysterious tones about her two white tablecloths.

Again she examined the garment. Yes, it could well have been made from tablecloths.

Circumstantial evidence began to pile in to support the hypothesis. Chastity loved white. She had been interested in Hannah's clothing and in Hannah's world. Maybe she had somehow found out about Hannah's clothing pail at the ledges and decided to hide one of her own.

Anger began to build. "I do not be*lieve* this! The little sneak! She's after Ephraim—no doubt about it. I've seen the way he looks at her. She'll get him up here on some pretext and head for one of those big wide oak trees over there, and then . . . Well, I can fix her wagon fast enough!"

She grabbed at the top of the robe to rip it apart, but her hands stopped midtension, frozen by two simultaneous thoughts. What if it were not Chastity's pail after all? And would she by this act destroy the "bucket of love" that God had poured over her so recently?

She remained immobile a moment longer, teetering on the edge of indecision, neither question enough in itself to pull her back. Finally, though, the strength of the double strand softened her face, and she carefully folded the dress in its homespun envelope and replaced it in the bucket.

The view toward Gilly from under the oak was not as good as she had hoped. Too many treetops stood in the way. On the back side of the hill in the opposite direction, though, a sheer, rubble-skirted drop-off made an excellent lookout with a view of Mount Rameau—minus its four radio towers, she noted. Also missing was one of the major highways she knew should have been off in that direction. In its place, a thin line wound through open pasture land. She shook her head in disbelief as she had after her first surprised glimpse of Ephraim's world. So many fields, so few trees!

But even that spectacular panorama could not erase the uneasiness she felt over the white dress in the sap bucket.

chapter 15

*H*annah and her brother Steve had never been on particularly amiable terms even during their younger years. Much more separated them than just the eight-year difference in their ages. Steve set himself above his siblings, especially the younger two, taking pride in his position in the pecking order, in his good looks and strength, and most particularly in his skill with machines. His swagger and bearing conveyed a general scorn that fell upon such disparate objects as Mike's gold neck chain and Hannah's method of doing dishes. Steve was a man! He knew how things should be.

Tom Valdegar viewed his son from a parental perspective. As heir apparent to Tom's life's work, Steve represented the sum of Tom's investment in his family. By and large, Steve had fulfilled his father's expectations. His interests lay in all the right areas, his mechanical gift met a particular need, and the two of them worked well together.

On the deficit side, Steve lacked the broad planning ability of a good manager. Tom sometimes wished Steve had some of Ardyth's talent along those lines and was less of an unimaginative plodder. But on the whole, Tom gloried in having at least one worthy son.

Hannah, though, saw much in Steve that riled her. She resented his continual carping over, of all things, the order in which she washed dishes. She despised him for boasting about his ability to hold liquor and then making a fool of himself in front of her friends. But above all other sins, a mean streak ran deep in his veins. Though he had kept it hidden fairly well from his parents, he had inflicted much misery on Peter over the years, compounding Hannah's anger account.

In her younger years, Hannah had often defended Peter with physical combat, which at best gained Steve's sadistic laughter, at worst some pain of her own. But she soon discovered her sharp, assertive tongue to be a more effective weapon against her dull-witted older brother, and she used it freely. So they had grown to a hostile standoff in which they largely ignored each other.

Now that Hannah's outlook on relationships was changing, however, this troubled her. In Ephraim's family, she had seen the fruit of interpersonal respect and love, even over the wide age and ability gap between brothers. Oh, how she wished she could bring some harmony to her homefront! She knew it would not be easy, but as one small step in Steve's direction, she began to wash the silverware first, instead of just before the pots and pans.

One day a moment of panic struck when Hannah neared the clearing. Before retrieving her skirt from her pail, she would often stand atop the ledge to look out at the opening just visible in the distance. This time, however, no opening appeared; she saw nothing but solid trees. Clutching her throat in dismay, she ran toward the wall. Still only unbroken woods. Her heart beating wildly, she turned—and saw Mike limping down the path toward her.

"Oh, Mike, you scared me!" She laughed, giving him a relieved hug.

"I just came to see who it is you're meetin' out here in the woods all by yourself."

"Well, you can see how many people are around, can't you?" She tried to appear nonchalant, but his teasing had shaken her.

"Prob'ly some Vahmont fellah wants t' invite you aout some toime to exercise some o' them paounds off jest a-lyin' under his patridge-in-a-poine tree." Mike affected an accent. "He'll have you so skwuz, betcha it'll take a yeeah—well, noine months, anaway—t'—"

"Oh, Mike, stop!" Hannah laughed. "There's nobody here and hasn't been. I just like to be by myself." *What a lame line!* "I . . . uh . . . like the ledges, and I sometimes sit and read." *A downright lie, unless you count Uncle Latham's "happineſs of virtue."* "And I . . . Oh, have you ever seen the cellar hole near here?"

Relieved by this convenient means of keeping uncomfortable questions at bay, she took him on a guided tour. To her surprise, they came upon the foundation, not on the slope where she expected, but up on the shoulder of the hill. *Am I mixed up again?* Then she remembered that neither cabin had a real cellar, only small root or storage cellars for barrels of applesauce and assorted vegetables. *This foundation must be from a later period. Ephraim's house, or one of his sons', perhaps?* she wondered wistfully. Right now, though, she couldn't handle the thought and put it from her mind.

Hannah tried to get rid of Mike, but it wasn't easy. First, he said he was bored at home just sharpening saws. Then he complained that his leg hurt too much to start back right away.

"Oh!" he exclaimed suddenly. "I forgot what I really wanted to tell you. A letter just came from Peter. He'll be here this afternoon. He decided to close at noon and come out for the weekend. So whadd'ya think of that?"

Hannah was ecstatic. She wavered between going back or staying, but she did want to check on Ephraim. After a bit of fancy dodging, she succeeded in sending Mike away. As she watched him limp toward home, she wondered what would happen if someone came along while she was weeding or tending the chickens in Ephraim's world.

Hannah found Ephraim up and hobbling around, playing with the peavey.

"Please be careful!" she pleaded. "I don't want to have to pull you from under another pile! Can't you wait till your leg has more strength?"

"In faith," he laughed, "your caution rings so like my mother's as to cause my eyes to wonder who it is that stands before me!"

Anxious to see Peter, she didn't stay long but hurried home for the long talk she hoped to have with him after supper.

By now, she had grown accustomed to the appearance or disappearance of the clearing according to her intentions. As soon as she set her face toward her own world, the trees closed in. An invisible line, however, seemed to lie somewhere between Uncle Latham's cabin and the clearing, for when she walked back from working in the garden or playing with Jonah, everything remained the same until she neared the edge of the opening. If she was with Ephraim and planned to stay a while, all remained normal. If she was indeed going home, the clearing never appeared, and she walked through slender birches to the gray, lichen-clad stone wall.

After supper Peter and Hannah went to the glen, mosquitoes easier to tolerate than family.

"As hard as it is to get along with them all, I think I understand Mom a little better now," Hannah reflected. "When you think of it, she's put up with an awful lot all these years, but still she comes and does what she has to. And who knows? Maybe a bucket of love will be dumped on her, and she'll change, too."

Peter looked at her, puzzled, and Hannah suddenly felt very glad that she had not responded to her anger by ripping Chastity's white dress.

She went on with her visionary dream of altered family life. "Maybe Mike and Ardyth—even Steve—will start thinking of ways to help her. I know I haven't contributed to corporate bliss a whole lot myself this summer, but I've ... been busy."

"Seems like you've done okay just keeping on top and not letting it get you down. What's happening on the God-front these days?"

"That's what I'm talking about!" Her eyes sparkled as she related her experience with Mike's accident. "And God helped me after that to do a very hard thing that I ... well, I can't tell you about right now. But it's funny—you know how Dad's always saying, 'Pay attention, Hannah!'? Well, he said that. I mean, I heard his voice saying it, and that's what helped me know what to do. I know it sounds funny, but that's what happened." She looked anxiously at Peter's face to see if he was laughing at her, but he was listening thoughtfully.

"Well, something's going on, that's for sure. By the way, before I forget, I brought you something. Remind me when we get back to the cabin. Whatever has happened to you seems real, I'll say that. But," he added, smiling, "I'm not ready yet to walk a sawdust trail!"

Hannah wriggled uncomfortably over a new line of thought. "There's something else ..." She hesitated, trying to give shape to what was basically illogical, even irrational. "Peter," she began uncertainly, "is it possible for time to change, for it to be now and another time all at the same time? Oh, what a geek!" She laughed self-consciously. "I guess I'm trying to ask if it's possible for a person to go backward and forward in time? I know that doesn't make sense either, but what do you think?" she asked, completely flustered.

Peter wanted to laugh but for her sake stowed the urge and considered the problem. "Well," he said finally, "if you had to choose one, I'd say you could probably go backward easier than forward. It's sort of like sound. When a jet goes over, you 'see' the sound in the sky way behind where the plane actually is, but you never see it ahead. It's my guess that—assuming, of course, that it was possible for this to actually happen—you could go back to something that has already occurred, but you wouldn't be allowed to go forward. The universe would crack apart from a gigantic cosmic boom or something. Maybe if everything began with a big bang, going forward would start the harvest before the world was ripe. Does that make sense?"

Hannah sat up. "Peter, why did you say just now that it *wouldn't be allowed?*"

"I dunno. I just did. Shouldn't I have?"

Hannah shook her head. "No, it's okay. Someone else said it recently, and I was just surprised, that's all."

When they were driven out by the night-shift mosquitoes, they returned to the house, and Peter pulled a new Bible from his bag for Hannah. "If you're going to read stuff, maybe this is the place to start."

"Oh, Peter! It's beautiful. Thank you," she said, giving him a big hug. She leafed through the Bible, glancing here and there. "Wow! No *thees* and *thous,* not even any f's for s's!"

chapter 16

*F*or several days, Hannah basked in her euphoria of good will. Each morning before going to see Ephraim and without the usual prompting, she washed the breakfast dishes and swept the entire cabin. She exercised extraordinary tolerance when her mother, instead of being appreciative, accused her of never being around when she could be useful. "You're always off on a spaceship somewhere, dreaming your life away."

Even when Tom and Steve made jokes—for Hannah's benefit—about Peter jump-starting a chainsaw, she contained her anger and said nothing.

Hannah read her new Bible eagerly but kept it under wraps, hiding it beneath her mattress while she was gone and smuggling it to the glen in a sweatshirt. It was a special treasure because Peter had given it to her and because it shed new light on the Catechism. She devoured it by the hour, taking in story and comfort but skipping temporarily over the harder parts. "I'll get Ephraim to help me with things like being holy and becoming like Christ in His death. He knows that kind of stuff, and he's got time, now that he has to take it easy."

Then she frowned. "*If* I can get his hands and mind off that darned ax and peavey! You'd think I'd given him a hydraulic tree cutter—something really high tech!"

Hannah's good will extended to Mike and Ardyth, as well, and they responded more benignly than the others.

"Hey, sugar," Mike hollered from the pickup as Hannah came back from the glen one evening, "who's the good fairy who put balsam needles in front of our tent? What was that for, to keep our b.o. from the rest of the camp?"

"Did you like it?" Hannah was pleased that they had noticed.

"Yeah. Smells great when you walk on it. How's about comin' along for ice cream? Ardyth's treatin' tonight."

"Can you wait till I put my sweatshirt in the house?"

"Just put it on. It's chilly."

"I'll only be a minute. Maybe I'll get a jacket."

She returned with a plausible substitute for the undercover sweatshirt, and the trio set off for town.

Both sun and thin-slivered moon set almost simultaneously, leaving behind the soft velour of a clear summer night. Rich black hills, silhouetted starkly against a yellow-green sky, groped down into the valleys as though to draw nourishment from the mist rising off the meadows. As the pickup wound back toward camp, the growing darkness arched over a tunnel of light fashioned by the headlights.

Hannah savored her black raspberry cone for as long as she could make it last. Her heart, wrapped in soft purple, also savored the effect of her new footing with her family and with Ephraim. Things looked good indeed. The love set forth in the Bible was different from anything she'd ever known, and while it had beauty in itself, it would surely usher in a new phase of relationship with Ephraim.

Haunting shadows still lurked over her like the miasma on the meadows. As yet there was no rational explanation of the two times, nor did she see how an eighteenth-century boyfriend could ultimately be incorporated into her life. Then, too, there was

Chastity. But even though July ended tonight, she had another whole month, plus Labor Day weekend, to work everything out. God would help her, even as He had with the log pile.

As the three of them headed into the cabin, Mike stopped abruptly. "Oh, shoot! I bet I left the TV out where we split birch this afternoon." He kicked the step in exasperation. "I wanted to watch 'Motorooter'!"

Ardyth sniffed. "Yeah, you snuck it out, and I couldn't watch anything—soaps, games, nothing! You know I don't like to miss—"

"Yeah. Roger and Ann and Tony and whose baby is whose, whose bed'll we sleep in tonight, and will the doctor fall for—"

Hannah broke in magnanimously. "Hey, it's all right. I'll go get it."

Ardyth glowered at her. "Oh, that's great! You'll go get it for Mike, but what good does that do me this afternoon when I needed it?"

Hannah swung around, a retort ready, then shut her mouth resolutely.

Mike's mocking laughter cut in. "What a dork! What will the can of beer I'm going to drink right now do for me five years ago? Maybe if you take sewing lessons this fall, that'd fix the big rip your pants you walked around with at Ziggy's ski lodge for a whole day last winter without knowing it."

"Ooh, I hate you!" She beat on him as he laughed his way into the cabin.

"Mike," Hannah called after him, "before you settle in, tell me where the TV is. Which woodpile?" She held the door open, but Ardyth yanked it out of her hand with a tirade about mosquitoes.

"Wait. I need a flashlight!" Hannah renewed the tug-of-war with the door.

Ardyth stalked off to join her mother on the couch.

"Why don't you take the truck?" Mike asked as he limped toward the refrigerator. "I'd drive you, but—"

[131]

"No, you should stay off your foot, and I need to walk off the ice cream. Hey, is this the good flashlight? It's not the one with the bad switch, is it?"

Her father looked up from a logging equipment catalog. "If it works, it's okay, dinglebrain. Even your favorite squash-head would know that."

With a grim set to her jaw, Hannah turned back to Mike, who was rummaging through leftovers for his beer. "Now, where exactly is the stack you left it by?" she asked.

Mike sat under the garish light of a propane lantern and twisted the tab from the can. "Okay, you bear left down the south road, right? When you get to the upper spur road, go right onto that a little ways, and the stack is over on the left, right? It's all white birch, so it shouldn't be hard to spot. The splitter's there, too. The TV is around behind the stack, and I hope to heaven the pile hasn't fallen over on it!" He made a face toward the living room crowd and winked at Hannah. "Y'all get back before ten o'clock, hear?" he sang in a mocking falsetto as she pushed through the door.

A long cricket chirped laboriously from the grass near where the vehicles were parked. Overhead, stars rained down brilliance on the little clearing, and Hannah regained the serenity that had been only slightly ruffled by the barbs.

Her little circle of light bobbed through the dark moonless night, smoothing the rough roadway. An owl huffed close by and was answered by a shrieked *hoo-aw* across the valley and a similar response from a more distant course of hills. A light breeze stirred the treetops and showered her with a gentle fragrance.

Oh, how beautiful! Hannah breathed in great drafts of night, lining her soul with its black velvet. *It works! It really works! I love them all in spite of what they do and say. Maybe someday they'll change, too, and I'll have a family just like Ephraim's.*

She stopped at a fork in the road. Which way had Mike said, left or right? She shined her light through the trees, trying to spot a stack of white birch, but shadows quickly swallowed the fragile beam. She moved uncertainly along the left track, carefully searching both sides.

The darkness seemed to be closing in, and she grew uneasy. *Help me find it, Jesus. Is this the road, or did he say to go right? Boy, the woods sure look different at night!*

She stopped and checked around one last time before heading back to the junction. As she turned, however, her foot caught an exposed root, and she fell flat. The flashlight went out. When she stood up again, it wouldn't go on, despite much earnest banging, twisting, and switch flipping.

"Hoo boy, what do I do now? Man, it's dark! I can't see a thing! Oh, well. I guess if I just follow the road, I'll get back somehow. Mike'll live without seeing his 'Motorooter.'"

But which way was back? Her fall had left her disoriented in the blackness. She groped along, trying to feel the lay of the road with her feet, but she tripped again, this time over a stump.

"Oh, no—I'm not even on the road! Where in the world am I?"

The darkness pressed heavily, a palpable weight upon her head and shoulders. When she raised her eyes to the lighter sky, though, the weight lifted temporarily. In this way she felt her way from one island of sky to the next.

"This is crazy! Why am I moving anywhere at all? I should just sit here and wait till Mike gets worried enough about his program to come looking for me. If I go too far, I'll miss him."

So she sat. Then a new set of fears began to clamor at her heart. This was a different kind of wilderness encroaching upon her. The night animals out there—coons, porcupines, foxes—what was to keep them from coming right up to her, now that she had no light? Even a mouse in the darkness ... She shuddered, her ears straining for the faintest sound, but there was only a more terrifying silence. Even the owls were still, presumably off hunting, and she fervently hoped they would carefully weigh her size against the easy pickings she offered.

She sighed nervously and looked around, then suddenly sat up straight. Off to her right, she saw what appeared to be pale splotches of light. "Is that the pile of birch?" she asked out loud.

She made her way carefully through the trees, drawn to the eerie spatter of light, until she nearly fell over a low flank of the sought-for woodpile.

"If it's birch, how come I didn't see this part of the stack? Maybe the moon doesn't hit over here." When she moved around the end, though, and passed her hand between the light and the theoretical moon, her spine tingled at the unbroken glow. She looked unbelievingly at the sky, then remembered the sliver she had seen set earlier. There was no moon now.

The light formed a random mosaic—some patches high, some low. Hannah felt a strange aversion to it. Finally, though, she squatted to touch a low spot and was surprised to find not a hunk of firewood, but the inside of a piece of bark. She investigated some of the other splotches. Those on the ground were upside-down bark; those on the pile were peeled logs.

It was the birch pile, all right, but what, or why, this strange infection?

Just then, two owls broke the silence with a wild screaming altercation almost directly overhead.

Hannah started. She lost her balance, tumbling forward into the scattered bark in front of the stack. Her cry mingled with the angry "wha-wha-wha" of the owls.

When she righted herself, though, and looked at her hands and arms, she screamed in terror. Specks and scratches of light glowed on her skin. She tried to brush it off, but it spread like a phosphorescent leprosy. In sheer panic, she jumped up and backed away, but the heavy darkness bound her tight to the blighted pile. She tried stomping on the light, but it only splashed onto her sneakers and wouldn't shake off. Screaming wildly at these unsuccessful attempts to rid her body of the contagious light, she hurled herself against the blackness and fell flat.

She lay with face buried in sawdust, sobbing, until an almost sacramental tranquility began its trembling visitation. It fluttered over her prostrate form like a dove, hovering just on the edge of her awareness, then settled with a peace that melted her rigidity, infused her with strength. She lay still for several minutes as the horror drained away like pus from a wound.

Sitting up, she looked again at the luminous display, this time with a sort of fascination. She reached out once more as though to touch it but drew back almost reverently and examined the remaining glow on her hands.

Finally, necessity drove her to her feet and set her thinking about how to get home. At least she was oriented now, or thought she was. The positioning of the pile and woodsplitter gave her the clue she needed to find the road.

She had lost the flashlight but didn't waste much time trying to locate it. "May the owls eat it for their midnight lunch," she invoked balefully.

She was about to shuffle blindly out of the little clearing when she remembered the television set. At first, she was inclined to leave that behind for the owls, too, but then a brilliant idea struck. The set was battery-operated. Why not use it as a flashlight?

She found the TV just where Mike had said, and its face glowed comfortingly in the surrounding blackness. The nine o'clock programs were just ending. She'd be late, but Mike would see most of his show.

She took one extra minute to shine her "flashlight" onto the glowing logs and bark. They looked like any other wood that had been cut and left lying on the ground for several months, decay setting in under the bark but the wood still sound. Why were these particular sticks glowing? Radiation out of decay, light out of death. She shivered and turned her spotlight toward camp.

Hannah returned to the cabin and described what she had seen.

[135]

Her father knew immediately what it was, having seen some as a boy. "Funny stuff, foxfire. You look at it in the daytime, and it's nothing but rot. Other wood that looks just like it won't glow even a little."

Hannah took everyone outside to look at her hands and arms, but not even a pinprick of light remained.

"What a liar!" Jane laughed harshly. "I'm too tired tonight for fantasyland. C'mon, Ardyth, I'll show you what's in that cosmetic kit that came today."

"Yeah." Ardyth yawned loudly. "Maybe Hannah could go into the makeup business—Foxfire Eyeshadow. It's just flaky enough to go with all her other screwy ideas."

The heavy night had lifted from Hannah, but so had the exhilaration that earlier cast such a rosy glow over her prospects. By means of the foxfire, something profound had happened within her that, as the Catechism said of baptism, "did signify and seal her engrafting into Christ." An exchange had taken place: instead of optimism she now saw only weakness—her own. But the heaviness had given way to strength, a cloak she didn't have the slightest idea how to wear.

That night when Hannah pulled her Bible from under the mattress, the words—even the hard parts—glowed and came alive like foxfire. Yet it didn't burn her heart in the same way the flecks had seemed to devour her skin. Radiation . . . light . . . death . . . decay. She finally had to close the book just to get her breath, and all night long the lump under her mattress gave off tiny warning blips that hooted like owls through her dreams.

chapter 17

*T*he next morning—the the first of August—Hannah's father announced at the breakfast table that they would begin logging the glen on Monday. "It's handy to the road, easy skidding, and there's big bucks in there. If the price of pine holds, we should net enough to start building a house. Are you listening, Jane? A house—a real one."

For the first time all summer, Jane's crabbed mask suffered ruin at the hands of a smile.

"So I don't want to hear one more bleeping word about bats or cupboards or johns or anything else," Tom went on. "You'll get your house, but the work has to come first."

Jane's face rearranged itself. "You said, 'start to build.' Does that mean you dig the foundation, lay a few timbers, and then run out of money? You're not planning to build a log cabin, are you? Because if you are—"

"Turn off your motor and listen for once. No, we're not building a log cabin, and no, we won't make enough to pay for the whole thing, especially if we hire out the construction. If Krechner mills the lumber for us, it won't cost a heck of a lot, but we'll still run short on money. We'll have to cough up a bundle just to get hooked into electricity. There's that whole hillside of gravel in the glen, though, especially over on the left, and once we get the trees out, I figure we can sell enough of that to—"

"You're going to log *where?*" Hannah banged out of her bedroom, clad only in underpants and a ski shop T-shirt. "Where did you say these house-building logs were coming from?"

"Hannah, go put some clothes on," her mother murmured automatically.

"Now, Jane, honey," Mike interposed, "don't go rushing the girl off. Sit down here by Mikey, Hannah, and have some homemade, fresh-out-of-the-oven, cold cereal. Mikey'll like that!"

But Hannah ignored them both, her eyes nailing her surprised father to his chair.

"Hannah, your mother's right. Go get dressed, and then we'll discuss it."

"We'll discuss it now, thank you, if I have to do it stark naked! That's *my* glen you're talking about, and there's no way I'll let you log that!"

"Now wait a minute, Miss High Hippopotamus! Whaddya mean, *your* glen? Since when have you been given controlling interest in that particular piece of real estate?"

"Well, if it comes to that, I figure I have a right to at least one-seventh of the property, or about forty-five acres. That glen couldn't be more than ten or fifteen—twenty at the most, and I'd gladly give up the rest of my forty-five in exchange for that!"

"You sure like top cream, don't you?" Tom retorted. "There's at least a hundred-thousand board feet over there without hardly lifting a finger to get it out. You've picked yourself a fine little plot to get rich on, while the rest of us—"

"I don't want to get rich. That's the whole point! That glen is more valuable just the way it is, but all you can see is dollar signs on every tree!"

Her father drew a deep breath, perplexed over such a reaction, especially from Hannah. Jane could be expected to find something wrong with the scheme, but Hannah hardly ever rocked the boat, even when things didn't please her. She had a healthy temper, especially in regard to Peter, but generally she went along with family activities, her griping relatively low-decibeled.

"Hannah," he said after a moment's pause, "we've all talked a long time about a decent house, and now we have a chance to—"

"I don't want a decent house, not at that price! You don't hear me complaining about the cabin. Why should I, who put up with it better than the whole lot of you, be punished by having logs come out of *my* glen? Aren't there enough logs on the other three hundred acres?"

"There you go again with *your* glen! It's not your glen, never has been. It's *our* property and has never been divided into yours or Steve's or anybody else's. We all do the work and all share in what comes off of it. It so happens that the logs there are concentrated and easy to get at, and we don't have time to pull out one log here and another there. You don't realize how hard it is to make skid trails. We'd have to make one for every two trees we took out. I'm sorry, Hannah, I know you like that spot, but we just have to log it, that's all. This is a tree farm, not a state park."

Tears streamed down Hannah's face. "You're sorry!" she screamed, kicking the table hard enough to slosh milk. "As long as you get money, you're sorry! After the house, you'll put a down payment on a skidder, buy a new sugar rig, put in a swimming pool. Why don't you cut down every tree on the property, and after you've sold the topsoil and gravel, you can mark it off into little square house lots!"

"That's enough!" Tom lunged toward his raging daughter, knocking over his chair. She kicked and swung at him as he manhandled her back into the bedroom and slammed the door behind her.

As he uprighted his chair, she opened the door for one final volley. "I'll tie myself to a tree! I'll lie down in front of the skidder!" she bellowed, slamming the door even harder.

After Hannah got dressed and left the house, sullen and without breakfast, she remained the topic of conversation until the men got ready to go to work. They were all so awed by her startling demonstration that its dampening effect on Tom's plan for building a house passed almost unnoticed.

Tom finally shoved back his chair. "I dunno, Mike. You might have the best chance at bringing her around. Maybe if you talk to her. Tell her she can have her choice of bedrooms, and with electricity, she'll have her own TV, stereo, whatever will sell her. Where do you suppose she went—to the glen to practice dying under a skidder?"

"Either there or over the ridge. I'll give it a try. You want me to go now?"

"Yeah. Steve and I'll finish cutting sugar wood on the cordwood saw. You can help stack it later."

Mike found Hannah mourning in the glen and stood watching her from behind a giant hemlock. Seated halfway up the needle-carpeted slope, she hugged her knees and stared out over the broken tumble of ancient moss-cloaked rock. The August trickle barely made a ripple on the tiered pools, and the only visibly moving elements in the tableau were water striders and dragonflies. High in a treetop a cicada endorsed the hot day with its long, strident crescendo.

Underneath, however, the moisture-breathing canopy gathered refrigerated air and hurled it down the sunless descent toward the warmed road from which Mike had just stepped. He breathed deeply of its coolness but at the same time shivered, and not just from cold. Perhaps it was the gloom or the dank smell. Or maybe some shadowy might dwelt here, protecting the glen from marauding loggers. He shivered again and moved toward Hannah.

"Say, ma'am. Are you Joannie Arc, gettin' ready for the stake?"

"Mike, go away."

"Is that any way to treat ol' buddy Mike? Here I've walked all these miles—could've come on my motorbike, but I didn't want to stir up a dust storm. Actually, I was gonna come on the dozer, but when I tried to start it, all I could get was 'boogity-boogity-boogity.' Couldn't get it to go 'RA-ARGHH!' just 'boogity, boogity.'"

"Mike, go away!"

"Aw, come on. Don't be such a grouch. Ol' Daddykins said you could choose your very own bedroom, and not be stuck with closet-attic-cellar-mop-and-broom-storage like it is now. And there will be—"

"I can't be*lieve* you're saying these things! I thought you were my friend, but you're going along with the charade just like the others! Mike, I don't want my own room. All I want is this glen. Is that so unreasonable? Look at it—the most beautiful spot on our whole property, even for miles around. People would pay money just to sit under these magnificent trees and listen to the winter wren and veery. It's a . . . a crime to destroy in a week what took centuries to grow. It's wrong to slice up a beautiful place like this!" Angry tears spilled once again.

Mike stood silent, watching her bent, graceful form, a new, surprised look in his eyes. He sat down and put his arm around her.

"Oh, Mike," she sobbed, "it's all so hateful! Why do they have to destroy everything beautiful just to get a little money out of it?"

He held her shaking body, stroking her hair. "Sh-h, sweetheart, it's all right. Money's not such a bad thing, y' know. It buys classy clothes like Leslie has, and lottery tickets that'll maybe fly you off to Hawaii or get you one of those cool sports jobs you've been hankerin' to drive around in. You can look at the glen till mud turns to chocolate ice cream, but all that bunch of beauty won't brighten your pocketbook by even one dusty little penny."

Hannah sat weeping quietly, not so much listening to what he was saying as soaking up sympathy.

Mike warmed to his task. "You're beautiful, too, y' know that?

[141]

You're not little kid sister anymore. How old are you now— seventeen? Seems like just last year you were nothin' but a pain in the butt, gettin' in the way of me 'n' Ardyth. You always did have a soft spot for ol' Mikey, didn't you? Chased me all over the lot. In those days, you had nothin' to show, nothin' to offer. Now, though, you got the goods, and I'm interested in makin' a purchase." His hand went from her head to her arm to her bare leg, and he kissed her forehead, all the while keeping up his gentle words.

Hannah's tears stopped and her body stiffened. "Michael Cramer, you lizard!" she shrieked, scrambling to her feet. "You stinking purple-nosed caterpillar!" She slapped his face as hard as she could.

If Leslie had been on hand to observe her pupil, she would have flunked Hannah on the spot. But Hannah felt a new and glorious victory in going against her friend's tutelage. Hannah could still see the surprised shock on Ephraim's face when she had first tried to touch him, and again on that awful day she had appeared in shorts and halter. Now his horror made perfect sense, protecting what was pure and good from the sort of bald proposition Mike was making. She knew that this type of offer was not unprecedented in her family. Steve had steadfastly resisted marriage, but he had his women. Even her father played around on occasion. But against the backdrop of Ephraim's world, Hannah saw such behavior as loathsome, repulsive, foul, monstrous.

It took only a few seconds for Mike to recover from the blow, turn livid, and strike her in retaliation. In his anger he lost all control, swearing as he knocked her around and ripped at her clothing. "You hit Mike once, and you don't do it again—ever! I wouldn't've hurt you if you'd been nice, but now you'll go down, like it or not!"

"Mike! Stop it! Stop!" she screamed, fighting, but not able to break away. "Jesus, help me, help me! Mike!"

Just then a loud crashing burst from the brush across the ravine.

Mike leaped away from Hannah, suddenly aware of how Tom might look upon his actions.

The noise was not his father-in-law, however, but an enormous ten-point buck driven from its midday resting place by the fight. After a few bounds, it turned from flight and stood motionless, watching the pair in a detached way as though responding to a call to act as referee. His eyes seemed capable of determining the outcome.

"Man! Would you look at that!" Mike's hunter instinct quickly overrode his unaccustomed anger. "What a sight! He must be granddaddy of 'em all! And me without a gun! You can walk around here all day, all night during huntin' season and never see a thing. But now with him so close and not movin', what a shot! And here I am without a gun!"

"Ohh—you *insect!*" Hannah's fury obliterated all fear. "Bad enough that you want to push me around, but you have to ravish and kill everything else, too—the trees, the ravine, the snake, and now the deer—*just because it's there.*" Her voice shook under the intensity of her wrath. "You wouldn't get anything from killing that deer. You don't even like venison—I heard you say so! Just kill and destroy for sheer fun! Go ahead—rape me if you want. What difference does it make? I'd let you if it would save the glen, but nothing can, *nothing!*"

She turned and ran up the hill, her agonized shrieks echoing among the dark sentinels.

Mike stood a moment watching her disappearing form. Then he turned slowly toward the heat of the road, half afraid still that Tom might step out from behind a tree.

The day dragged endlessly as Mike waited for the second shoe to drop. At first he didn't know what to do, whether to go back to work as if nothing had happened or to pack up and run. He knew Tom well enough to write the script of his father-in-law's wrath if and when Hannah told her story. He worked out a story of his own, but Hannah had the advantage of being a Valdegar, whereas his position in the family was shaky at best. To run would be a clear admission of guilt and would cut him off from hearth and livelihood, no further questions asked, unless, of course, the family's own hanky-panky were to give Tom a cooler perspective.

Once Mike decided to stay, the next hurdle was to try to carry on as usual, provided Hannah had not gone straight to her father. He approached the tractor-powered cordwood saw with considerable trepidation, especially jumpy when Tom saw him and stopped the machine.

"How'd it go? You get anywhere?" Tom asked.

"Naw." He could breathe again. She hadn't squealed yet. "No, she's upset. Prob'ly best not to say anything to her for a while. What do you want me to do, take this load to the sugar house?"

Tom squinted at him. "You okay? You look like you just saw your great-grandmother's ghost."

Mike's heart thudded as he tried to put on his usual cocky smile. "I'm all right—just havin' cordwood withdrawal symptoms. Everything'll be fine once I start stackin' again." He sauntered casually to the jeep and backed it toward the trailer hitch. But a sharp smell of cold decay assailed him, to the point where he almost cried out and gave it all away.

Hannah, too, knew about her father's wrath, having lived with it far longer than had Mike. At first, she could hardly wait to add his fuel to her bonfire, but as her anger cooled, she began to weigh the consequences of telling him. She knew she had a case, but what would it do to Mike? Surprised at the question, she wondered if she would have considered it even two weeks ago or before last night's foxfire "baptism."

She began crying again as she reflected on the avalanche of events that had ripped her good feelings to shreds. That "bucket of love" wasn't protecting her from anger, hatred, vengefulness, or self-pity. Bad enough that her beloved glen was to be destroyed and that a person she liked so much and trusted had betrayed her. But on top of that, she had to do something with this volcano of emotion boiling within her.

Before her encounter with God, her fury would have blistered everyone within range. Things had changed, though; she was being squeezed between the tactics and the demands of a God who was somehow Love. God seemed to deal out the circumstances of life, but no longer could she just blow up over the unpleasant ones. She had to learn to operate under a whole new set of rules. At this moment, her specific task was to figure out the best course of action—not to benefit herself, but to benefit Mike.

Could she do that? Anger still smoldered within, fed by the pain in her body. It was not fair of God to place that burden, that choice upon her. Mike had wronged her, and she should have satisfaction. What would happen to him, though, if she claimed her rights?

Indignation and mercy sawed back and forth for the rest of the morning and most of the afternoon. It wouldn't be right to just let him get away with it, would it? God took such actions seriously; why shouldn't she? After all . . .

Finally, though, she felt once again the soothing balm of the Scripture Ephraim had poured over her shame at being "scantily clad": "The grace of our Lord was exceeding abundant. . . . For this cause I obtained mercy."

If Hannah were to turn Mike over to her father, she would be no better than the much-forgiven debtor she had read about in the Bible, who scalped the fellow owing only a couple of bucks. After all, Mike hadn't raped her. He just made a fast play, probably feeling sorry for her and wanting to get her mind off the glen. And then he got mad when she slapped him. Who wouldn't? But what if that deer hadn't come along?

Supper was a quiet, tense affair. Hannah sat with the family in restrained dignity. No one asked or even made mention of her several bruises and scratches, no one took notice of Mike's uneasy glances in her direction, and most particularly, no one said a single word about the glen or a new house.

Later that evening, though, as Hannah emerged from the outhouse on her way to bed, Mike spoke softly out of the darkness. "Hey, Babes, thanks for not rattin'. You're a cool kid, you know that? Pretendin' you were frosted but leavin' the door open for ol' Mikey to give you a good time, huh?" He started to put his arm around her, but she writhed out of his grasp as though he were some vile reptile.

"Don't touch me ever again!" she snapped. "My father is twenty-five yards away. If I holler, you're dead! Now get off my back and stay off!"

Mike shrugged and went on into the little shack. "Well, no harm askin'!"

chapter 18

The glen gained at least a week's reprieve when Tom and the boys went shopping for a skidder. Not a new one—that would have been out of the question. If they could find a used machine, though, subject to only one breakdown per week, they would consider their money well invested.

For fast, heavy-volume woods work, a skidder would compare with their tractor and dozer as a snowmobile to a team of sled dogs. It had high flexibility with its hinged midsection and independently suspended wheels that rode easily over stumps and rocks, plus greater safety with its cage and roll bars. They would all rest easier about that. Tom was glad that Jane had no interest in watching them work with their old equipment. She would have a rich supply of new horrors to feed her daily hand-wringing routine.

Hannah found out about the plans to buy a skidder quite by accident. When she stated her desire to go into Gilly to buy a new blouse, Ardyth gladly relinquished the care and feeding of the gas cans into her hands. As Hannah waited by the fuel pump for the cans to be filled, the name *Tom Valdegar* floated through a haze of cross conversations. She sat up and looked into the side-view mirror. A burly bison of a man with a lump in his cheek seemed to be asking directions to the Valdegar camp. The station attendant scratched his head, trying to pull together what sketchy local geography he knew.

Hannah opened the pickup door and jumped down. "Hi. I'm Hannah Valdegar. You're looking for my father?"

The man examined her, not one to toss off words without careful consideration. He turned and fired a stream of brown juice at the base of the island. "Ayup. You know where he lives?"

"Guess maybe I do." She smiled. "What do you want to see him about?" She was suspicious of strangers, of demands they might put upon the men and indirectly upon her.

Again he weighed his words. "Wal, he's lookin' fer a skiddah, an' I'm lookin' t' git rid o' one. Thought we moight git t'gether an' talk bizness."

So her father was going to get a skidder out of the glen proceeds. Hannah's anger rose, and she was tempted to vent it on this logger who loomed phlegmatically before her. Then she almost giggled out loud, remembering a private joke she and Peter had over "Robut," a tobacco-chewing dozer operator who had done some work for them. That man was similarly buffalo-chested and hard as nails, a dozer among men, towering over everyone both in size and skill. Even Steve had marveled. "The guy can practically ice a cake with that thing!" he exclaimed.

Peter had stayed well away from Robert, though the man gave no cause for fear. Afterward, however, when the two children were alone, Peter swaggered up to an imaginary dozer operator and announced in as deep a tone as his changing voice could produce, "Robut, if you spit on m' shoe, I'm gonna have t' hit ya." Then they both laughed hysterically at the incongruity of Peter standing up to such a titan.

Remembering that laughter of years ago defused Hannah's anger now, and she grudgingly gave directions to their place.

"Not loikely I'll make it up theyah roight naow, though. I got a caow about t' freshen, an' I need t' git on home t' hold 'er hand. Her fust one, an' they take a lotta hand holdin'. Y' git t' thinkin' it's gonna be at least a yeeah before it comes aout, an' then it's right theyah, no toime 't all." He grinned at Hannah. "Caows an' wimmin are a lot aloike." With another juicy shot at the gas pump, he turned and climbed into his truck.

Hannah shook her head, wished him well with his cow, and went on to the little dress shop on the village green. She had not visited Ephraim for several days, but before she went again, she wanted a different blouse, one that was loose and frumpy and not apt to stir unwanted fervor. Trying on one over which she would normally have exclaimed, "Me wear that?" she surveyed the effect with grim satisfaction. She even tried pulling her hair back in a stubby ponytail, but it didn't make any appreciable difference.

She wished her hair would grow out quickly so she could do it up in a neck knot or something equally ugly. Perhaps good looks were in fact a handicap and the Thecla Turners of the world were, after all, the lucky ones. Because of their unattractiveness, Thecla, and Peter as well, were automatically protected from the temptations and power struggles that go along with being beautiful. They had been forced to develop a dimension of beauty that would serve them the rest of their lives, rather than betray them in the end. Hannah, Ardyth, and even Chastity were definitely among the deprived on that score. Most fortunate of all were the Tobiases of the world, happy in themselves, caring not a whit what the world thought of them.

Hannah kept asking herself a bothersome question: Suppose it had been Ephraim who had made the play for her, and not Mike; would she have been so upset? She thought back to her daydreams of the ways Ephraim might come to her.

Perhaps on an especially hot day, he would lead her to the cool grove of young pines just up the hill. She would lie back on the scented carpet, and he would sprinkle needles over her face and neck, then laugh and blow them off, getting closer and closer. . . .

[149]

Or maybe it would come after she had said something extremely funny—the perfect putdown of Chastity, perhaps. In spite of himself, he'd give her an appreciative hug. Then the laughter in his vibrant eyes would turn into the glow of love, and his tentative, tremorous kiss on her ready lips would be the right response to the catalytic joke. . . .

Or after she had hauled brush, his gentle hand wiping off grimy perspiration . . .

There hadn't been much recent fantasizing, though. She'd been too busy processing accidents and Mike's treachery to think specifically about her longing for Ephraim. Now the imminent execution of the glen had put everything else out of her mind.

Just how much was the doomed glen tied up with her reaction to Mike's attempted seduction? The two were so close in her mind that to think of one was to dredge up the other.

One thing was clear, though. Her designs on Ephraim had been wrong, patterned after the cheap sexual currency on exchange in Darbury High. She had not simply been trying on the relationship in preparation for marriage, even if that were a real option under the circumstances. No, at first she had gone after him with conquest in mind, to win him away from his religious straitjacket, to prove that oddball Hannah could land her prize.

It had taken Mike to bring her up short, to make her see the stark, pitiable ugliness of her schemes. Ephraim's puritanical attitude toward sex kept the field clear of weeds so the crop could grow toward the unselfish love that Daniel and Abigail displayed so effectively.

Hannah was not about to present any further temptations to Ephraim if she could help it. His resolve already showed unsettling signs of erosion from Chastity's capers, and maybe her own. Just how much damage had Hannah already done? Well, she couldn't do anything about Chastity, but she could put a lid on her own enterprises. Her projected scenarios were all in the basket now.

Hannah made another purchase while in town, a small King James New Testament to store in the pail at the ledges. The Bible Peter had given her was just what Hannah needed, but she wanted something that was like the Wards' Bible, yet easy to carry and read. She had been studying things that she wanted to talk over with Ephraim—a much better use of their relaxed moments than pine needles and perspiration.

Ephraim was delighted to see her and had missed her. His warm eyes took in the new blouse, and she thought she detected just a hint of disappointment. *Good. May it be well with your soul because of it!* she invoked silently.

"You must come observe my proficiency with your ax." He pulled her excitedly to a ring-side seat and proceeded to give a prodigious demonstration of felling, chopping, and splitting. Never before had that ax been in such masterful hands. He had honed it to extraordinary sharpness, and its modern qualities put an extra edge on his own native strength and skill.

Hannah clapped in genuine appreciation, but he stuck the ax in a stump and moved to the log pile for a peavey exhibition. He had thought of maneuvers she had never seen before, and again she clapped.

"Well done! You have earned a trophy of high honor," she exclaimed, tucking a tiny bouquet of ferns into his shirt front. "Now sit down and cool off for a minute and tell me how your leg is doing. You don't seem to be limping much."

"It is much improved, I thank you. And you have been well?"

Hannah looked away and poked at the dirt with a stick. "Ye-es, I have been well . . ." She wasn't sure how much to tell him, but it soon came pouring out: the plans for a new house, the logging and sale of gravel to pay for it, and her grief over the desecration of what was to her a sacred temple. She omitted, however, any mention of Mike and his attempted lovemaking. "So you see," she finished up wryly, "the war in my family is what's going well."

"I am heartily sorry to hear of your distress. However," he

added with a twinkle, "you seem fair to bid defiance to their schemes!"

He went on to talk of his own building plans. Having changed his mind about the need for a stock shed, he wanted to have his logs milled out so he could start working on a frame house. He wished he could afford a brick dwelling, like the finer houses in town, but it could not be, at least right now. Perhaps in a few years, if some ideas forwarded by Uncle Latham materialized, they could well afford a brick house, post and beam barn, and a team of fine horses.

"Morgans they will be," he boasted, "a new breed of much promise originated by a singing master close at hand." They were fast, Ephraim said, good pullers, comfortable to ride, and splendid. He had his eye on one over in Harfield, but that, too, would have to wait "until their subsistence became more tolerable."

Hannah looked over at Ephraim's drowsing horse. "Good old Captain," she said. "How long have you had him? He's older than your other horse, isn't he?"

"Yes, he is even more years than I by several. He and Major have served us well, but only yesterday I had to make use of the oxen to remove a great oak, a fine one for the foundation." He stretched his arms to demonstrate the size, then shook his head and grimaced. "Molasses! They move about so slowly that I was not done until midafternoon, missing my midday victuals."

"Poor baby!" Hannah laughed. "Tell me, is your mother happy about getting a new house?"

He smiled. "She knows naught yet; however, I doubt not that the prospect will excite astonishment and delight. She and my father's mother before her have labored under much adverse circumstance, and now at long last she shall receive her just recompense."

Before leaving for home, Hannah picked a few late raspberries and black caps along the pasture edge and took them to Jonah. The two had become fast friends, and Hannah marveled at the child's intelligence and wit. He loved stories and clamored for as many as she could recall.

She considered buying a few books for him but decided against it and instead dredged through her own childhood memories. A trip to the Gilly library had supplied additional grist, and she even developed some skill in tales "of her own manufacture," as Jonah would say. The two shared Bible stories as well, and the child was spiritually perceptive beyond his years. Hannah learned much from him, while he believed himself to be taught by her.

They compared notes on what birds still sang in early August. Hannah, from her bedroom deep in the woods, could hear hermit thrushes, peewees, an occasional wood thrush, and the ubiquitous vireo. Peter had once said, "There are so many of 'em, they have to sing a lot to hang on to their few cubic feet of air space!"

Jonah, listening in more open land, added goldfinches, cedar waxwings—"You can scarce hear them, they pipe so high"—and blue jays. He showed her his collection of bird feathers, some brought by Ephraim, some spotted by his own sharp eyes on their piggy-back walks.

Hannah found herself praying for Jonah on the way home. He was not well, and his weakness and pain seeped into her own heart until she could scarcely bear it. She poured out anguished "whys" but then got twisted up in the complications of praying for someone who didn't exist or who was long dead.

"Oh, Jesus, there are so many things I don't understand. I don't know why this other world opened up to me alone. Was going back in time the only way I could find out about you? And what about Peter? He's a better person than I am. He believes in you, but he just happened to be born in a horrible family. You're the only one who can help him. You're the only one who can help any of us. Please, Jesus ..."

She began suddenly and unaccountably to cry. Jonah's twisted limbs, Peter's soft flabby body, the Catechism's stiff formulations—all writhing and melting in her mind before the piercing, all-encompassing love of God. In the unbearable intensity of that love, her own body seemed about to crumble, but her soul was drawn and protected and given eyes to receive the unfathomable, even with little understanding.

> God moves in a mysterious way,
> His wonders to perform;
> He plants His footsteps in the sea,
> And rides upon the storm.

> Judge not the Lord by feeble sense,
> But trust Him for His grace;
> Behind a frowning providence
> He hides a smiling face.

The words as Ephraim had so often sung them came back as though written in flaming letters, and she knew without doubt that the faulty, seemingly contrary perceptions of God's ways that she now held would all come out right in due time.

> God is His own interpreter,
> And He will make it plain.

chapter 19

*E*phraim was not alone in his desire for a new horse, or better still, a matched team. Chastity took up the cause on behalf of a light, fast conveyance. "It need only be large enough for two," she said with a significant look past Hannah to Ephraim. "You shall take me out for a quick trot all the way to . . . Ephraim, how great a distance shall your new horse be able to travel in one day?"

The boy cocked his head with a lofty air. "Oh, perhaps we should reach the Connecticut River, with time enough to cross over, or in the opposite direction, we should travel beyond the height of land and perhaps on toward Manchester."

"That far!" Chastity's eyes shone as she looked off through the trees toward those far reaches of geography. "What shall their names be? The horses, I mean."

Again Ephraim rocked back and forth with some importance. "The sort of horse I intend to procure will already have a name— Gaylord's Glory, or some such, but of course one could not assign that for everyday usage. Now, if I were not intending to purchase a stallion, we could perhaps call it *Chastity*." He smiled playfully. "But that would never do for a sire, would it?"

The girl turned away in utter confusion.

Ephraim looked immediately contrite and went to her. "I apologize, dear sister. My thoughtless words have given offense. Please forgive me!"

Hannah fumed silently. *Dear sister! Listen to what she has him saying! She oozes sex and then acts shocked at a mere play on her name! When it comes to men, she's got a built-in guidance system that rivals NASA. What an operator!*

Chastity looked up at Ephraim with a strange sort of pain. "You should not speak such words, even in jest. 'Every idle word that men shall speak, they shall give account thereof in the day of judgment,'" she quoted. Again her eyes searched the ground.

Ephraim stood uneasily, obviously touched by the beauty of her bowed head with its long golden hair framing her transparent skin and finely sculpted features. He cupped his hand under her chin and lifted her eyes to his. "Will you grant me pardon this day for my sins?" he entreated.

A ghost of a smile returned his, and she nodded almost imperceptibly. They both relaxed, and the conversation went on. It seemed to Hannah, however, that from then on, Ephraim's eyes followed Chastity's every move.

A short while later, Uncle Latham made a dramatic entrance to the clearing. "Aha, thou hussy! 'She lieth in wait at every corner. Her house is the way to hell, going down to the chambers of death. I beheld a young man void of understanding. And, behold, there met him a woman with the attire of a harlot, and subtle of heart. She is loud and stubborn; her feet abide not in her house. My son, keep thy father's commandment, and forsake not the law of thy mother. It will keep thee from the evil woman. Lust not after her beauty in thine heart; neither let her take thee with her eyelids.'"

At first, Hannah thought his tirade was aimed at her, but then Chastity leaped away from Ephraim and stood trembling in guilty confusion. For once, Hannah was just a little pleased at Uncle's interference.

Chastity picked up her skirts and ran down the lane like a

frightened rabbit. Her father frowned after her and spoke to Ephraim about "consorting with such a jade, her mind taken up with naught but gay gewgaws and unprofitable dalliance. In truth, she bids fair to merit the flames of sulphur and brimstone!"

As he went on to talk of other matters, Hannah decided this might be a good opportunity to register with Chastity her own opinion of the girl's behavior around Ephraim. Ephraim had grown up in a context of brothers and little girl cousins, but with Chastity becoming a woman right under his nose, it wouldn't be long before his appetite became an uncontainable brushfire. With a hasty "I'll be back in a minute," Hannah gathered the front of her skirt higher even than Chastity had (glancing back to make sure Uncle Latham wasn't watching) and followed after the girl.

She was surprised to come quickly upon Chastity strolling leisurely toward the Latham cabin and humming a little tune, all terror seemingly gone. Hannah's eyes narrowed. *This cookie is something else!*

"Chastity," she began, falling in step, "I think your father is right about this. You've been fooling around with Ephraim, putting ideas into his head that aren't good for him, and they're sure not good for you."

Chastity looked puzzled. "Ideas?"

"You know, thoughts that boys have about girls. He looks at you, and where he once saw a sweet, innocent child, now he sees a flirt."

Chastity stopped walking, her eyes widening in alarm. "I do not understand."

"Oh, come on, honey. You know perfectly well what I'm talking about. You can play your little innocence game with Ephraim, but you can't pull it off with me! You're a flirt. You slink up to him and bat your big blue eyes and pretend you're interested in horses and carriages and stuff he likes, when all the time you just want to get close enough to touch him. That's not good. The Bible says, 'Blessed are the pure in heart, for they shall see God.' Well, that's not the way to a pure heart."

Chastity cringed visibly and began to shake.

Ignoring warning signals deep within, Hannah went on relentlessly with yet another weapon. "He's your cousin, and cousins shouldn't marry. And besides, even if you could marry him, only sluts meet guys in the woods. What do you think his mother and father would say if they knew?"

Hannah took one final look around her arsenal and leaned close. "I know about your tablecloths!" she whispered dramatically. She stepped back to observe the impact of her words but was totally unprepared for the actual effect they had on the girl. Chastity's skin turned whiter than ever; indeed, she seemed about to faint. She stood frozen, utterly stunned, then dropped to her knees and buried her face in her lap.

Hannah bit her lip, at last conscious of the inner whistle that had been blowing persistently. What was it warning of, though—Chastity's designs on Ephraim, or her own tactics? The girl was now weeping uncontrollably. Hannah wasn't sure what to do next. She couldn't even be certain that it wasn't all a big show just for her benefit.

"Come off it, Chastity. God wants you to be pure, to live up to your name, and I'm only trying to help." Somehow the words fit like a pig in a doghouse.

Chastity raised her head, her face devastated by anguish or guilt—Hannah wasn't sure which—but terrible to look upon. Hannah drew a shaky breath, trying to say something that would make them both feel better. Before she could pull her thoughts together, however, Chastity leaped up and ran howling into the trees.

"Whoosh! I hit some sort of raw nerve. That's for sure! Was I right or wrong to say what I did? Maybe she'll go off a little way and start singing and strolling like before. What ails that girl anyway?"

"Hast thou found the wench?"

Hannah jumped at the voice behind her.

Uncle Latham was frowning and looking closely at her. "I thought I heard her mindless wail. Hath she acquainted you with some improbable melancholy?"

Hannah looked down, feeling less and less sure of herself. "Well, I . . . uh . . . talked to her, but she was still upset." *If I had your scrofulous breath down my neck every step I took, I guess I'd be upset too,* she added silently, noting her inner contradiction of sympathies at the appearance of Uncle.

He set his mouth grimly. "I'll be sworn, I know not the height nor depth of her lustful depravity!" Then he turned on Hannah. "In thy discourses with her, see to it thou excite not further unlawful passions by flaunting thine own vanity and heathenish conduct. Much of the world, the flesh, and the Devil still remaineth upon thee!" With that he went toward his house, leaving Hannah even more confused.

When she returned to the clearing, Ephraim straightened from the wedge cut he was finishing. "You were absent for too long a time. I feared you had found a better object of charity." His laughing eyes looked her up and down.

This close inspection made Hannah uncomfortable. *I was right about Chastity's effect on him,* she decided. *The last thing he needs is a flirt to wake up the Mike inside him. That much is clear.*

Yet the difficulty with Chastity still perplexed her. Hannah felt distinctly uneasy about her shabby treatment of the girl, especially when measured against her own motives and goals. Had she really been any less provocative than Chastity? Well, perhaps not in the past, but things were definitely going to change from now on. Maybe she was seeing in Chastity what was hard to look at in herself. The desolation in the girl's face hung starkly before her and made her uneasy. She determined to make amends as soon as possible.

Her chance came the following day when she was walking past

the Latham cabin and saw Chastity scrubbing clothes with her usual earnest devotion. With only slight hesitation, Hannah turned to Ephraim and excused herself. "You go on. I need to talk to Chastity. I'll catch up in a couple of minutes."

Chastity was pathetically eager to patch things up and overrode Hannah's embarrassed apologies with a torrent of her own. "Forgive me for thus straying into temptation through youth and ignorance of the proper thing. I beseech you, do not hold me in contempt. I am sensible of my sin and ill deserve your cordiality. I shall—I *shall* turn from my wicked ways." She wrung her water-wrinkled hands and groveled like a contrite puppy.

"Hey, it's okay!" Hannah responded with relief. "We both have a lot to learn, I guess. Don't worry about it. Come on—I'll help you wring out that big sheet or blanket, whatever it is."

Hannah had wanted to have her say and then run on after Ephraim, but when the wringing was completed, Chastity seemed unwilling to let her go. At first, Hannah thought she might just be trying to keep her from Ephraim, but it became apparent that she had something on her mind.

"Mistress Hannah, I wonder . . . do you . . . ?" She looked down at the ground.

"Say it, Chastity. What do you want?"

Her eyes flicked upward momentarily. "I am sorry. I keep you from joining Ephraim at the clearing."

"It's okay. What is it you want?" Hannah was getting nervous about what might be coming, but when Chastity requested, with much hedging and apologizing, that Hannah read something from the New Testament in her skirt pocket, Hannah laughed in relief. "Sure. Anything in particular?"

"I believe the book of Titus."

"The whole thing?"

"No, something about obedience . . . or disobedience . . . I do not recollect."

"Well, let's see . . . 'Exhort servants to be obedient—'"

"No, that is not it."

"How about 'For we ourselves also were sometimes foolish, disobedient—'"

"No."

"Here. You find it." Hannah held out the little volume. "You know what you're looking for."

Chastity blushed and put her hands behind her back. "I am not taught in reading as you are."

Hannah was aghast. "You don't know how to read? You're kidding! Chastity, I'm sorry. I shouldn't have said that." The girl seemed about to crumble again. "I was surprised, that's all. Do any of your sisters read?"

Chastity shook her head dumbly and then spoke so softly that Hannah could hardly hear her. "It is not the custom for girls to be thus taught."

"Hey, I'll teach you. No problem! It'd be fun."

But again Chastity shook her head. "Father would not allow . . ." Her voice broke off, trembling.

"Oh, pish!" Hannah was silent a moment, thinking through the implications of this revelation. "Not even your mother, or Ephraim's mother . . . ? No, I know she can read. She teaches Jonah. Oh, well. I'll read anything you want. Now—" She looked back at Titus. "We were looking for *obedience*."

"I believe 'twas *disobedience*, yes, and *purity*, near the commencement, but not altogether near."

"Uh . . . how about this: 'Unto the pure all things are pure: but unto them that are defiled and unbelieving is nothing pure; but even their mind and conscience is defiled.' Is that it?"

Chastity's eyes shone. "Yes, and the next as well."

"'They profess that they know God; but in works they deny him, being abominable, and disobedient, and unto every good work reprobate.'"

"Yes, will you read it again and again so I may be instructed by it and bind it to my heart?"

[161]

She seemed so excited and eager that Hannah didn't have the heart to abandon her for Ephraim. So while Chastity scrubbed, Hannah lined out the verses until they both could say them without error.

Leslie Streiken dropped by camp with the latest gossip about who was going with whom, what Cindy Drummond had dared wear at Drew Harney's pool party, the latest teacher scandal, and who had recently gotten in and out of pregnancy.

"And how is it going with . . . what's his name again? Did you get him yet?" Leslie asked.

It was fun talking with Leslie about people back home, people they both knew. Despite Hannah's new view on sex and morals, this was familiar, comfortable territory—the words, the innuendos, the putdowns. She reassured herself even as they talked that she was above this now; it all lay behind her.

Leslie persisted in her interrogation. She wanted to know if Ephraim was still a virgin, who he hung around with, if Hannah had any competition.

Since controllable competition made the object seem all the more desirable, Hannah told her about Chastity. "She's pretty—this cloud of blond hair, y' know, skin you can see right through to the veins. But she's not your classy lady—definitely immature. Kind of weird, really. You just never know what she'll come out with next. She cutesies up to Ephraim, cool as you please, then the next minute she'll be crying or playing embarrassed. One day, we were talking, and out of a clear blue sky, she goes, 'I have two tablecloths!' Just like that! And I go, 'What are you talking about?' But she wouldn't say anything more. Really strange! I think she might even be a witch!"

Leslie nodded solemnly. "Yes, you definitely need to keep your eye on somebody like that. Guys sometimes get turned on by weirdos. Your best defense is to play cozy with the girl when both of you are with him but paint her as a waste when she's not there. You gotta keep one jump ahead of everybody, honey!"

Hearing her own strategy coming from Leslie's mouth was as good as getting an *A* on a term paper, and Hannah smiled. When her friend left, though, taking the comfortable froth with her, Hannah felt flat, hollow, her soul suffocating under a thick layer of scum.

chapter 20

*H*annah ran down the trail, annoyed with Ardyth for dawdling while they shopped in Harfield, annoyed with the van for developing a radiator leak that compelled them to visit every gas station on the way home, and annoyed with herself for going along in the first place. It was past two o'clock, and Ephraim would be gone from the clearing, probably scything grain with his father in one of the lower fields.

Well, if she didn't get waylaid by Chastity, Hannah could entertain Jonah and maybe see if the herb garden needed weeding. Abigail had been teaching her the names and uses for the more common plants. Horehound for colds and coughs; tansy for stomach ache, worms, and bladder complaints; camomile for ague; and the bright yellow and orange calendulas for dyeing yarns.

And lavender. Abigail was partial to her three silvery blue-spiked plants tucked close to the house for protection against the bitter Vermont winter. Already she was clipping foliage and flower stalks to hang from the log beams near the fireplace. When they dried, she would lay the stalks among her clothing and bed linens, to which they would lend their gentle fragrance.

Scarcely had Hannah gotten her skirt on at the ledges, however, when her neck tingled at the sound of wailing sobs close by. With thumping heart, she scrambled up the ledge to check once again on the clearing. Before reaching the top, however, she spied a young, enormously pregnant girl lurching through the trees. Her long skirt identified her with the other world, but who was she, what was she doing on this side of the wall, and what was wrong? *Maybe,* considered Hannah, *if I stand perfectly still, she won't see me.* But quicker almost than the thought, she knew what had to be done.

The girl's distress made her oblivious, so Hannah stepped cautiously into her path.

"Hi, my name is Hannah. Is there something I can do to help you?"

The girl shrieked at the sudden apparition and wailed even louder. She was younger than Chastity, fourteen or fifteen, perhaps, her face plump and pleasing to look at but vacant of any great intelligence. She was dressed more poorly than any of the Wards or Lathams, cap and hair disheveled, shawl ripped and falling off.

"Oh . . . oh . . . oh. I be dying!" she gasped, doubled over, her face contorted with pain.

"What's the matter? Are you sick?" Hannah put her arm around the trembling shoulders.

The girl groaned and clutched at the nearest sapling. "I must die. I've no place to go but to hell. He consigned me to hell, he did. Ohh!" Again she writhed in pain.

"Are you in labor?" Hannah asked anxiously. "Is your baby on the way?"

The girl nodded, but another spasm, this one accompanied by unmistakable pushing signs, sent Hannah into near frenzy.

"Good grief, what'll I do? She's going to have that baby right here! What can I do?" Hannah looked frantically about, but no help was at hand. She would have given anything to have seen Mike, or anybody, walking down the trail, but no one came.

[165]

Each contraction brought new screams from the girl, and after a particularly bad one, she started running, crashing blindly into trees.

Hannah grabbed her arm and jerked her around sharply. "Hey, cool it! Knock it off! Come over here and lie down on this moss." She spoke with more imperiousness than she felt, but it worked. The girl lay down obediently.

Now what do we do? The childbirth section of her first-aid course had been required reading, and though she had been interested, she couldn't remember a great deal. Well, first and basic to anything was to calm and reassure the patient, and this one would certainly need a lot of hand holding, like the skidder man said of his "caow."

"Everything's going to be okay. You're going to have a baby, and I'm here to help you. Is this your first one?" How could it be anything else? At least it was something to say.

"Yus, ohh! I be dying!" She pushed and panted wildly.

"No, you're not dying." It was high time, though, to find out just what was going on, so with commands to relax between contractions, Hannah lifted the layers of skirt. There was indeed a baby on the way. In proper position, too. Just the thought of a breech birth . . .

But how long would it take? Was there time to go for help? No, the girl would never stay alone, and either direction was too far. Hannah would have to deliver the baby by herself, even if it took all night. If the girl was already pushing, though, it might not be long. The time had already passed for "hoo-ha" breathing, as her first-aid instructor had called it. "Just relax. It's all right. You'll be okay. Hold tight to my hand. You haven't told me your name. Mine's Hannah. Do you remember that?"

"He . . . called me Grace . . . but I be named Nancy."

"Nancy. That's a nice name. Who called you Grace?"

The girl burst into tears again and would only shake her head. "Nancy, what are you doing out in the woods like this? Is someone after you, trying to hurt you?" *Another gang, perhaps, like Tobias's avengers?* she wondered.

"He consigned me to hell. I be wicked. I have no place to go!" Her voice trailed off in another high wail.

"Is this . . . the baby's father you're talking about?"

The girl nodded forlornly.

Hannah's indignation rose sharply, then took a sudden leap of alarm. If Nancy was wandering in these woods, the father from whom she had unsuccessfully sought help must be nearby. And of the males close at hand, the most likely possibility . . .

"Nancy, who's the father? You must tell me his name!"

But she would only rock her head and moan.

Hannah wanted to shake her. "Don't play games!" she snapped, regretting it immediately. The poor girl had problems enough. This was serious, though. *Ephraim* playing fast and loose with a girl like this? Chastity she could believe, but not this girl. It just couldn't be. Who, though, if not him?

A mix of anger and hurt boiled up within her, but she couldn't bring herself to ask outright if it was Ephraim. And her veiled questions got only a vague response of "Ma'am?" and "Ephraim, he were a-scythin'." After that, her mind had quite enough to do just grappling with the goings-on at hand.

Much more of the head was showing, and Nancy agonized through every contraction. Taking deep breaths herself, Hannah reviewed what to do when the baby came out. How would she get it to breathe? Maybe it would be best if it didn't. Would Nancy have to go around with a scarlet *A* on her dress? Baby Pearl . . . What would they do? Maybe Hannah should take them home to her mother and Ardyth. Ha! Wouldn't that cause an earthquake! No, the only real help lay in the other direction, but given the scruples there, the picture looked less than promising.

Man, what a lot of work to have a baby! This wasn't exactly the idealized natural childbirth setup with loving husband bravely cheering on a toiling but joyfully sanguine wife. Hannah was doing her best, but she herself needed cheering. Why didn't the baby come?

Suddenly a voice cut through her nervousness, almost as clearly as when Ephraim was under the log pile.

"Fust ones take a long toime."

This time it was the bovine midwife. Hannah smiled and was cheered.

The skin holding back the baby's head was stretched tight and beginning to tear. Didn't they cut that skin? If only she had scissors . . . Aha, the toadstool's knife! She pulled it from under her skirt and wiped the blade, hoping the bacteria on cloth was less harmful than that of her fingers. She slipped the smallest blade carefully behind the tear, gritting her teeth against the blood. She had no time to worry, though. After one more tremendous heave, the head popped out. In a few seconds more, Hannah found herself with a slippery, blue-skinned, wailing baby boy in her hands.

"Oh—oh—oh!" was all she could say. After the initial shock, she plugged in her first aid once again, wrapping the baby in the receiving blanket she had prepared from Nancy's underskirt. The afterbirth came next, and with pained mutterings of "Gross! Oh, gross!" Hannah simply ripped up handfuls of moss and covered it, moving Nancy to a clean spot.

She was glad to see the baby's face and extremities turning pink, now that she had time to worry about how blue they had looked. And it was time to tie off the cord. With stained and sticky hands, she looped a strip from Nancy's tattered shawl close to the baby's belly and severed the cord, then sat back, well satisfied with her afternoon's work. She rather wished Jane or Ardyth had been on hand to watch her performance, but there were other things to think about, like getting help.

After propping Nancy as comfortably as possible and helping her start the baby nursing, Hannah headed for the clearing, promising to return quickly. Her mind churned convulsively as she ran. Was the child really Ephraim's son? She hadn't thought to look closely at its eyes to see if they might betray kinship. No, it couldn't be. She just wouldn't believe it.

There was an immediate problem, however. If Abigail wouldn't come, where could she turn? Mrs. Latham would certainly not be any more compassionate, and Patience was a carbon copy of her mother. Chastity might not be as rigid, but she wouldn't be any help. Daniel? Mr. Latham? *Jesus, help me convince somebody.* Nervously, she began to marshal her scanty store of biblical arguments for mercy.

By the time she panted up to the cabin doorstep, her voice was hard to control. "Mrs. Ward, I found . . . this girl out in the woods . . . and she had a baby . . . and I delivered it, but . . . I need help. She's . . . she's not married, but someone had to help her, and she was . . . so scared, she was smashing into trees, and I thought Jesus would've . . ."

With one look at the distraught, bloodstained girl, Abigail took in the situation, pressing her lips together in a way that frightened Hannah. She drew her inside, though, and pushed her toward the sink. "Do wash, child, whilst I gather what will be needed. Is the babe well?"

Relief washed over Hannah along with the cold water and homemade soap. "Oh, yes. It's a boy. He's awfully tiny but seems to be all right. He started crying the minute he came out. I expected I'd have to spank him or something. I guess I really didn't know what to expect." Again her voice quivered, and she was annoyed.

With a brief word to Jonah, Abigail swept out the door, arms full of linens and blankets. Hannah carried a small crock of warm water from the teakettle on the hearth and had to practically jog along the dusty lane to keep up with Abigail. As they went, Hannah told the woman the little she knew of the baby's father but kept her own conjectures to herself against the hope that the older woman might have a reasonable explanation. Again

[169]

Abigail's lips pursed ominously, and Hannah quaked. Did she know who it was? Certainly not Daniel, and the only other male on the hill was Uncle Latham. Hardly. He, at least, had been busy enough with his wife to have kept out of trouble. Might Tobias be the culprit? As when he set the fire, he wouldn't have thought he was doing wrong; he would just consider it "frien'liness." No, Hannah decided, he couldn't have done the deed. It would break his heart to consign anyone to hell.

They found Nancy and the baby both asleep. Nancy was frightened at first sight of Mrs. Ward, but the latter's gentle and kindly competency set her mind, and Hannah's, at rest. With the water and cloths, Abigail soon had everything put to rights until they could get back to the cabin.

After considering fetching the men, she decided instead to try walking the girl, at least as far as she was able to go. Hannah, conditioned as she was to hospitals and proper care, was appalled by the suggestion, but Abigail seemed to look on it as quite practical.

"Indeed," she remarked, "there are some few women, remote from family or society, who have not opportunity for ease. How should the toddlers do with their mother in bed? If such mothers can step forth soon after birthing, so shall Nancy."

So they made slow procession through the clearing, Hannah carrying the baby in one arm and supporting a blanketed Nancy with the other, and Abigail on the opposite side with her load of pharmaceutical goods.

All went reasonably well until they drew opposite the Latham cabin and Nancy again began crying. "Oh, I daren't walk here! He said I be wicked to come nigh. He wouldn't call me *Grace* no more—just wicked!" She trembled violently and seemed about to faint.

Abigail looked not at all surprised, but the line of her mouth grew even thinner, and her formidable eyes flashed blue lightning. Her voice, though, remained gentle. "Come along, Nancy. There is naught can harm you while I walk at your side." With a grim glance at the ramshackle dwelling, she drew the parade along to the safety of her own home.

Before Hannah left, Abigail held her arms with compassionate understanding. "This has been a distressful piece of work for you; however, you have demonstrated fortitude and skill and love for the unfortunate. May our Lord give you calmness of spirit as you go, and"—she looked directly into Hannah's eyes—"a tongue disinclined to prattle. For reasons you may not understand, this unhappy affair of passion must remain betwixt you and me and the holy God who will most certainly bring justice to bear on both parties."

Hannah understood that the justice meted out to the simple, gullible Nancy would be of a different sort than to the sanctimonious old lecher. With a warm hug that might easily have precipitated Hannah's pent-up tears had it not been so quick, Abigail pushed her out of the door and on her way.

She had not yet reached the line of demarcation near the clearing when she heard a shout from behind.

Ephraim panted toward her from the lane, but his eagerness quickly turned to alarm when he saw the state she was in. "Hannah, my . . . dear!" He reached out a hand as though to touch her, but it hung in the air, pulled from one direction by habitual restraint and from the other by pent-up longing. This gesture of compassion, combined with her own relief over his innocence, became too much. She dissolved in exhaustion.

Immediately Ephraim's arms were around her, and her sobs blended together the kaleidoscopic emotions of her eventful afternoon with the sun-baked, dusty smell of his solacing body. He held her tightly and kissed her bedraggled hair and face, concerned, frightened for her, whispering her name over and over.

Finally she drew away, wiping her nose with a blood-stained piece of Nancy's shawl that she had stuck in her waistband. "I'm sorry, Ephraim. Did your mother tell you what happened?"

He shook his head. "I saw you as I came over the rise and ran to overtake you. Surely something dreadful is amiss. Were you attacked? Are you ill? What can I do to give succor?" His anxious eyes searched her face as he smoothed her hair with his strong, gentle hand.

She fought off renewed tears. *Oh, Ephraim,* she thought, *this isn't anything like how I imagined it would happen. No sprinkled pine needles, no laughter turning into love . . .*

She shook her head. "I'm awfully tired. I can't explain. I'll let your mother tell you." She held his hands tight against her face and looked up at him, her chin trembling. "Thank you," she whispered. "Thank you!" With a soft kiss to his lips, she turned and ran through the trees.

chapter 21

*H*annah reached home in physical and emotional tatters. She did manage to get to her bedroom, though, without anyone noticing her or the bundled-up clothing she had brought back to wash. She was marked by more than bloodstains, however. Mike found that out rather quickly when he tried out a pleasantry and she burst into tears.

"Uh-oh. She's still got it in for ol' Mike. You been off in your woods thinkin' up ways to get even? How much longer do I stay in the dog house?"

Angry with herself for crying, she turned on him. "Oh, shut up! Why would I waste tears on a geek like you? Get out of my way!" She pushed by him, heading for the glen and the quiet of the twilight hours.

She couldn't get the baby out of her mind. Even with Leslie's detailed instructional sessions in the sexual arts, plus her mother's lone embarrassed recital on the subject and the monthly reminders of her body's capabilities, she had never come even close to comprehending the astonishment of an actual birth. What a mixture of wonder, horror, and gore. And what incredible completeness in such a tiny person! Something within her own breast had leaped at the infant's first clumsy attempts to suckle. And that head when it first emerged—eyes closed, a blood-smeared blue mask of death, yet so quickly alive and squalling. How sober and old newborns look! Hannah thought of Mike's grandmother, a person far too old. She never smiled either. Was laughter limited to a few brief years in the middle?

Uncle Latham lurked in the corners of her mind, a splinter in her already inflamed emotions. She didn't want to think about him, not with Mike's trespass still painfully etched on her heart. At least Mike wasn't a hypocrite. His activities came naturally—an opportunistic game. Uncle, though, was an outrage, a rank weed on cleared land. The two of them seemed to be advancing on Hannah from both directions, a noxious cloud threatening to pollute the pure love that God had planted within her.

That brought her thoughts around to Ephraim. All summer long she had hoped and dreamed of being in his arms. Now, on the far side of her reveries, everything had turned upside down, inside out. It wasn't just the circumstances and her disarray. One of her alternate scenarios, in fact, had included sweat and dirt as a lure for his attentions. Why, then, should she feel uneasy? He had done exactly what any boyfriend would have, but maybe that was the problem. She had had enough experience with boys to know what was on their minds at any given moment. Was Ephraim fundamentally no different from other boys? Just what could he have done that would've been right?

The sun had set, baptizing the grove with a luminescence that burned around the edges of her heart. "Oh, my Lord Jesus, the only thing I'm sure of now is Your love. Each new wrinkle—Chastity, Nancy, Uncle Latham—hurts terribly, but it's a kind of pain that seems to make Your love plainer. I don't understand it, Jesus. I don't know why any of this has happened, but the darker everything gets, the brighter Your light seems to be.

"Jesus, I'm tired—so tired. I wish I could just bring Ephraim here where it's safe under these trees, and we could sleep on the moss and watch the waterfalls and—oh, I didn't mean that *sleep* part like it sounded. I really did mean sleep.

"God, what does Your love mean? I thought at first it would make everything okay, but the foxfire showed me that sometimes Your love hurts. I don't know what's ahead, but You do. Your love is greater even than the strength of the glen and the beauty of Ephraim's life.

"Dad and Steve think they can harvest logs here, yet the harvest will be just like them—grab what you can, kill if you have to—but it won't be forgotten, for You are unchangeable in Your justice.

"And Ephraim—oh, I love him so. But I see now that real love is so much more than the silly disease that turns every high-school kid purple. I get this feeling that his holding me this afternoon was really more sex than love. Lord, am I some sort of 'Department of Scrofulous Disease Control,' or . . . or am I the carrier?"

In the ensuing days, Hannah's fears appeared well founded. Back when she first started going to the clearing, Ephraim had been unwilling to spend extra time with her. Now while she was around, work seemed low on his list, forcing Hannah to seek creative ways of keeping his hands busy with tools instead of with her.

In the middle of one particularly trying episode, she simply gave up and went home, leaving Ephraim to puzzle over her manufactured excuse.

After changing her clothes at the ledges, she fell to crying. Not wanting her family to see her in that condition, she departed from her well-worn trail and meandered aimlessly until she could rein in her emotions.

Now, Hannah knew about woodland bees. She had studied the particular habits of wasps, hornets, honey bees, and yellow jackets. She tolerated their nosy interest in whatever food she carried outdoors. She had even learned to spot nests and avoid confrontation.

This day, however, her hard-earned education betrayed her, and she came to grief at the hands, so to speak, of yellow jackets. At the very moment when the warning buzz finally cut through her consciousness, she tripped over a branch and fell flat, right onto the bees' front porch. She scrambled up as quickly as she could, but not before being blessed several times.

When she reached home, Mike saw what had happened and offered sympathy and a wet washcloth.

Hannah, angry with herself, accepted the cloth ungraciously. "Okay, I'm a klutz—you don't need to rub it in!"

"I'm not rubbin' it in! Man—you're touchy! It's like tryin' t' walk blindfold through a whole yellow-jacket minefield!"

He glowered silently, the previous events looming anew. His footing in the family would be precarious indeed, should Hannah decide to cash in her chips and tell her father what he had done. Being at a disadvantage, especially with a woman, stung him hard. Hannah's insult to his kindness only fed his mounting anger.

"You think you're Miss Priss—playing 'Queen of the Mountain' over us barn rats. Well, I'll tell you somethin': you'll find this rat won't just snap to attention every time you waltz by. How much stock do you suppose ol' Daddy-o will put in your story now that you've let so much time go by? Everybody knows you've been about as much fun lately as a swamp full o' nettles. What would one more little grouch amount to?"

He had a point and Hannah knew it. Every day that went by weakened her hold over him, and should he decide to follow her to the glen again, her case, even in a court of law, would look pretty sick. She had told Peter what happened, explaining why she kept still, but his testimony, considering his position in the family pecking order, would certainly be of no advantage to her.

Mike had still another weapon in his arsenal. "I've seen what you been readin' lately up at the glen. And you snuck off to church last Sunday, too! You didn't think anybody would know—that line about needin' stuff at the drugstore. Well, I went to town, too, and saw the van parked by the church. That juicy tidbit should be good for a few laughs around here, just in case you get too uppity!"

Hannah shouldn't have been ashamed of being seen reading a Bible or going to church, but a lifetime of ridiculing such things was hard to counter. "Well, I don't care—laugh all you want!"

Yes, Mike had found her out and knew where she read her Bible; yes, he might even follow her and attack her again. Despite all that, she would not—could not—stay away from the glen.

Tom had taken no action there yet, although a deal with the buffalo-chested skidder owner had inspired a bottle of champagne nearly a week ago. Hannah knew better than to take heart over a delay. The glen was definitely on death row, and by continuing to go there alone, she might well be, too. But perhaps death was what the harvest was all about.

chapter 22

At least one problem seemed to have resolved itself. Evidently Chastity had taken Hannah's reprimand to heart and seldom went close enough to Ephraim even to speak to him. She appeared to be deliberately repairing a fault previously unknown.

Hannah felt good about that, more convinced than ever that Ephraim didn't need further stimulation. She tried to reward Chastity by spending extra time with her, especially in reading Scripture portions that the girl requested. Almost all of them had to do with purity and obedience.

No matter how much Hannah did for her, though, Chastity seemed to withdraw more and more into morose depression. She clung to Hannah, her eyes pleading for something that words could not express.

"What's wrong, Chastity? What is it you want me to do?"

But the girl would just shake her head, always on the verge of tears, and look off across the valley to the hills beyond which she still longed to travel. Never again did she mention Ephraim as her traveling companion, but she sometimes spoke of Ethan Cobbleigh or John Gatson as possibilities.

Were these town boys leading her on in some way? Hannah

wondered. She asked Ephraim if either of them were serious about Chastity.

He snorted. "What lad is not serious about Chastity? They flock about her thick as pigeons in spring."

"Well, are they giving her ideas, making promises they don't mean to keep? She's so sad all the time, and I think she's lost weight since the beginning of summer."

Ephraim laughed it off. "I'll warrant it is the gallants that are the worse for their attachment. What female has pity on her swains? Beauty is relentless on every occasion." With that he swooped her off her feet and over his shoulder. He carried her screeching over to where his keg lay buried under a protective layer of leaves.

He took a cooling swig. "Ah—'tis intolerably warm this day; I find even my shirt excessive." He held the cask to her lips. "Verily, 'tis too oppressive to labor longer." He lay back on the needled carpet.

Hannah almost choked. "You big fake! It's not nearly as hot as that day . . . as other days when you wouldn't stop for anything! Who are you trying to kid? You're getting just plain lazy!"

He grinned mischievously, then sat up, a gleam in his eyes. "I have hit upon a goodly scheme. Let's walk about in the woods."

This time Hannah heard not a quiet inner whistle but clanging bells. *Oh, no you don't, Buster!* But before she could say anything aloud, she saw he was pointing over the wall. Her mouth snapped shut, and she sat back, thinking. This was the first time he had suggested entering her world. She had often wanted to draw him over the wall if only as an experiment, yet she hesitated to bring it up. But now it was his idea. Would it work? Maybe he would disappear as soon as he stepped across. Abigail hadn't when she went over, nor had Nancy. Well, they could only try.

Where would she take him? There was nothing close by to show him but heavily cut woods and an empty plastic pail. If they stayed long enough, maybe a plane would fly over. How about her family? Should she—? No, that would be disastrous. Maybe they could walk to where the men were working, though, and watch from a distance, provided she could keep him away from the machinery. Or they could stick to things like the sugar house and sugar bush. He knew the land well and would be interested to see what had become of the "tolerable syruping place just before the mire."

And the glen ... Of course! No one would bother them there. Terrific!

"Hey, what a great idea!" Hannah responded at last. "C'mon, I'll show you our sugar house and evaporator, and we'll walk along the ridge trail and sit by the brook in the glen. You'll have a chance to see it before it gets wrecked." The prospect of sharing its beauty with him tempered the dull pain she felt whenever the glen came to mind. She pulled him up, and hand in hand they moved out from under the trees. Hannah's palms became moist with nervous perspiration.

As they crossed the clearing, Ephraim looked up at the sky, anxiety in his face. "The heat ... No, it comes not from the sun but from beyond the wall. Can you not feel it?" He put his arm up as though to shield his face.

They stopped, and Hannah looked at him. "What's the matter? It's hot, but not that bad. Don't be a baby!" She tried to drag him on, but he was not joking. Some sort of invisible furnace was not only driving him back to the relative shade of the sun but reddening his skin as well.

He stumbled back to his buried jug and dumped its remaining coolness over his face and arms. Then he lay still, eyes closed.

"Ephraim, are you all right? Please say something!"

He opened his eyes and smiled weakly. "Your world offers a rough welcome. I am not at all astonished that you feel not the heat of the day if that is the sort of warmth to which you are accustomed!"

"Come on! Our temperature's the same as yours! But something sure burned you. What'd it feel like?" She patted a few stray drops of water onto his red cheeks.

"Like Nebuchadnezzar's furnace!" He made a face. "Shadrach, Meshach, and Abednego were not tried in hotter fire!"

He sat up and became serious once again. "On one other occasion I attempted to cross the wall. Oh, I frequently go back and forth in the course of my labor, but this time I desired as a deliberate act to repair to your world. Though not hindered by any great heat, I could not, despite extreme effort, negotiate the wall itself. The stones seemed resolved to impede my progress."

Hannah got up and walked over to the wall. She looked at it curiously, stepping back and forth over it. The trees remained the same, even when she walked some distance on the other side, and she could feel no extraordinary heat or resistance from the stones. "Hmm. It knows I'm not really leaving for home. There's something strange about this wall, and I don't doubt for a minute—even if I hadn't seen your skin burned like it is—that it could keep you from crossing if it wanted to."

She frowned and shook her head. "Every time I come over, especially these last few days, I get a funny feeling, as though the wall were *allowing* me to cross, but that I shouldn't take it for granted. A lot of times I've wanted to go with you to Gilly, just to see what it looked like, but almost as soon as I thought it, this strong ... *thing* ... would come over me, y' know? Now I'm wondering if I might get burned, too, or stumble over rocks or something if I tried it. I'm able to be here in your world, but there are fences around the pasture. Maybe Peter was right: it's okay to go backward but not forward."

Ephraim looked perplexed. "Backward? Forward?"

Hannah shook her head and sighed. *He still doesn't understand the time business.* Aloud she said, "Oh, you know. I can come here, but you can't enter my world."

Ephraim nodded absently. "It is not allowed."

[181]

Hannah frowned at the recurring phrase. *Why does he keep saying it's not allowed?*

Ephraim made a pretense of working a little longer but soon gave up and headed back with a few sticks for firewood. Hannah went with him, chiefly to get a drink before leaving for home, Ephraim's water supply having been drained for cooling purposes.

Abigail was outdoors dumping fireplace ashes into the soap-making barrel. She greeted Hannah affectionately. "Such a warm day! May I get you a drink, my dear?" Without waiting for an answer, she hurried inside and returned with a tankard of cold spring water and a wooden mug.

Hannah drank greedily. "It really is hot, especially for this time of year. You'd think it was July, instead of the middle of August. Wouldn't a snowstorm feel nice about now? I'd love to just roll around in it."

Instead of agreeing, however, Abigail frowned and shook her head. "No, I think not. Snow brings great suffering with it, and I would not burden August with the pangs of January."

Hannah's thoughts of snow were diverted by the appearance of a horse and buggy, different from Uncle Latham's, on the road below them. Daniel had intercepted it and stood talking to the driver, both of them gesticulating in seeming disagreement. Finally, Daniel appeared to prevail, even to prohibiting the fellow from driving up to a wider spot in the road for an easier turn-around. The rig jockeyed back and forth with some difficulty and then went back down the hill.

Wiping his face on his arm, Daniel shouldered the wooden hay fork and walked toward the cabin for his turn at the spring water.

"Ahh!" He smiled at his wife. "There are some that say water is drink fit only for beasts, but I say Mr. Washington himself could find no finer draught than that which you offer us on such a day as this, my dear!"

Ephraim turned to his father. "Who was that in the gig? I did not recognize the horse—a spare and bony nag."

"Yes, and ganted up with thirst. But I would not allow the scoundrel closer access."

"Who was it?" Abigail and Ephraim spoke in unison.

"Colby the limner whom Deacon Ellsworth cautioned us has been gadding about the region. Wanted to talk with my wife and daughters. I told him I had no daughters, and my wife was a woman of sensibility—good day, sir!"

"What's a limner?" Hannah asked. "I never heard of that."

Daniel scowled. "A limner is a rogue who preys on a female's vanity by painting her likeness. He travels from house to house, stirring the emotions of silly women by showing them portraits of grand ladies who want only a face. We have already sufficient frivolity abroad to occasion an unhappy effect on the tempers of our young ladies."

Under the prompting of an uneasy conscience, Hannah's face turned red.

But Daniel seemed to be frowning toward the Latham establishment. "I fear the scoundrel has already been about. He inquired most particularly of Mistress Chastity."

Abigail nodded her head. "You did well, Daniel, to send him off, although my very being is disquieted by not proffering so much as a draught of water on such a day."

"He knows well where to find water, I'll warrant! But he'll not find what he seeks here if I can forestall his schemes!"

As Hannah left the little group to return home, Abigail's smile and hug refreshed her soul like the coolness of the glen. Both Daniel and Abigail were steady, unchangeable—solid rock upon which she could stand and be strengthened at a time when everything around her was crumbling. Uncle Latham, Nancy, Chastity . . . even Ephraim was changing almost daily as though a protective veil of holiness had been ripped from his eyes and he now saw as other men. And of course the glen itself, the bedrock of her inner life, was soon to be shattered.

But Hannah began to understand that the endurance, the

substance of Daniel and Abigail in the face of overwhelming drudgery was not a thing to be relied on, in and of itself, for she knew the uncertainty of their lives. It was merely an indicator, a symbol of something beyond them that in turn would never let her down.

She drew the little Bible from her pocket. "Truly my soul waiteth upon God: from him cometh my salvation. He only is my rock and salvation; he is my defense; I shall not be greatly moved. How long will ye imagine mischief against—"

Hannah jumped as Chastity touched her arm. "Oh! You scared me! I didn't see you coming. You were so quiet!"

"I'm sorry, I'm *sorry!*" Contrite, Chastity wiped her wet hands on her apron as though they were somehow at fault.

Man, you can't say anything to this kid without her going on a big guilt trip! "It's okay," she said aloud. "Are you doing laundry again?"

"No . . . I mean, yes . . . yes, laundry." She looked directly into Hannah's face—something she seldom did—with such anguish, desperation even, that Hannah caught her breath. It lasted only a few seconds, though, and again she looked down and fumbled in a pocket.

"I . . . made this for you, that is . . . if you like it." Chastity drew out a small square of fine white linen, hand embroidered around the edge with an intricate floral design in pale lilac, and the letters *H N A* done in tiny, almost microscopic stitches.

Hannah examined it, at a loss for words, while Chastity wrung her hands in uncomfortable suspense. "'Tis not very good, and I don't know if the spelling came right. I copied letters from the Bible, and—"

"Chastity, it's beautiful! I've never seen anything like it! I just don't know what to say!"

Chastity relaxed visibly, a rare smile appearing on her face. "You do like it? I laid it in the sun for hours and hours to make it white, and I saved the purple wrapper from the sugar to dye the thread. I asked Jonah what letters were in your name, and he said there be just three. Did I get it right?" Her anxious expression returned, and Hannah didn't have the heart to say anything but "It's just fine. You got all the letters right."

It was truly beautiful, and Hannah looked at it appreciatively. Mike's grandmother knew about such meticulous stitchery. The only handwork done by anyone in her acquaintance—mostly bored housewives—came in numbered, color-coded kits.

Hannah studied Chastity, trying to see through the tangled threads that made up the fabric of her life—the flirtaciousness and waxlike beauty, her obsession with cleanliness that made even Abigail look like a coal miner, the habitual gloom that hung over her, the way she hung on Hannah to the point of being a nuisance. Now this new twist—a present that in terms of love and labor was worth every bit as much as the dress by Garachi.

Impulsively, Hannah reached out with a heartfelt hug. After an instant of surprised stiffness, Chastity responded with a clasp that nearly squeezed the breath out of Hannah. But then her body began to shake, and she broke away and ran off into the woods, weeping as uncontrollably as on the earlier occasion.

Hannah stared after her, her jaw hanging in astonishment. "Chastity!" she called. She took a few steps to follow but then abandoned the idea as useless. With a sigh, she looked down once again at the handkerchief. "*H N A,*" she murmured; "the letters of Hannah but only half the name. Is Chastity something like that?"

chapter 23

*H*annah's concern for Ephraim grew as the situation in his world deteriorated. She felt torn between two crises. Uncle Latham, it seemed, had been busy with more than just making babies. His interests, far from being confined to the "happine∫s of virtue" as Hannah initially thought, ranged through the business world and real estate. He had lined out for Ephraim an elaborate scheme to market peaveys, plus a long-range land development plan that promised to give the New York land barons some stiff competition.

"Uncle has acquaintance with upwards of five worthy fellows who aspire to farming. Three are able to purchase outright, while the others would tenant farm until such time as their gain enables them to purchase also."

"And where is the land that you want to sell coming from?" Hannah wanted to know. "While your father's alive, you can't just go selling parcels all on your own, can you?"

A brief shadow darkened his eyes, but he brushed it away as a fly. "Of course, I would of necessity work out the details of my inheritance, but the scheme is as much to his advantage as to mine. Much of our claim lies in wooded waste for want of labor, and this will bring a sure reward to all concerned. This paltry pile of logs here," he said with a disparaging gesture, "will be as broom straws. We shall have logs sufficient to construct a worthy and prestigious dwelling, as well as a hay and grain barn with clay threshing floor and two mows on either side, plus another for the fine herds I shall accumulate. As a considerate man, Father will most certainly accede to my earnest recommendations.

"And then," he continued, "within the span of a year, we shall be enabled to purchase a prime tract north of here for which we already have three potential—"

"Ephraim—," Hannah interrupted.

"Now, hold. Hear me out. Three parcels will be sold, each for more than the initial purchase price. And that money may make plausible our investment in a brickyard, as there is none such within a span of thirty miles. Uncle believes that the growing market for brick, as well as a certain one for the peavey, would soon bring great wealth to our door. Now, what think you of that?" His eyes scattered blue shards of excitement. "Frequently you have said, as does Uncle, that we suffer from want of rest, and now this will of a surety afford the means of a more agreeable existence."

Thus his theme was carried along: "You said . . . You described . . . In your world are many avenues for pleasure . . . In your estimation these goods are ill-contrived . . . You wear finer stuff than this wretched homespun . . ."

At this point, Hannah exploded. "Wretched homespun! After all the hours your mother puts in cleaning and carding, spinning, and sewing, you have the gall to call it *wretched*? I'd gladly wear it for no other reason than her hands made it!"

Hannah's anger took him aback, and with a sheepish expression, he changed the subject.

With a stab, Hannah recognized in the mirror before her not Ephraim's image, but her own. Her selfish, status-seeking attitudes, sown in ignorance and immaturity, had been fed and watered by Uncle Latham and were just now coming into bud. With a sense of horror, she saw in his face not so much the presence of something evil as the absence of something good. The light within him that had overcome her own darkness had been turned down like the wick of an oil lamp. She tried to think when they last talked about things in the Bible. He frequently mentioned church affairs or people, but these references were no more than weak seedlings from last year's pumpkin crop. When she tried to discuss some new scriptural insight she had discovered at home, he dismissed her excitement with "Of course. Everyone is sensible of such matters."

She sighed.

"Hannah, what is it? Why do you look so?" He put his arms around her and held her tightly.

"Ephraim, I don't like to see you caught up in all these money-making plans. The things you want—more land and money, an easier life—are not bad in themselves. But there's something wrong with the *way* you want them, the way you turn good things to bad and then pretend they're okay. It's like . . . like trying to make *Playboy* out to be nothing more than a dating service. Yah, yah, I know. What's *Playboy*? Well, forget it. Don't even ask!

"You talked to me once about all the good-time stuff I thought I needed to be happy," she continued. "You said then that it was no good if it pulled me away from God. Do you remember? And that's just what's happening to you. Oh, Ephraim, I only want you to love God and tend to your work. You say your log pile will grow, but lately you haven't even—"

He kissed her to stop the flow of words. "Dearest, I am working, and I do love God. Have I ever not presented myself at meeting? And only twice did I miss evening prayers at my home, and those I joined with Uncle, Aunt, and cousins after speaking on matters of business with Uncle." He chuckled. "Certainly you can find no cause for censure in such company."

There was cause enough, but she couldn't speak of it without going against her word to Abigail. And trying to make him understand on other grounds was difficult. Then, too, time spent in Chastity's company, her new restraint notwithstanding, could only add fuel to his fire.

She sighed and pulled away from his arms, so unwilling to release her. His words of love were gentle, but she sensed in him the same ravenous hunger that stalked the corridors of Darbury High. Getting him to touch her was no longer the problem. How long before he became a Michael?

That night she searched her Bible and the next day retrieved her little Testament from the pail, taking time to mark certain pages for quick reference.

Ephraim was with Uncle Latham, so she had to wait. Her time was well spent, though, observing the highly skilled old piper as he drew the boy down his own dissolute pathways. His patter, well seasoned with Scripture, laid out the good life, from ale house to multiroomed mansion.

At one point when Hannah tried to break into the conversation, she was immediately dispatched with "Let the women learn in silence with all subjection. I suffer not a woman to teach, nor to usurp authority over the man, but to be in silence." It had the ring of a well-worn tool.

When they were alone again, Hannah dodged Ephraim's grasp and tried to keep a respectable distance between them as they walked back to the clearing.

"Hannah dearest, why do you remain so far removed? Do I excite your displeasure in my outward appearance? You know other men who are more finely appareled. I lack, perhaps, the fragrances of your world, of which you told me. My breath, perhaps—what is it that you say?"

Hannah smiled in spite of herself. "No, you don't have zoo breath, if that's what you mean." But her amusement quickly faded. "Ephraim, I was wrong in telling you all those things I thought were so important. I didn't know any better, but now I do. You must forget the things of my world and turn back to the Savior who loves you and gives you all you need right here.

"Ephraim, please, *please* don't listen to your uncle. He's simply trying to make you think that money and fun are better than what God offers in Jesus Christ. Listen to this—" With shaking fingers she found her first argument.

" 'Love not the world, neither the things that are in the world. If any man love the world, the love of the Father is not in him. For all that is in the world, the lust of the flesh, and the lust of the eyes, and the pride of life, is not of the Father, but is of the world. And the world—' "

" '—passeth away, and the lust thereof: but he that doeth the will of God abideth for ever,' " Ephraim's voice joined hers, but with a hint of mockery. "And in James," he continued with a supercilious grin, "chapter four, verse four, 'Know ye not that the friendship of the world is enmity with God? Whosoever therefore will be a friend of the world is the enemy of God.' What other would you read me?"

"Ephraim, you're not serious, and I want you to be. This isn't funny at all. In Romans, it says that, 'To be carnally minded is death.' Ephraim, I'm afraid for you!"

"But," Ephraim shot back, "the Scripture also saith, 'Every man also to whom God hath given riches and wealth, and hath given him power to eat thereof, and to take his portion, and to rejoice in his labour; this is the gift of God.' And again, 'Be not righteous over much; neither make thyself over wise: why shouldest thou destroy thyself?' "

"Oh, come on. That's not in the Bible! You're making it up!"

"No, I protest! Ecclesiastes, chapter seven, verse sixteen."

"I'll look it up when I get home. But I don't believe it's what you make it out to be."

"And Ecclesiastes eight, fifteen: 'Then I commended mirth, because a man hath no better thing under the sun, than to eat, and to drink, and to—' "

"All right, Ephraim, you've read the Bible longer than I have, but there's one thing I do know: your uncle just stirs up the 'old man' inside you, and you're disobeying God when you listen to him. Now, you can throw something else from Ecclesiastes at me, but you know in your heart that I'm right. You are to put that old nature to death. You must, Ephraim! I say this because I love and respect and admire you, and I want you to have life and peace—not death."

The blithe smile disappeared, and he looked long and sorrowfully into her anxious eyes. "My dearest," he said, drawing her gently to himself, "I heartily wish that I could undo the wrong which has wrought such an inharmonious effect upon your spirit." His hand smoothed her hair and caressed her shoulder and arm. "Those times when first you came, desiring only to be friendly and offering yourself ... I have ofttimes pictured in my mind the beauty of your limbs, how unencumbered and pure. My desire is for you—to see once again that which you covered in obedience to my hasty instruction, but which is for us to enjoy as a gift from—"

She wrenched herself from his hold, tears streaming down her face. *"Ephraim, what have I done to you?"*

chapter 24

The following day, after waiting in vain for Ephraim to appear, Hannah finally abandoned the clearing and found the Wards and Lathams all in a dither in front of the Ward home. Abigail and Daniel stood tight-lipped and somber as the Latham women wailed and wrung their hands.

Uncle stomped about, all but frothing at the mouth. "A plague on them both! Fie! How came we to such an end? She hath the mark of the beast upon her; we have cherished the spawn of Satan in our midst!" He ripped at his clothes and threw dust into the air.

Aunt Latham cried out. "Oh, husband, dear, treat tenderly of your clothing. How now shall they be ment or laundered?

Hannah looked around anxiously. "What's going on? Where's Ephraim? Where's Chastity?"

Daniel's face grew darker. "Chastity has departed."

"Departed? Where?"

He shook his head grimly. "That is the nub. We know not where."

Hannah felt the blood leave her face. "And Ephraim?" Her voice squeaked.

"The lad has been these three hours searching out the woods

and swales. He has the gun to signal if she be found." His eyes traversed the surrounding acreage as though to help his son. "But we have heard nothing."

Hannah drew a relieved breath. Bad enough that Chastity had disappeared; at least she hadn't disappeared with Ephraim. In view of his recent frame of mind, anything was possible.

"Are you sure she's not up on the hill or hiding somewhere?" All of Chastity's strange behavior came back to Hannah in a rush. The hidden bucket and white robe, her sudden departures into the woods, her emotional instability. Maybe she should have told someone about these things when they happened—Abigail, at least.

Daniel shook his head. "Our brother has searched everywhere. We believe it to be the doing of the limner. Ephraim relates that Chastity cherished the vain hope of escaping her lot by means of some conveyance, especially a fine one. In truth, the limner's gig and steed were not so very fine, but he has been about, and it seems the most likely explanation."

Now it was Hannah's turn to shake her head. "Poor Chastity! What will become of her?" She sighed and was silent a moment. "How long has she been gone? Any hope of catching them?"

"I rode early into town to inquire about the rascal, but no one has seen either him or the lass. My brother discovered her absence when he arose during the night. He straightway took up a lantern to search about for her."

"Yes," Uncle chimed in. "She had retired with her sisters as was her wont, but before day's light, she had escaped with the miscreant—may God's wrath fall upon him!"

"Yes, but how do you know it was him if nobody saw either of them? How do you know she went anywhere at all?"

Daniel raised his eyebrows and shrugged. "If not he, then who—or where? The limner has been around—two or three times, it appears. And the hill you speak of that she frequents, Mr. Latham searched it carefully but found no sign."

"Yes," added Uncle, "I even descended to the base of the sharp pitch for fear she might have fallen."

"Or thrown herself over!" wailed Aunt Latham with fresh vigor.

Just then Ephraim trudged wearily down the lane from the clearing. His mother poured some water for him and took his gun in exchange. There were no questions from anyone, only distressed silence.

After Ephraim had rested a bit and eaten some cold pigeon pie, he set to work on the necessary Latham chores so Uncle could ride to town to make his own inquiry. Hannah, after momentary indecision, went off to check the hill for herself. She was pretty sure Uncle didn't know about the sap bucket, and she wanted to see if anything had changed there.

It had. The white robe was gone, and in its place she found a cloth packet, tied carefully with the same bark cordage the girls had used to string the beds. Strangest of all, the packet was charcoal labeled, *H N A.*

Hannah turned it over and over, trying to determine what it was. Finally, she worked the string loose enough to unwrap it, but even then, she couldn't make it out to be anything more than a bunch of rags—clean, but with stains of some sort. The material was different from the tablecloth robe—not as white and much coarser. But what were they?

Something gnawed at the edges of her memory, and she frowned in concentration. Finally, with a shake of her head and a sigh, she took one last look in the bucket. Had she not done so, she might have missed what was, perhaps, the most significant discovery of all.

A stiff cardboardlike object had been wedged tight against the contour of the bucket. As Hannah pulled it out, she saw again the shortened version of her name on the exposed side, and on the other a crude, almost primitive painting that she readily recognized as Chastity. For all its artistic shortcomings, it captured the porcelain beauty of the girl in a way that stabbed Hannah's heart. The face especially radiated a serene joy that Hannah had never actually seen. This was the *completed* Chastity.

Looking again at the back, Hannah spotted some faint handwriting that had been eclipsed by Chastity's charcoal letters. She examined it closely.

This bee no Portrate of a Fin ladee I mak you all Mysef yor to buteefull To fit a portrate I Wisht it war beter.

Yor fathfull Sarvent,
Elias Colby

"Oh, wow! An autographed work of art, yet! But did Chastity know what it said? He must've told her. Well, I guess that pretty well settles what became of Chastity. But why didn't she take it with her? Why did she leave it for me? And whatever are these rags?"

Another thought struck her: was Mr. Elias Colby, and not Uncle Latham, responsible for Nancy's baby? It could be, especially if it were true that he made a habit of hanging around the vicinity. Maybe that's why Abigail didn't want to make waves over Uncle Latham. "But why would Nancy come up here? Oh ... I don't know!" She shook her head and gathered up the objects.

After tucking everything back into the bucket, she went on up the hill for a look around. Under the big oak she found signs that something, or someone, had been there recently. Grass had been trampled, shrubs torn, dirt and stones kicked up, but nothing that couldn't have been done by a deer or a skunk.

From the lookout her eye took in occasional splashes of color against the green march of hills. She peered straight down, but the precipice was too irregular to see more than sparkling rubble that had been cleft by years and weather from the shiny rock face.

She went back and sat against the big green oak. As she mulled over all the facets of the strange situation, her eye played with the design of her velcro sneakers.

Ephraim had made fun of them. "I am astonished that burrs should turn to the task of fastening apparel! I shall make a cloak of them that will never depart from my back!" At least her feet mirrored each other, unlike his "unifoot" boots.

She moved restlessly as though the tree bark were digging into her back. The tingle remained, however, even when she leaned forward away from it. She looked up and down. Deep within her was a feeling that the tree held some terrible importance, whether for good or evil, she didn't know. Moving out from under its spreading branches, she lay back on the soft hilltop grass and was gratified to find ease once again.

She thought back to the last time she had seen Chastity, when the girl's eyes had pleaded silently for understanding. Had she known then that she would be leaving? Was that why she had given Hannah the handkerchief?

"Oh, Chastity, I didn't understand. Even if you had told me, what would I have said? Wherever you are, may you at last have peace. May the love your artist has for you be enough to feed and clothe you and keep you safe. And may God be your happiness."

Hannah returned to the Ward cabin, having retrieved the picture and bundle of rags on her way. She kept them out of sight while passing the Latham establishment and brought them out only for Abigail to look at.

The older woman nodded and clucked at the painting. "Yes, 'tis as we thought." She turned the board over and looked curiously at the charcoaled letters.

"You mustn't laugh at that," Hannah admonished. "It was Chastity's way of spelling my name. Jonah evidently gave her only the three basic letters, and this is the way she put it together. She embroidered a handkerchief for me, so that's how I know."

Jonah, who had been unusually quiet all this time, began to cry, smitten by an attack of conscience. "I did not bear false witness. There are only three letters that make up Hannah's name!"

Abigail looked at him sternly. "But you did not think it fit to instruct her in the arrangement of those three letters, is that not so?"

The boy nodded miserably.

Hannah tried to comfort him by displaying her handkerchief. "Never mind. See how beautifully she embroidered those three letters!"

Abigail pressed her lips together but said nothing more. She went on to read the limner's tribute and shook her head with a sigh.

Hannah thrust forward the rags. "What do you make of these? They have my name on them, too."

Abigail's eyebrows shot up, and she looked inquiringly at Hannah. "Were they as they are now, or—"

"No, they were tied in a neat bundle. I had no idea what it was. I still don't, for that matter. So I opened it."

Again the woman's eyebrows went up, and again she looked sharply at Hannah. "You truly know not the significance of the packet?"

"No, honest! Is it something I should know?"

Abigail pursed her lips and lowered her voice so that Jonah would not overhear. "Do you not use such material during your . . . time?"

Hannah's eyes widened, and suddenly it came to her where she had seen these rags before. Chastity had them all laid out for laundering that day the girls had first met. "But why—?"

"My sister-in-law has observed the custom of tying up her cloths each time she found herself with child, and it seems that Chastity as well may have affected the procedure."

Chastity pregnant? Could it be? Hannah did some quick figuring. *That must've been late June . . . July, August . . . yes, it could be. Why didn't I think of that?* "That explains a lot," she said out loud. "No wonder she was upset and sad! Why didn't she tell somebody?"

The sound of a horse sent them to the door.

Uncle Latham appeared over the hill, his horse in a lather. "News at last!" he shouted as he trotted by. "The rogue hath been seen leaving early this very day—a woman with him! A pox upon them both! 'The Lord revengeth, and is furious; the Lord will take vengeance on his adversaries, and he reserveth wrath for his enemies.'" His voice faded into the trees.

"Well!" exclaimed Hannah in the silence that followed. "At least the guy had the grace to take care of her after he got her in trouble. Not like poor Nancy at the hands of somebody else we know!"

As Hannah crossed the wall on her way home, she whispered, "Please, Mr. Elias Colby, deal kindly and gently with her!"

chapter 25

At least part of the reason for the logging delay in the glen was the weather. Queer, some of the local oldtimers called it. Tom and Steve used stronger words and grew progressively out of sorts at each new development.

First it was rain, greater and lesser amounts, but continuous moisture that rusted the very souls of those whose only shelter was not much better than that of the forest creatures. So said Jane.

The rain also set Hannah up for getting Ephraim into trouble with his father.

The two men had sought shelter from the nagging drizzle, Daniel bagging grain to take to the mill, Ephraim repairing the wagon. Abigail, however, needed a chicken. Normally, this was accomplished easily enough by luring the bird into the coop and then cornering it. The rain, however, had turned the yard into a quagmire, and Hannah and Ephraim skated around ineffectively, screeching with laughter. Hannah slipped and fell to her knees in the mud, and when Ephraim careened over to help her, she grabbed him and pulled him down, too, pelting him with handfuls of muck.

Ephraim returned the fire with enthusiasm just as his father stepped out of the barn to see what was going on.

"Son!" Daniel thundered. "Have you no better employment than to burden your mother thus with unnecessary labor? Has she not quite enough to do? And what of Hannah's clothing? What unhappy effect will your treatment of such fine stuff have on her mother?"

The two leaped up in chagrin, but before Hannah could explain and apologize, Ephraim had taken the entire blame onto his shoulders. "I ask your pardon, Father. I shall seek my mother's and Hannah's as well. You justly reprobate my conduct, and I stand with no excuse. We shall go at once to emend what we are able." He immediately dragged Hannah off to the water barrel, effectively cutting off any opportunity of her sharing the reproof.

After the rain came wind. Not the heady, refreshing sort that sends fair-weather clouds scudding across an azure sky. No, this wind accompanied a lesser episode of rain and became an invisible, capricious Attila the Hun that stomped about noisily down in the valley before making a thunderous, driving attack up the hillside.

Mike had always claimed to like wind. It reminded him of Paul Bunyan, able to straighten twisting rivers, corral stampeding forests, uproot trees by the hundreds. This wind was different, though. Just hearing its express-train approach from below was enough to make him look to the rafters and count the nails holding everything together. Felling trees was out of the question, so he decided to haul sugar wood. But when the rotted top of a dead poplar landed close by and a hemlock blew down in front of the jeep, he headed back to the cabin with a sudden interest in saws that needed sharpening.

After the wind came an eerie stillness: hot, steamy from the saturated earth, building anger, adding further outrage to tried spirits. When enough anger had gathered in both man and sky, gigantic thunderclouds hurled mortar shells in ceaseless barrage, again driving the fainthearted to cover.

While Hannah was with Ephraim, she tried not to be caught by storms and usually headed home if one threatened. This one, though, gave little advanced warning until the sun was blotted out by a crash that tore a great rip in the clouds.

They were not at the clearing. Ephraim had wanted to show her another potential house site, the third that week. This one, he told her, was on one of the flat shelves of the big hill. "A fine situation for sun and protection from elements."

Hannah sighed and went along but kept reminding him of all the jobs he should be doing instead of playing dream house. When she realized, though, just where he was taking her, the hair on her neck prickled, and she became even more opposed. She knew the place well from her cellar hole tour-guide experience. Just the thought of Ephraim's house overrun by wilderness made her shiver. It too closely paralleled what she saw happening in Ephraim himself.

With each of them busily trying to reshape the other's mind, they hadn't even reached the spot before rain began spilling over them. The discussion curtailed, Ephraim grabbed her hand, and they ran down the hill and into the lane, dodging thunderbolts and puddles until they tumbled gasping and laughing into the Ward cabin.

Abigail gathered them in and drew Hannah to the fireplace to dry herself with a linen towel. "The rain has scoured you thoroughly, child! But if it does not extinguish our blaze, we shall have you dried in a trice." Abigail moved her steaming kettle from its hook over the low flame to one of several others off to the side. With added fuel to the fire, she soon had steam rising from Hannah's skirt.

Jonah gabbled ecstatically at the unexpected entertainment from Hannah and Ephraim's arrival, but Abigail moved uneasily from window to window, starting at each detonation. Finally, Daniel appeared from behind the barn where he had been seeing to the comfort of the frightened sheep. Abigail flew to the door to welcome him with relief and a fresh supply of towels.

"Whoosh!" he exclaimed, shaking himself like a dog. "A storm of no mean proportion, one to put the fear of God into both man and beast! And it appears not likely to soon pass." He pulled off the cord holding back his hair and rubbed his head vigorously. "The large pine hard by the road was struck and shattered, but in the other direction there appeared a singular, unaccountable phenomenon. I watched what appeared as a great ball of fire forming over our brother's house. Then the extraordinary light lifted and moved off. It struck me as quite like the departure of the glory of the Lord in the vision of Ezekiel and effected much astonishment as I watched."

Hannah looked wide-eyed at Ephraim and shuddered, but Daniel went on.

"Storms such as this ofttimes produce strange effects. I recall as a boy hearing tales of fireballs visiting first one, then another dwelling within the span of a mile or so. I can still see within my mind the stripe left in the darkness after the passage of some small part of lightning in through one wall of the cabin and out the other. I can avow that my mother heard some mighty wailing on that occasion!"

"What happened to the cabin?" Hannah asked.

Daniel shook his head. "No damage done to it or us, and like Shadrach, Meshach, and Abednego, not even the smell of fire was upon us." His eyes twinkled. "After that, however, I paid close heed to my parents' instruction and correction, at least throughout the remainder of the thunder season."

The apocalyptic storm seemed determined to keep Hannah from returning home. Abigail was already preparing supper, and she pressed the girl to stay and eat with them. "I have always desired a daughter if for no other reason than to have her set table for me," she said, her eyes laughing, so like Ephraim's. "Sons lose enthusiasm for such chores as soon as their fathers entice them off to more exciting adventures out of doors. So"—Abigail gave Hannah a warm squeeze—"you may serve as my daughter for the duration of the rain and do my bidding until your limbs fail for weariness. Will you remain?"

Hannah was delighted at the invitation, although she worried momentarily over what her family might think. But after another crash shook the cabin, she quickly decided that there was really nothing she could do about it. They would not likely come looking for her in this weather. They probably figured she had found some sort of shelter until the storm let up.

Hannah helped Abigail spread the snowy-white tablecloth and set out matching napkins. This linen, unlike the homespun towels and sheets she had seen in the household, was more like Chastity's tablecloths, of fine even weave.

She needed instruction, however, with the strange dishware: three wooden "trenchers," as Abigail called them, each a combination platter and bowl hollowed out of poplar. "Grandfather manufactured a collection of six when first he settled on this acreage," Ephraim told her during the meal, "but with just four of us remaining, we normally make use of only two, excepting, of course, for the addition of guests," he added, obviously pleased at her presence.

Another mystery was the one large mug, also of wood. Hannah herself decided that if the plates were shared, so must be the cup, just as they had all used the same mug on that hot day when the limner first appeared. A high salt cellar in the center of the table and pewter spoons at each place completed the setting. "Had I but known you would be our guest," Abigail remarked, "I would have fetched the glassware from behind Ephraim's bed in the loft, but since you are today my daughter, you will be served as family on common stuff."

Hannah could think of no better compliment.

As Abigail bustled about preparing the meal, Hannah marveled at her skill in adjusting the fire to several levels: flame under the bubbling stew, hot coals under what looked like an assortment of stir-fried greens in a "spider" or fry pan on legs, and a third pot of unknown content semiburied in hot ashes.

Hannah couldn't help but wonder what kind of meal would come from her mother's hands under these conditions. Even with a gas stove, Jane's menu was severely limited, and Hannah's father complained a lot about unvarying *"soup toujours."* Even cookouts were more than she cared to tackle, and they seldom used the stone fireplace that Hannah and the others had worked so hard to build. "If you think I'm going to stand in smoke all day with no shower afterwards . . . And you never pick cold days to cook over a fire. It's always the hottest day of the year . . ." and on and on.

Hannah turned off the carping refrain in her mind with a question. "Mr. Ward, how hard is it to keep the house warm in winter? I mean, even with a big fireplace, it must get awfully cold." She looked at the chinks between the logs, fitted and daubed carefully enough, but at best no more than a windbreak.

Both Daniel and Ephraim grew grave, and immediately she had her answer. Winter was indeed perilous and the small cabin a pitiful defense against the forces of biting wind and driving snow, as Abigail had hinted on that hot day.

But Daniel's weatherbeaten face crinkled in a smile. "Not so hard as you might think, lass. Why, come December the first, we pile half the cabin full of firewood, whole green oaks on the bottom, stout back sticks right up to the rafter poles, knotty foresticks on a cushion of brush. Then we move our beds nigh and invite the creatures in to fill the remaining space. With a goodly supply of sausage, pickled cabbage, and a barrel or two of cider close at hand, we set flint and steel to the tinder, creep under five feather beds, and wait for the singing of birds and the voice of the turtledove to call us forth."

Jonah could hardly contain himself. "But Father," he piped, "you have left out Christmas! We must not forget such a day as that!"

"Oh, yes," Hannah joined in, "where will you put the tree in all this? It wouldn't do to put balsam or spruce too close to the fire, and the oxen and sheep might eat the ornaments, especially if you string popcorn and . . ." Her voice trailed off as she noticed four puzzled frowns.

"Oh, dear," she moaned, "I . . . guess you don't have Christmas trees. I'm sorry . . . I should've—"

But Daniel went on with the game, ignoring her embarrassment. "Why, of course—Christmas! That is the one day in the whole of winter on which we emerge from the cabin, wrapped each of us in a feather bed, walk to town for service (for we would not impose upon the horses on such a day, would we?), and return to our former place with a strong infusion of lovage root to cure whatever inward disease we might have incurred by venturing forth."

"And Father, there's syruping, too! If we remain abed until the birds sing, we should miss syruping!" Although Jonah's eyes could not match the blue of his brother's, they sparkled and snapped like spruce kindling.

This time Ephraim answered him. "Ah, little Grasshopper, had we Hannah's fine eight-foot boiling contrivance, with sap drawn from the trees through long spouts that communicate directly to the kettle, we should creep out of our bed for only such time as would be required to waken the trees and light the fire. Then our sleep could indeed continue until the singing of the birds, and when at last they shrill us into spring, we should find our sugar all manufactured and packed into crocks."

Ephraim's words fit the fantasy so well that Hannah was prepared to laugh with the others and simply pass off this unexpected reference to her world. But neither Jonah nor Daniel laughed. They both stared at her in wonder, and Ephraim's eyes held a glint that matched the edge in his voice. Before anything else could be said, however, Abigail ended the play by calling everyone to the table.

As Daniel carried Jonah to his place, Ephraim whispered to Hannah, "Tell me more of this tree so nobly clothed at Christmas. If such adornment could find place in our house, how we should be looked on by all the townsfolk!"

chapter 26

The new skidder arrived at camp on the crest of the storm. Tom couldn't believe his thunder-battered ears, but he looked out to see a truck with a low-bed trailer whining unproductively in the mud at the foot of the driveway. "Who in his right mind would deliver anything in this kind of weather?" He opened the door in welcome as the sodden farmer-logger abandoned ship and trudged toward the house, a stolid hulk indifferent to the celestial fires sizzling about him.

"How do," he said, nodding universally. "Kinda wet, ain't it? Good fer gittin' skiddahs noice an' clean."

Tom shook his head in disbelief. "You said you'd bring it today, but you might've waited till the storm let up."

The man shrugged. "What else is theyah t' do on a day loike this? Your duff sets as good as moine."

So they sat. And waited. Jane handed out beer all around and dug out the crumbled dregs of several nearly empty bags of pretzels, chips, triangles, and salted nuts, which then necessitated more beer. And still the heavens growled.

No one gave thought to where Hannah might be taking shelter. The men fell into a comfortable swap of logging tales that served nicely to block out Jane's running commentary on the rapidly deploying leaks in the roof. By the time the beer, pretzels, and conversation had run dry, there was enough of a letup outside for them to slosh down the driveway to conclude the transfer of property.

After the men had maneuvered the skidder to its new berth alongside the other machines and scraped an inch of mud from their legs, an exhilarated Tom suggested they dine out in celebration. "Jane and Ardyth will be glad to get out of the ark, and we can afford to splurge a little. This skidder is gonna make plenty bucks outta that glen!"

At mention of the glen, Hannah popped into their minds. "Hey, where's she been all this time?" Steve wondered aloud. "You'd think she'd have sense enough to come in out of a storm like this."

"Aw, she can take care of herself," Tom replied. "She's found a rock overhang somewhere and is holed up till it quits." He looked up and winced as yet another flash prodded them toward the cabin. "Man! I've seen some lightning in my day, but it seldom sticks around this long! Like it's parked on top of us. If she's not home by the time we're ready to leave, she can shift for herself."

" 'God is jealous, and the Lord revengeth; the Lord revengeth, and is furious; the Lord will take vengeance on his adversaries, and he reserveth wrath for his enemies.' " Daniel Ward read to his little storm-beaten flock from the book of Nahum in his well-worn Bible.

" 'The Lord is slow to anger, and great in power, and will not at all acquit the wicked: The Lord hath his way in the whirlwind and in the storm, and the clouds are the dust of his feet.

" 'Who can stand before his indignation? and who can abide in the fierceness of his anger? his fury is poured out like fire, and the rocks are thrown down by him.' "

A fierce flash and simultaneous clap of thunder seemed to Hannah an extravagant use of visual aids.

" 'There is one come out of thee, that imagineth evil against the Lord, a wicked counsellor.

" 'For now will I break his yoke from off thee, and will burst thy bonds in sunder.

" 'Behold upon the mountains the feet of him that bringeth good tidings, that publisheth peace! O Judah, keep thy solemn feasts, perform thy vows: for the wicked shall no more pass through thee; he is utterly cut off.' "

Daniel returned the volume to the modest holding of books along the front wall and raised his arms in a gesture of prayer that lifted them all to a place of safety.

"Almighty and sovereign God, we Thy frail creatures are helpless before this awesome manifestation of Thy might. As the prophet hath said, Thou wilt indeed have Thy way in the whirlwind and the storm. Nevertheless, we cry to Thee, Oh our Father, and put our trust in Thee. Forgive us our sins; withhold Thy judgment and Thy wrath. Now bless to us the food that cometh from Thy bountiful hand. May we live before Thee in purity and holy love, according to the riches of Thy grace in our Lord Jesus Christ. Amen."

Pulling out the benches, they settled themselves at the table. Ephraim, who had held Jonah during the reading and prayer, shared a trencher with him on one side. Daniel and Abigail sat together opposite them, and Hannah with her own dish was next to Abigail—positioned away from Ephraim with maternal deliberation.

A huge pewter platter of stew steamed before them. Next to it, a smaller plate held the "salad" that had been fried in fat and garnished with pickled nasturtium buds. A fragrant crusty loaf of dark bread lay in a white napkin in the middle of the table. A great tankard brimmed with milk, and throughout the meal Daniel filled the common cup as it was emptied. Two tallow candles sputtered oily smoke, and at long last, only an occasional rumbling flash outside broke the encompassing gloom.

In honor of Hannah's presence, Abigail had made two shy amendments to the normal table. After a bit of last-minute rummaging and polishing, she substituted a silver spoon for the pewter one at the girl's place and set out a glowing silver mug of intricate design, along with a bottle of homemade blackberry wine.

It was this last touch that flooded Hannah with a wave of humility. Here she was, sitting at a crude plank table in homely surrounding. The Wards possessed no more than basic survival equipment, few comforts, and no time to keep even the little they had neat and clean—according to Hannah's modernized standards, anyway. Even Hannah's mother on her laziest day would not have put up with such dirty clutter, to say nothing of flies covering everything.

In this place, however, such luxuries as a neatly stacked woodpile, sanitized dishes, and a well-swept floor crumbled beneath the over-burdening weight of work. And because they couldn't do anything about it, it just didn't matter.

The truly important things were their dependence upon God for life and salvation, enough food on the table, shelter against the elements, and, binding all things together, their deep love and respect for each other. Yes, they owned and prized a silver cup, but significantly, it was brought out, along with their best beverage, only to honor a guest.

Thus, this rustic setting displayed handsomely a jewel of hospitality far more gracious and elegant than the most lavish mansion Hannah could remember seeing. She gave Abigail's hand an appreciative squeeze.

The family put away a prodigious amount of food. The pewter platter was filled again and again with a stew that consisted of meat and at least six different kinds of vegetables. When Ephraim was dispatched to the crock for a resupply of milk, he brought back a jug of cider—hard, Hannah noted, wrinkling her nose— for serving when the milk gave out the second time.

Normally, Hannah had a healthy appetite, but in this company she seemed a poor feeder in comparison. Only Jonah ate less than she, and Ephraim played games with him to encourage more food into his frail little body. The younger boy could feed himself, but only with much spilling and smearing of gravy over face, hands, arms, and tablecloth. His napkin was brought into frequent use, but hardly less than those of the rest of the family. Apparently fingers were acceptable substitutes for the missing forks.

Daniel broke off a chunk of bread to sop up gravy. "Well, lad, how goes the work in the opening?" he asked. "It seems you've spent less time there of late. Nearly done, at least for the nonce?"

Ephraim flicked his eyes furtively toward Hannah and busied himself with another mouthful before giving answer. "Nay, not done, but other tasks intrude."

Hannah glowered at him. *Other tasks, my foot!* As Ephraim adroitly shifted the conversation to safer ground, she wished Daniel was less blind to what was happening. Why couldn't Ephraim's parents see? Immediately, however, she realized that outwardly, Ephraim had been behaving much the same as always; the hollowness was all on the inside.

"Father, relate to Hannah your recollections of the land clearing you have done on change-work. Only take heed lest you embroider your tale beyond reality!"

Smiling, Daniel nodded and moved into a comfortable replay of past labor shared among neighbors. "Ay, the cut-down for Matthew Barlow's cabin; that was a good one. Perhaps it made strong impression because of my youth; however, many an older man still talks of it to this day.

"Thirty men came together on that occasion, and when the circle was marked out, we commenced preparing the drive. The king tree was selected and thus the direction of the fall. We each had two or three trees to undercut on the side away from the master tree. They had to be done with great care, that neither too little nor too much be chopped away.

"When all was in readiness, Matthew Barlow himself cut

through the back of the great five-armed pine that fell onto the others, sending the whole crashing to the ground with such force that the rock on which I stood split beneath my feet. I tell you, not a man among us could but shout and whoop and slap backs. Much rum was drunk also, but it was well earned.

"We praised God, also, that no man was injured. I have heard tell of drives that gave way with choppers caught in the midst. It is not to be undertaken lightly." He looked pointedly at Ephraim. "It does, however, combine agreeable diversion with labor."

Abigail contributed to the conversation her recollections of her early life as a clergyman's daughter. As such, she had been instructed in Latin, Greek, rhetoric, penmanship, Jewish and Church history, chronology of the Bible, and prayer.

Along with her feelings, both good and bad, about sitting at the front of the church with her mother each Sunday, she gave Hannah a detailed sketch of life in a small community.

"Perhaps, though," she finished, "my most agreeable recollection is of my father presiding over the Lord's Supper, an occasion particularly momentous, as it falls only every third month. It was his finest hour."

"What was the Lord's Supper like?" Although Hannah had read about Jesus' last meal with his disciples, she had only vague notions about modern-day procedures and no idea at all of those early New England celebrations.

As Abigail gave her description, Hannah closed her eyes and saw, almost as though she were there, the little church with its rows of benches, women on one side, men on the other. Abigail's father's church was not grand enough to have the enclosed square pews of churches in larger communities. In front, however, were special seats for the minister's wife and the deacons.

Through Abigail's eyes, Hannah saw a child squirming through long hymns of twelve to fifteen stanzas, long prayers of up to an hour, and even longer sermons. When the moment arrived for the holy feast, however, even the child sensed a solemn readiness and spiritual hunger as the small group focused on the words of the pastor:

Having thus warned the profane, the ignorant, and scandalous not to approach the holy table, I now invite such as, sensible of their lost and helpless state of sin, depend upon the atonement of Christ for pardon and acceptance with God; such as desire to renounce their sins, and are determined to lead a holy and godly life.

Our Lord Jesus Christ, on the same night in which he was betrayed, having taken bread, and blessed and broken it, gave it to his disciples, . . . "Take, eat: this is my body, which is broken for you: this do in remembrance of me."

Here, Abigail reported, the round loaves would be broken into chunks and apportioned to solemn black-clad deacons, who, in turn, served the communicants.

After the same manner our Saviour also took the cup; and having given thanks, as hath been done in his name, he gave it to the disciples, saying, "This is the new testament in my blood, which is shed for many for the remission for sins: drink ye all of it."

The young Abigail had watched with awe as her father poured wine from an ornate tankard into each deacon's polished pewter cup. As they moved slowly among the rows of worshipers, words of exhortation hovered over them:

Recollect, then, the grace of God, in Jesus Christ, held forth in this sacrament; and of your obligation to be the Lord's. Walk worthy of the vocation wherewith you are called; and as you have professedly received Christ Jesus the Lord, that you be careful so to walk in him, and to maintain good works.

Hannah shivered under the stern warning, but Ephraim seemed unmoved and filled his trencher yet another time. Abigail rose to clear the table in preparation for pouring the wine. Before she removed the bread napkin, though, Hannah reached for a remaining crumb and set it carefully by her own napkin.

As she sat back on the bench, her mind swirled in an ecstasy of pain, sorrow, inadequacy, hope, and the glory of grace. She was here at this table and had eaten real food that nourished her body, yet she saw everything as through a veil, suspended in time: Ephraim—loving, courageous, and virile, but with cracks issuing from feet of clay; Jonah—a factory reject, second-quality body but first-quality spirit; Daniel—the provider and spiritual sustainer of his little flock, but blind to danger on his doorstep. He had seen Chastity's peril but couldn't recognize the same symptoms in his son.

And Abigail—how could Hannah characterize such a woman? Plain, but with eyes more piercing than the lightning now past, her work more arduous than either Ephraim's or Daniel's. Still she found time to know and care.

The little cabin with its meager store of creature comforts, yet with enough to mark it as *belonging* to these particular people. They, or Daniel's parents before them, had made most of the items. A few special treasures, such as the old clock on the mantel with its stained and smoky face, linked them with an even more distant past.

Now Hannah was sitting at their table, loved and sustained by them, shown the way of life. As her father harvested trees that had been mere seedlings in these people's day, so she was reaping what they had sown of salvation and love.

At the same time, she was contaminating them, bearing seeds of death. Gain from her father's harvest meant death to the glen. In like manner, seemingly as a result of her salvation, what had once held back the wilderness of sin was now crumbling in Ephraim. Was terrible loss inevitable to such gain? And how soon was the harvest?

As Abigail set out the leftover two-thirds of an apple pie, Hannah groaned in protest. "I can't possibly eat another bite! Let Ephraim have my piece. He'll have to work hard tomorrow to make up for the rain." But she tried a small corner, surprised at the flavor lent by dried apples and maple sugar.

As the wine was poured into the silver cup and passed around, Daniel and Ephraim laughed over the "rough welcome" offered by the blackberry patch last summer as an obstacle to their wine-making. Hannah, however, was emotionally sequestered, her thoughts on thorns of another sort.

This is my body, which is given for you: this do in remembrance of me. As she ate her tiny crumb, she felt nourishment proceeding to her from Jesus, the compassionate Source of redemption. Yes, to *her,* the sorry source of contamination.

This is the new testament in my blood, which is shed for you . . . shed for you . . . shed for you. As thorns crowned Christ's sacrifice, so briars pierced Hannah's heart, mingling her own blood and tears with the blackberry wine.

Ephraim's voice brought her private communion to a close. "If the rain continues thus, Hannah, we shall be obliged to bundle you overnight, is not that so, Mother?" He got the expected frown from Abigail, but his father joined the playful thrust.

"Ay, lad, and before we know, you will have us procure a sofa for your sparking. Now, that would of a surety provoke the wrath of the entire church upon your head!"

"But Father, Hannah's world is such that bundling is considered a trifling affair, more cause for laughter than scruple. Do we not lend weight to unseemly thoughts by reprobating such innocent practices until they do indeed have that unhappy effect? Is not the exercise of honor by two people in bed a more convincing sermon than continually railing against it?"

Daniel pursed his lips, nodding thoughtfully, and then winked slyly at his son.

Hannah could feel her hot face throbbing and wanted to cry out, "Don't listen to Ephraim! *Please* don't listen!" How far would the infection spread? Daniel? Jonah? Was even Abigail safe?

Mr. Ward started to answer Ephraim, but Abigail broke in

sweetly. "Daniel, my dear, has not the rain abated sufficiently to tend to chores before light fails us? It is gloomy in here already. I do wish we had but a little of the illumination in Hannah's world!"

Numb, Hannah looked up at the mantel clock. "What time is it, anyway? I need to be going before it gets darker. Hey, that clock can't be right. Isn't it a lot later than five o'clock? It must be closer to seven." But in trying to figure the time from the Roman numerals on the dial, she discovered that the whole thing was backwards, as though she were seeing it in a mirror.

chapter 27

*T*omorrow we begin logging." Hannah's father looked steadily at her. "And there will be no interference—of any kind."

Hannah's skin prickled in the booming silence. She felt surrounded by so many snakes, each one tasting the reverberating air for her reaction. Her need to say something froze the passing seconds, but what could she say? "No, I won't let you"? Not to her father she couldn't. "Wait just one more day"? What would that gain? Besides, once her father set out to do something, he would not put up with avoidable delays. Mechanical breakdowns he could only fume over, but the desires of his children were never an obstacle.

Finally, Hannah rose slowly from her chair and raised her hand in a formal oath-taking gesture. Mike started a smile, but it broke immediately under the weight of her pale seriousness.

"I, Hannah Valdegar, do solemnly swear"—her voice trembled almost uncontrollably—"that I have done everything within my power on behalf of the wilderness area entrusted to me, to preserve it from men bent on ruin and exploitation. I pray God will hold me guiltless in the day of judgment, for I hereby separate myself from the goals and values of this entire family, save for my brother

Peter. May God have mercy on us all!" With contorted face, she fled from the house into the cool stillness of the late-August evening.

Her first thought was to simply withdraw from the scene of carnage and find solace with Ephraim, if only by substituting one pain for another. After a mostly sleepless night, though, she decided that one thing still remained for her to do: she could watch and weep in silent demonstration. Were she to stay away, she would bear the guilt of a rape victim who submits to violation without protest.

The next day, the equipment parade, led by the new skidder, made its way along the base of the glen. Mike spotted Hannah huddled at her lonely post off to the side, her Bible now in plain sight. He took advantage of a lengthy debate between Tom and Steve on the layout of skid trails to amble over with some awkward but well-meant consolation. "I . . . uh . . ." He cleared his throat. "You shouldn't sit here and watch all this, Snooks. Why don't you go buy yourself a new outfit for school?" He dug into his pocket for the roll of bills he liked to flash at effective moments. "You'll be a senior this year, won't you? And—"

"Cockroach!" Hannah screeched venomously. "On top of everything, you try to buy me off. Get away!"

"Mike!" Tom roared. "Leave her alone!" He swore. "You got nothing but a balloon in your head! Get over here and start hauling saws or tools!"

Hannah bit her lip as Mike slunk off under the double attack. Belatedly, she recognized his kind intention and regretted her hasty fusillade.

As her father had predicted, the logging was nearly as easy as tipping the logs onto the truck. They first cleared a log-yard below the road and then began to chop their way uphill, the mighty trees falling into the slope and sending seismic shudders through Hannah's heart.

As each monarch came down, the crew fell to with saws abuzz, limbing, measuring, and cutting them into log lengths. Then Steve, proud and trying to camouflage his skidder inexperience, pulled his full twitch of logs down to the yard and pushed them with the stacking blade into a neat pile. Tom hummed a gloating tune as he marked the cuts on long, thick trunks that sometimes yielded as many as seven twelve-foot logs.

The higher they worked in the glen, however, the more difficulties they encountered. With Hannah as audience, they were trying hard not to damage the young trees that would remain, but the heavy-crowned giants had a way of bringing down everything in their way. Steve kept skinning trees with a skidder wheel, and his hefty twitches scraped and tore off bark as they threaded through the standing timber. Huge ruts began to develop along a wet contour, and by noon the hillside resembled a battlefield.

So different from logging with a horse, thought Hannah. Faster, to be sure, but at such a price. Ephraim's horse Captain could never haul these logs, though, not even with Major helping. The oxen might, but their tongues would be hanging out in exhaustion, and it would take them forever. Ephraim, though, could skid the logs with scarcely a scuff mark on any of the other trees. Gentle logging, kind to the land.

As another tree crashed to the ground, Hannah suddenly wondered whose side Ephraim would be on in the controversy over the glen. She felt sure that a couple of months ago, he would have joined her in protecting the glen, but now . . . would big business override other values? Would he and Uncle Latham start drawing up plans to market a skidder, provided they could invent the internal combustion engine?

She tried to get some perspective on it all. Logging, she knew, was necessary and good in its place. Trees were a renewable resource, useful in hundreds of ways from fuelwood to food. And the work her father did was good, clean work, nonpolluting, self-healing. She had no objection to cutting big trees as such, scattered through the woods or even a large stand.

The glen, though, was different. Here, where time was marked in rings measuring thirty-seconds-of-an-inch, big trees joined with the foundations of the earth, the primordial springs of life and wisdom, to become a temple where God Himself was pleased to dwell. Now the structure was being razed, the city sacked, the inhabitants put to the sword. And her mother was to blame with her wearisome carping about the cabin and a swimming pool.

No . . . her mother was not to blame. Hannah had been quick to echo her mother, to model her desires after her sister and hanker for the trappings of the rich, the party crowd. Less than a month ago, she would have jumped at Mike's offer of money to buy that Garachi, not simply because she liked it, but because the designer name signified power. She was different now. She didn't care about the dress or money or influence. The damage, though, had already been done, the germs had spread.

The infection had first taken root by means of the heavy pill. She saw that now. The Pepsi had tempted Ephraim; why else would he have kept it so long? But he blew the pill test, and she had been the pusher, forcing it on him against his will. Why hadn't she listened when he told her it wasn't allowed? Why hadn't she stuck with his Simpler's Delight, or whatever it was called? It had seemed so obvious that her ways were better. And they were. He did get fast relief from his pain. At such a price, though!

With shame, she saw again his look of defiance as he stated the rule and then deliberately broke it. Then after that first act of rebellion, he got hooked on the ax and peavey and all the other ideas she had dangled before him.

Perhaps Peter was right: dabbling with the future does make cracks in the universe—moral cracks, at the very least.

The backward clock on the mantel haunted her as a possible key to the whole question of *why*. There was some opposite connection between Christ's holiness and her own sinful nature. Would Ephraim have remained strong if she had not stumbled into his world? And if she were responsible for his downfall, to what degree was she responsible to turn things around? Should she simply stay away and forget him? How much could she really do by going back, or was it already too late? Maybe she should go and just stay there forever. Would giving up her life in this world be "killing the old man within her," setting them both free?

Oh, Ephraim, Ephraim ... For the fourth time that day as she watched the destruction mounting around her, she opened her Bible to some lines that at first had seemed curiosities but that now took on terrible meaning.

Before she had read more than a few words, however, her attention was diverted to a pickup truck bumping along the logging road. It wasn't Mike's, and she didn't recognize the little man who jumped out and bustled about with an armload of tools and other items.

The skidder had stopped just a few minutes earlier, and the men hovered over it anxiously. With no logging noise to direct him, the stranger spied Hannah and headed toward her. He was a thin, wiry man, middle-aged, with the bright, sharp features of a fox.

He greeted the girl with an eye-crinkling smile. "How do? Lookin' for Tom Valdegar's skidder that needs fixin'." He looked around and spotted the machine that Hannah hadn't even realized was disabled. "Ah! There 'tis. Won't take but a minute to get 'er goin' agin."

He started off across the slope but turned back to Hannah, holding out a small plastic juice container half full of some unknown beverage. "This bein' a dry sort of day, you might be needin' a bit of this t' keep your strength up. Here. Take an' drink it."

Hannah shook her head, suspicious of unlabeled potions, despite the stranger's friendly manner. She could have used a drink, but she wasn't *that* thirsty. The man nodded his blessing anyway and whisked off to his repair job.

With a remote sense of wonder, Hannah watched him work his
way through the logging slash to keep an appointment that no one
seemed to have made. He was right, too, about the job taking but a
minute. With a few quick turns of his huge wrench and some
well-focused hammering, he soon had the skidder roaring once
again. After shaking hands all around, he headed off downhill.

Hannah responded to his brisk wave as he trotted past and then
turned her attention back to Hosea.

"I know all about Ephraim;
    Israel is not hidden from me.
Ephraim, you have now turned to prostitution;
    Israel is corrupt. . . .

"Though Ephraim built many altars for sin offerings,
    these have become altars for sinning. . . .

"The prophet, along with my God,
    is the watchman over Ephraim,
yet snares await him on all his paths,
    and hostility in the house of his God. . . .

"Ephraim boasts,
    'I am very rich; I have become wealthy.
With all my wealth they will not find in me
    any iniquity or sin.' . . .

"It was I who taught Ephraim to walk,
    taking him by the arms. . . .
I led him with cords of human kindness,
    with ties of love; . . .
For I am God, and not man—
    the Holy One among you. . . .
I will settle them in their homes,"
    declares the Lord.

Peter came and sat beside her. As she sobbed in his arms, she
wondered what he was doing here at this time of the week, but she
never did get around to asking.

"Oh, Peter, I kept wishing all day that one of the trees would fall over on me, and that would be the end of it. But they're gone and I'm still here."

Peter looked ruefully at the broken and skinned tops. "Well, they didn't cut every stick, or at least they tried not to. Before you're a grandmother, the glen will be recognizable again, even though it won't be the same."

"Huh—birch and poplar. Some glen!"

"Well, you could do worse. A lot of people like birch."

"Yah, what do they know? Peter, don't try to make me feel better. It won't work."

He nodded and was silent a moment. "Hannah, you're angry and hurt. I am, too. But maybe . . . now and again . . . I've had more . . . uh . . . opportunity to deal with anger than you have. I heard something awhile back that helped me, and maybe it'll help you. There was this lady who'd been through the Holocaust, lost her family and all. But her response was to say over and over, 'Forgiveness is the only remedy for history.' She endured more than either of us will likely have to bear, yet she knew that vengefulness can never heal, no matter how big the hurt. Can you see that, too, Hannah?"

Now it was her turn to be silent. "Yes . . . no . . . I don't know," she finally said. "I don't think I feel vengeful, but I'm not ready to forgive. There's too much . . . emotion tied up in the glen." Again her tears started. "But revenge, no. There's a bigger battle, somewhere else, and I can't think about getting even right now."

Peter sat back and studied her face carefully. "Hannah, there's more to this business than you're letting on. Some things you've told me and some you haven't. I am trying to make you feel better, but you're hiding something that I can't get at. If and when you want to talk about it, I'll listen."

She looked at him gratefully. "Peter, who have I got but you? Everything's so . . . mixed up. I'm right in the middle of a storm with two fronts, maybe even a third that I can't even see. And I

[223]

feel like I'm about to be blown away." She bit her lip and fought to control her voice.

His eyes moved to the Bible beside her. "You like it?"

"Oh, yes. It's super! When I'm reading it, though, it's like I'm in the eye of the storm, a place where it's calm and safe, but I never know when I'm going to bounce off again into the screamers. I want to show you some things in it, maybe after supper. Now that the guys are gone, though, let's walk up the brook to where they haven't cut."

They talked late into the night, and at first Peter had to pick through her oblique remarks in an attempt to discern the shape of the crisis between the two worlds. In the end, however, she told him everything, as well as her struggle over what to do.

"You were right, Peter, about going forward and backward in time. For some reason, I've been allowed to go back and be part of Ephraim's world, but by trying to sell my world to him, I've unleashed some horrible infectious virus, a 'scrofulous humor,' they'd call it," she laughed. "Now somehow it's up to me to stamp it out before it goes beyond Ephraim. Uncle Latham can't be helped. I don't believe he ever did belong to God. He's just there fertilizing the weed seeds I brought in.

"I'm convinced I need to go to Ephraim, something specific I have to do, maybe involving the ax and peavey, but I don't know what it is. Something's pushing me, and if I stay and be safe, I'll have missed the most important thing in my life."

She hesitated a moment, then went on. "Not even the glen is holding me back anymore. When I first got here this morning before the men came, I stood near the bottom of the brook where it goes under the culvert. I saw something way up at the top of the hill, and as I watched, this filmy . . . glow . . . seemed to gather the beauty of the whole glen and draw it down over the rocks and waterfalls. It came down just like those old movies on television where the vampy woman floats down a wide staircase while violins play in the background. Only it wasn't vampy, and there

[224]

weren't any violins. It got bigger and bigger, and at the same time, it seemed that the glen was getting smaller or losing its strength. Then it went under the culvert and was gone. I felt like part of me went with it, and it didn't matter, because what was left had to do this thing ... whatever it is."

Peter was trying hard to understand, to give support, but he was shaken by her intensity and abandon. The easiest explanation, that the glen crisis had pushed her over the edge and she had flipped out, made more sense than did her strange tale. And though it would be painful to face such a problem, he could accept it except for one thing: the humming night surrounding them upheld her compulsion, and he too felt the pricks of her necessity. No, he decided, she wasn't crazy.

Nevertheless, he tried to persuade her to stay. "You're not responsible for somebody's life nearly two hundred years ago. Your family needs you, and I ... I need you."

"No, Peter, you're cut from better cloth than the rest of us. Leave, go away, become a monk or missionary or a worker with purple sea tortoises—anything. Just give Jesus and the Bible a chance instead of the grab-what-you-can business around here. But I have to go. I must not betray the harvest, that thing that is like me and cannot be forgotten."

chapter 28

*H*annah was out of bed early, hoping to get away before anyone else stirred, but she found Peter up. Through pantomime he tried to convince her to eat some breakfast, but she refused. They went outdoors, finding behind the outhouse a place for whispered conversation.

"Please don't follow me. Will you promise? You'll wreck everything if you do. Peter, do I look all right? I mean, am I covered and decent, not apt to stir even a whisker in guys if I walked down Main Street?" She turned around to display her unpretentious slacks and loose-fitting shirt. Indeed, her costume, though neat and harmonious, quite likely would sneak her past even the most dedicated girlwatcher.

With a nod of satisfaction at Peter's dubious appraisal, Hannah put her arms around him and held him tightly. "I love you, Peter. Vushondio!" she whispered, and with a quick teary kiss she was gone. Peter stared after her, trying to keep his own face in order.

Hannah thought she had gotten safely away, but Mike stepped out of his tent, stretching and yawning loudly. "Hey, what bedbug drove you out so early? You goin' out to set mines on the skid trails?"

Hannah stopped, turned back with a piquant smile, and put her hands on his shoulders. "Yah, Mike. About what I said yesterday. I realized right after I lit into you that you were trying to cheer me up. I'm sorry." And she kissed him, too.

"Well, I'll be . . ." Mike rubbed his head as she headed off into the trees.

The sky, bright overhead, hung close and heavy above the trees. Darkness seeped from the earth, and Hannah had the sensation of walking on squishy, slippery ground, yet everything was dry. A rank smell of war tainted the fall air. Wood asters and white goldenrod bent away from her dogged tread; hay-scented fern turned yellow in her path. At her approach, birds fled south, leaving behind only the steady thrum of a thousand lacewings.

Summer had ripened, the harvest had come, and Hannah slogged laboriously through viscous smoke distilled from centuries of autumn leaves. It clung like tar to her legs, and soon she was panting from the effort. Over and over in her mind ran a line from the Scripture Daniel had read at the table: "Keep thy solemn feasts, perform thy vows . . . perform thy vows . . ." She pushed ahead with all the strength within her.

When she reached the ridge trail, she stopped for several moments, then wheeled and shouted into the emptiness between her and the camp. "I forgive you!" With a small smile of satisfaction, she resumed her march.

As she passed the ledges, the elemental conflict became so intense that the ground beneath fairly shook. Her legs trembled and buckled.

But the physical struggle to get that far paled to insignificance when she saw the figure at the wall. No ordinary man, he seemed all of burning bronze, though his great cloak flowed soft and supple. Even more alarming, he was one person, yet his shadow traced other shapes—a nervous, bent tree; a mushroom; a ten-point buck; a bison; a fox—all moving as multiple images in his train.

Hannah fell to her hands and knees, overcome and speechless. Was she to die right here, her mission aborted? If so, she would perish at the hands of a terrible holiness, like ice before a blow torch. Her chest felt bound with steel; she could scarcely breathe.

"Ephraim, help!" She tried to cry out, but her voice, locked in weakness, would not carry beyond the wall. She turned it inward. "Jesus, please, help me!" Devastating sobs wracked her body until she was spent and lay as dead.

The figure in bronze looked pityingly on her prostrate form. "Hannah, you who are highly esteemed of God, I am a Sent One, commissioned to guard your passage through time, through wisdom, through pain. Rise up now, keep your feast, perform your vow." He reached down and laid his hand on her.

She recoiled in agony. "Oh, please, keep away! I can't stand it! How can I do anything? You've taken every ounce of my strength!" she cried, unaware that a moment earlier, she couldn't have uttered a word.

"You speak rightly. In yourself you have no strength, but infinite power dwells in weakness. Come now. Rise up and drink." He held out the same plastic juice container that had been offered her the day before.

She looked into his face and recognized the foxlike features of the skidder mechanic. But with it were all the other faces as well—the historian, the old lady, the deer, the man who sold them the skidder. She rolled back, overwhelmed by this revelation of both natural and supernatural backup throughout the summer.

"Had you accepted the drink yesterday," he went on, "you might have been spared a greater part of this cup of suffering. But you will be upheld. Come. Drink. This is blackberry wine, your heart's blood shed by you. Peace! Be strong now. Be strong."

As she sipped the dark liquid, the secret of the mirrored clock came instantly clear.

Hannah sat alone, a new vitality within that nearly equaled the tempest still tearing at earth and sky. After she had risen slowly to her feet, she could scarcely remain upright on the heaving, thundering ground. But when she stepped across the wall, everything became suddenly still, as though the whole universe hung in a state of suspension.

chapter 29

*P*eter took a long walk before breakfast, conflict of a different sort tearing at him. He desperately wanted to abandon his promise to Hannah and even hiked the length of the ridge, stopping at her trail junction to stare out toward the ledges. Her plea held, however, and he walked on through yellowing bracken, a singular sadness feeding on his own personal turmoil.

He had been shaken by their conversation the night before, by the strangeness of her experiences, to be sure, but even more by her comments about his situation that seemed an audio replay of his own mind. She had not asked, and he had not told her, why he had come on Tuesday. (Tom had said remarkably little, too. "Just be sure you head out early enough in the morning to get the store open on time.") But from what she had read to him out of her Bible, he felt she had an uncanny grasp of his frustrations. Two things in particular kept hammering at his thoughts:

> "If you want to be perfect, go, sell your possessions and give to the poor, and you will have treasure in heaven. Then come, follow me. . . . Everyone who has left houses or brothers or sisters or father or mother . . . for my sake will receive a hundred times as much and will inherit eternal life."

"Do not suppose that I have come to bring peace to the earth. I did not come to bring peace, but a sword. For I have come to turn."

"a man against his father,
a daughter against her mother . . .
a man's enemies will be the members of his own household."

"Whoever finds his life will lose it, and whoever loses his life for my sake will find it."

Was that what Hannah was doing—losing her life for God's sake? Peter wondered. If so, she'd be okay. But what about him? How should he go about losing his life for God's sake?

. . . For God's sake. Now there was a familiar phrase, the leitmotif in all his father's reprimands. The irony made Peter smile until with a chill he recalled Hannah's "Pay attention!" experience while trying to untangle the log pile. Were even their father's colorful blasphemies used by God?

Peter was afraid of his father. Strange that after all these years he should suddenly become aware of such an obvious thing. Tom had never been a child beater, and although Peter had had his fair share of spankings as a child, he had never been singled out for physical abuse. Perhaps he would have suffered less had that been the sum of his ill treatment. The actual damage, though, had gone far deeper.

Now the time had come to sound his real-life "Vushondio!" and to make a stand for the preservation of what little wilderness still remained to him. Had it not been for Hannah, he perhaps would've gone on for years, cringing and submitting and hating himself all the more for his weakness.

He could do one of two things: if he stayed, he would have to declare his independence in large block letters, and then fight for it, and in all probability be routed anyway. Or he could play the coward's role and run, leaving the inevitable explosion for other spectators to appreciate. His chief concern there, though, was that Hannah would become victim of the fallout.

He went back along the ancient path of the ridge trail, again hesitating at the junction, then on to the top of the glen by a circuitous route, keeping well away from the logging crew. He sat with his back to the mayhem below, observing instead the rocks and ferns and mosses and the water course that had just traces of moisture left.

Yes, the glory had departed, and his path was clearly laid out just midway between martyrdom and capitulation. After a lingering farewell to the trees, he returned to the empty cabin, scribbled a brief note, and left it with his ski-shop keys on the table.

chapter 30

*E*phraim and Uncle Latham were both in the clearing when Hannah came over the stone pile. Neither was working or seemingly had any intention of doing so, having neither horse nor tool for woods work. *But that's not true.* Hannah frowned. *The ax and peavey are here, right next to Ephraim.*

She was correct the first time, however. The stage was set, the props in place, the actors ready; now that she had arrived, the play could begin.

To his costume, Ephraim had added the first fuzz of a beard, along with Mike's hat, worn at exactly the right angle to make Hannah's heart leap in spite of herself. The hat and wavy hair framed his sapphire eyes, and with his loose open-necked shirt and work-stained breeches, the effect would have worked up a small mob of teenage girls anywhere in the country.

The three stared at each other, Ephraim cocky and eager for Hannah's reaction, Uncle Latham a bit off balance by Hannah's change of attire, and Hannah trying to channel her first impressions toward some purposeful dialogue. Uncle spoke first.

"Aha, Missy, thou art once again clad to provoke godly men to the abandonment of virtue and to recommend thyself by thy heathenish garb—"

"Don't say another word, you scrofulous old begetter and abandoner of babies! I am not of your world and have been coming here only as a guest. As such I've worn clothing that would make me acceptable, but I don't care about that any more. Dressed in clothes that are fitting and modest in my own world, I stand here to make you accountable. You are the one who provokes godly men to sin by hypocrisy and selfish money-making schemes, and I command you in the name of Jesus Christ to leave this place once and for all!"

Hannah knew even before his startled look became a malicious smirk that he wouldn't give up as easily as all that, but she felt a rightness about what she had said and done so far.

"Ephraim, lad, what think ye of the hussy, that mayhap she hath a fair amount of unpresentable parts under all that modesty?"

For once, Hannah rejoiced over so many years' exposure to her family's loose banter. Mike especially, for all his appealing qualities, had served as a sort of mirror image of the old reprobate. This was not the time to be embarrassed, and her steely eyes scarcely blinked as she turned from Uncle Latham to Ephraim.

"Ephraim, you are a child of God's love, but you've let yourself be drawn in by this dirty old man. I realize I started it all—and may God have mercy on me. I pushed that pill on you, even though you said it was not allowed. I brought in seeds of sin that have grown all summer into acres of weeds. Uncle, though, has been busy watering and fertilizing the weed patch, keeping you from working, filling your head with silly get-rich-quick ideas. You're so used to him that maybe you didn't notice at first what he was up to.

"Ephraim, the things you've actually done aren't all that wicked, but you're standing on Thomas Allen's log, ready to start your own little war of independence against God, and Uncle is trying to get you to fire that first shot. You know what the Bible says about these things a whole lot better than I do, but you've stopped your ears and chosen to be sucked in by promises as slippery as watermelon seeds. Hey, I know firsthand all about this kind of stuff, and I can tell you, you're chasing a fistful of smoke!"

With a look of annoyance, Ephraim picked up the peavey and leaned on it, but Hannah went right on.

"You know what carpenter ants are—those big tanks that tunnel through trees?" She ignored the blank look on his face. Never mind that he wouldn't know a tank if he sat on one. This was hard enough without having to translate everything she said. "Well, it's like you're letting them loose in your house, and now the cabin is ready to fall down around your ears. Soon trees will start growing out of the foundation, and people will come by and say, 'Too bad we couldn't see it like it was!' Ephraim, you were once a beautiful person, but now you're shot through with rot, all because you listen to Uncle Latham."

She glanced in Uncle's direction, hoping her words were having some sort of effect on him. If he were out of the way, she felt sure Ephraim could be brought around. The older man, however, was rocking on his heels, looking confident and well pleased with the loyalty of his protégé. As Ephraim tossed the peavey aside and responded to Hannah, Uncle's smile grew even larger.

"Dearest—" He took her hands and spoke with gentle persuasion.

With the hat and those eyes, Hannah's heart quailed within her.

"Beloved, my inner being sees naught but beauty in you. Even when your anger gathers, you are lovely to behold—your eyes, your hair—" He brushed a stray wisp with the backs of his fingers. "I desire you to be with me always. I am sensible of your world being vastly different from mine, but if you will but consent to marry me, I will have done with such menial labor as log cutting and will utilize my time in constructing a fine dwelling— perhaps even of brick—as comfortable and worthy as can be contrived. With the increase of means which I envision, you shall have fine garments as befits the wife of a man of influence and power such as I shall be, and we shall entertain a host of persons of high estate. You must consent, my dearest. I pray you, marry me and stay here forever."

Hannah stood in a state of shock, appalled not only by his brazen proposal in front of Uncle Latham, but most of all by the full flower of corrupted piety opening before her eyes. Beauty, wealth, man of influence—indeed!

Ephraim continued his pitch. "I should strive to ease your lot, perhaps with a servant lass." He gave Uncle a quick wink. "We have acquaintance with one who would feel herself well used in such office, even with no wage but a crust of bread thrice a day."

"Oh, I'm sure!" retorted Hannah. "A real bargain! And since your charity is so great, I suppose her baby will benefit, too— maybe even inherit a portion of all this wealth you're going to generate—especially the Latham part," she added with a scathing look at the older man.

"Ephraim, Ephraim," she went on, "when you were a child, God taught you to walk, taking you by the arms. He led you with cords of kindness, with ties of love. When I was a child, you taught me. You instructed me in the Catechism and led me away from the outlooks and values of my world. I used to think we had so much in my world, and I told you about our houses and cars and fast deals. I compared your life with the future, and that made you dissatisfied. Now when I look backwards into your time, I see that it's you guys who are truly rich. You don't have a lot of gadgets, and you have to work hard, but that's just the way it is here. Everyone works hard, and everyone puts up with pain. In return, you've got more than enough to eat and wear and keep you warm; you have more freedom than we do, and you don't need locks on your doors or tranquilizers or antacids.

"Ephraim, don't you see what you have? God has set you about with stone walls of protection and love. It's only in Him that you can be fruitful."

Her voice took on authority. "Ephraim, take off the hat. Give back the peavey and the ax. It's too late to do anything about those pain pills—they were the first things to catch you—but you can get rid of the other things. Those temptations from my world that you fully understood to be *not allowed* have become idols to your destruction. You let them in, and now sin controls you. The only way out is to kill the old nature."

Hannah shifted, and her words softened. "Do you remember that day when you stood up to the men who were after Tobias? That's when I first began to truly love you. It wasn't just your courage, awesome though it was; no, you were willing to risk your life for a nobody. Hey, I've got a friend at home who's *somebody*. You know what she'd do with a person like Tobias? She'd step on him, grind him into the dirt. You're not like that. You care about Tobias and Jonah; you'd gladly risk your life for them.

"Ephraim, you're a strong oak, but there are vultures in your branches. Get rid of them! Turn back to God; crucify the 'old man' within you!"

The battle raged in earnest now, between earth and sky, tree and field, growth and decay. Hannah's legs trembled violently, but she felt an unshakable calm within.

Uncle's smile vanished, and he moved behind Ephraim, speaking softly, yet audibly, in his ear. "God hath not commanded such austerity as she would have thee believe. Doth not the Word, say, 'Forget not, my son, the instruction of our Lord. He giveth a goodly life to those who follow Him'?"

Ephraim, too, had lost his jaunty air, and Hannah was encouraged that the conflict was no longer just in the elements but had finally moved to his face. He looked at her with tortured longing. "Hannah, please. I love you. If what I have offered vexes you, then I would lay it all aside to regain your affection. It means nothing apart from my love for you. Pray, consent to marriage and abide with me for alway. I beg of you, dearest!" He drew her into his arms.

Dear God, what is this temptation? It would be different if I hadn't known him as he was, so full of love for You and consideration for his family. Oh, Ephraim, how can I give you up, turn you over? Maybe this is just a temporary thing that would change if I did stay. Peter is the only one who'd care. Hosea does say, "I will settle them in their homes." Maybe the decision to stay—like the way the clearing comes or goes, depending on my intention—would snap the chain that holds me to my time, and I would spend the rest of my life here.

Could I live like Abigail and spin wool, scrub clothes with homemade soap, kill a chicken for supper, bear babies and bury most of them? Abigail is a strong woman, strong with glory, a lot stronger 'han I am, but I could work at it. Ephraim, though, isn't strong, even with all his muscles; his looks can't make up for the terrible cancer he got from me. Oh, Ephraim, I am your weakness!

She pulled away, her eyes steeled with new resolve. "Ephraim, if I go, you must give back the ax and the peavey. If I stay, I must die, and you must kill me. Only then will you be free. There is no other way."

Ephraim had been set to argue, but her ultimatum stunned him. Uncle, too, was taken aback, but he recovered quickly and paced about the boy, his nervous directives rising to a shriek. "Pay no heed, lad, pay no heed! 'Twould be the greatest folly. She hath no power over thee and would only bind thee tighter in the name of freedom. Take care, though, lest she attempt to escape by turning back. Thou knowest she has but to—"

"Ephraim, listen to me." Hannah stopped in irritation and lashed out at Uncle's jabbering din. "Shut up, will you?"

Strange that Mike should come to mind at such a time. He could always talk the tail off a monkey, according to her father. But even beyond that, was he linked in some deeper mirrored way to Uncle Latham? Would Hannah's fight with Uncle affect Mike as well as Ephraim?

She couldn't stop to figure it out now, though; enough that Uncle had quieted down.

"Ephraim, the rules of this time game are weird. Somehow I know that if I turn toward the wall today—even with no intention of leaving—I'll blow the whole thing. I'm no coward, though. You've seen that. I'll stand here till I turn into a beech tree unless you give me the ax and peavey."

Unlike Ephraim, Uncle seemed to understand the time aspect of the encounter, to be acquainted with the mechanics of her comings and goings. He circled to safety behind her, knowing full well, despite his words, that she wouldn't turn.

Uncle Latham began a new line, his voice dropping to more persuasive tones. "If she will not have thee, lad, there are other means of procuring the desired end. Thy passion gnaws hot within thee and needs find release. Thou art safe here from prying eyes. Or if this suit thee not, the hill beyond offers a fair enough place, there under the spreading tree. Lie with her, and she will marry speedily enough. She is a ripe grape, yea, meat enough for more than one!"

Hannah could hear him fairly slavering behind her.

Something clicked in her mind, but she dared not break her concentration to pursue it. Her only hope of overriding anger and fear was to keep her eyes steady and fixed on Ephraim's face. He was difficult to read, and she couldn't tell how he would respond to this new approach. That he had become aroused was obvious, but he remained motionless.

The three stood as though in position for a stately dance, waiting only for the music to begin. How much longer could this go on? In sheer desperation, Hannah fell back on a weapon of the past to break the deadlock, beginning a soft, almost irrelevant recitation:

"Question: What is the chief end of man?

"Answer: The chief end of man is to glorify God and to enjoy him forever.

"Question: What is adoption?

"Answer: Adoption is an act of God's free grace, whereby we are received into the number, and have a right to all the privileges, of the sons of God.

"Question: What is sanctification?

"Answer: Sanctification is the work of God's free grace, whereby we are renewed in the whole man after the image of God, and are enabled more and more to die unto sin, and live unto righteousness."

Infuriated, Uncle screamed vilifications and amended his orders from rape to murder. "Drag her forth from the city gate and put her to the sword! Take her to the high place and there offer sacrifice to the Lord thy God, even as did Samuel and Solomon! However, offer first thy seed by lying with her, then pour forth her blood with thine own right arm!"

Hannah drew in her breath sharply, her vision spinning as though icy water had been dumped down her back. Just in time, she checked herself from wheeling around to face Uncle Latham and thus losing everything by turning toward the wall.

"*You!* You murderous old fiend! You killed Chastity!" Her voice echoed against the surrounding trees. "You got her pregnant, then you killed her! That line about searching the base of the cliff and your trips to town—all a big sham. You took her out that night for one last orgy, didn't you, before doing away with the evidence!"

Uncle's screeching had stopped, and he began to chuckle.

Hannah could scarcely contain her rage.

"Ah, Ephraim lad," Uncle Latham said, a loathsome smile infecting his voice, "You know not the pleasure of such an one. But you shall, you shall. Mistress Hannah here will bid us defiance, but we two shall prevail. 'Two are better than one; because they have a good reward for their labour.' Thou shalt indeed have good reward. She hath no white robe to inflame thy passions, but youth needs not such artifice."

"You even made her wear her white dress?" Hannah's fury made her voice unsteady.

"Ah, no!" he tittered. "'Twas her own affectation. I acquainted her with my design to offer her to the Lord as did Jephthah his daughter. As that good woman did make a request of her father, so Chastity made supplication to attire herself fittingly. I'll swear, the vision was worthy of an angel in heaven! Where she acquired or had it concealed, I comprehend not, but 'twas a generous bargain on her part!"

All during this recital, Hannah kept her eyes on Ephraim's face, and for the first time, she detected a flick of uncertainty. But why wasn't he crying out in horror at the grisly confession? Was he so deeply in bondage to Uncle that he no longer had any sense of outrage—he, who had been so upset when she appeared in a halter and shorts?

Hannah spoke as to a child. "Ephraim, Chastity is dead. Most likely, you'll find her body at the foot of the lookout, maybe under the crumbly rubble. She'll be dressed in white, a robe washed in blood. Even though her body is soiled and stained by this man's lust, her heart is pure and her name, Chastity, is complete—not just a bunch of letters. She lived up to her name by hiding her virtue in the *Name*."

She covered her face. "Oh, Chastity, I never knew! I never understood any of it, why you were so anxious to get away, through Ephraim at first, but when I got on your case about that, by whatever means. I didn't know why you were always washing, why you liked white so much, why you made the robe in the first place, why you loved all those verses on purity! You're the only person my influence didn't get to. I might have been able to do something if I'd known, but even if I could've rescued you from your father's clutches, I probably would've ruined you like I did Ephraim."

She lifted her eyes again to Ephraim's face. "Oh, Ephraim, don't you see? Uncle has played the game to its final end. He took his fornicating to the high places under a green tree, even to the point of sacrificing his firstborn. He brought worldliness around full circle to where it becomes worship once again, an abomination, a loathsome, defiled idolatry. He wants to draw you as well into his evil circle. Ephraim, don't let him! I can see in your face that this is a horror to you, that you want no part of it. Come away from this terrible wickedness and put off the works of darkness that have grown up in your soul!"

Uncle Latham could see Ephraim's face, too, and again he began to howl.

"She is a sorceress and would turn thee from the path of life! Thou hast an ax at thy right hand; it is the sword of the Lord. Kill the strumpet; slay her who opposes Mount Zion. 'If thine eye offend thee, pluck it out; if thy right hand causes thee to sin, cut it off.' Take thy weapon and use it against her!"

"Yes, Ephraim, for once he speaks the truth. I am the one who caused you to sin. I am the 'old man' that must be put to death, and you must do it!

"The Lord has shown me—through that old clock on your mantel—why I'm here. My time somehow mirrors yours. I don't know how or why, but the tree farm accidents, the way each of us looks at wilderness, even Chastity and Leslie—all these are mirror images." She folded her hands out like a book opening.

"In the same way, there's an opposite kind of sacrifice. My rotten nature—the 'old man'—is the reverse of Jesus. In some way I don't understand, if I am killed—a sinful sacrifice, like His was a righteous sacrifice—then you and I both will be alive to God in Christ Jesus."

She straightened, her voice hardening. "The only alternative to killing the 'old man' is to give back the ax and the peavey, and I will leave you forever. Ephraim, you must choose!"

The trees groaned under the midday sun, though no wind blew.

Three jays wandered too close and screamed in terror, unable to escape the charged area.

Ephraim stood trembling, ashen, his breath coming in gasps. His eyes locked into Hannah's. Uncle continued his fomenting shrill, but the silence between the two young people blocked it as effectively as a sound-proof wall. Ever so slowly, Ephraim reached down for the ax, and his eyes shifted from Hannah to the tool.

But he was not alone. As he straightened, Hannah saw—faintly, but unmistakably—another hand upon his and a bronze-like cloak swirling around him in shimmering, distorting waves of heat. On this occasion, however, unlike the time Ephraim had tried to cross the wall, he seemed not to feel it.

Hannah could just barely make out the glimmering face, but the thunder and lightning in it made clear what Ephraim's choice would be. She knew right then that just giving back the tools would not deal sufficiently with the infection she had brought in, the wilderness she had sown. A different remedy was required, and she saw it to be right and just and good. From the moment of her foxfire baptism, she had been set apart, tutored by extraordinary means, tried by the destruction of her dearest possession, strengthened by a storm-girded sacrament. She had been brought to this moment of death so the two of them could be free. Ephraim must perform the act; he must kill the "old man," the corroder of his soul. But the Avenger was handing him the ax.

It looked graceful and familiar in his callused woodsman hands, its edge glittering from affectionate honing. Without a word and without again lifting his eyes, he stepped behind her.

Shaking violently, she bowed her head and clasped her hands before her face. The harvest had come, and she was ready. *Just don't dawdle!* she implored silently.

The blow fell, and Uncle's frenetic goading broke off suddenly.

Every nerve in Hannah's body shrieked, but the silence held a velvet tranquility, and she opened her eyes in time to see the shimmering presence move off.

At the same time, however, another figure fell away from behind her—a scurrilous shadow, bent, twisted, with seven heads, adorned variously through thousands of years from paint to punk. One of the heads hung lifeless from a long-ago wound; four others bore injuries of varying degree, and from a sixth streamed a purple sporelike cloud as from a mushroom or puffball. Only the seventh remained intact. As the figure slunk away, it hurled such intense, distilled hatred at Hannah that she would have fallen had not the vision been suddenly eclipsed by Ephraim.

He came back around the astounded girl, wiped the ax head with his handkerchief, and placed it with the peavey in her hands. As the color began to seep back into Hannah's face, his eyes once again found hers. She saw in them the exhilaration of triumph glowing beneath the worn, spent look of a conquering general returning home after an apocalyptic war.

They found her body early Thursday, not a mark on it except for finger imprints on the back of her hand, as though it had been squeezed lovingly for years on end. Her eyes were open, but they looked beyond with delight and joy, and her face was becomingly framed by a man's hat.

"Hey, that's mine!" Mike yelped, surprise interrupting grief. "Where'd she find it? I been lookin' all over for weeks!" It was Mike, too, who spotted the rusted remains of an ax and peavey half buried in the duff, handles long rotted away.

They might have found the body Wednesday night. Mike, though, who knew exactly where to look from his excursion while recuperating, had been struck down at noon with a terrible headache. "Like I'd been hit with an ax," he groaned. It eventually went away as suddenly as it had come, but according to Ardyth, from the very instant it happened, all the spice that had made him worth having around seemed to have died out of him.

epilogue

*E*arly October in Vermont. Sugar maples that six months ago bled sweetness from naked veins now shake the hillsides with exploding color. Gift shops, motels, restaurants, all dust off welcome mats and cash registers. New England in its finest array plays host to admiring hordes.

These gawkers, though, choose only surface beauty. They don't stoop to peer beneath centuries of leaf mold, to search out the lives and legacy of people who hammered the hills into community. Nor can the tour-bus folk be lured from balsam pillows and mugs stamped "I ♡ VERMONT" to contemplate the network of old stone walls basting together the fabric of the countryside.

Beyond those walls lie the ancient folk who made the syrup, grew corn, fished the pristine waters, chipped arrowheads from bedrock, decorated their deerskins with porcupine quills. There came upon them a fateful overshadowing, quite like the first appearance of a gypsy moth or killer bee. A curiosity at first, the white invaders overran ancestral hunting grounds and raised their flag of "freedom" over the bodies of the ancients. The hills, however, still echo the keening wails and ceremonial rhythms from bark huts and smoky fires. The land never forgets.

Those vast reaches of multicolored wilderness mean something to hunters, perhaps. Before the leaves begin to fade, they ready their guns and gather their beer. For many of them, though, the forest is little more than a place to escape boredom and play out the tribal rituals of "real manhood."

For the Carleton Bufords and Ziggy Baretskis of Vermont, October is the prologue to financial life or death, depending on the vagaries of winter snows on slopes laid open by some spiteful giant's claw. They are beholden to well-heeled beautiful people and cater to assorted appetites, praying always to the god of pleasure to ensure a gilded bottom line.

Life—and the mix of human participation in it—goes on, even after a death. The Leslie Streikens, the Abraham Lincolns, the Uncle Lathams, the Janes and Ardyths, the Hitlers, the Daniels and Abigails, the Platos, the Mikes, Steves, Toms, the King Ahabs, and Jonahs. These all dwell side by side, separated by a deceptive line we call Time. They live out their simultaneous existence, not in a chronological time-line, but in a tight circle around the judgment throne, waiting for the trumpet blast that will rip away the illusion of the past, present, and future.

For now, however, death remains a persistent reality.

In the intervening weeks, Peter had seen only decay whenever he walked the blighted swath that marked Hannah's passage. From the crossroad on the ridge, down past the ledges to the wall, ferns were curled and leaves hung limp. Now, though, like frost spreading over a window, the darkling shadow of autumn was assimilating this narrow path of premature death.

Life, though, still hung in the air, and the earth thrummed almost visibly beneath the golden carpet, feeding on the bones of man and beast that once roamed the hills, the ridge trail—the well-worn path between camp and the wall.

Now that the glen was gone, Peter spent his visits, not with the family, but at the cellar hole, reading, groping through the mystery. Had Hannah somehow pulled off a magnificent coup?

She had unlawfully dangled the future in front of Ephraim. Had she resolved the problem by dying according to the present and, at the same time, by remaining alive in the past? Perhaps her body and the ax and peavey remains were only husks, and the real Hannah still existed somewhere, somehow.

Yes, that must be it. In what other way could she have stayed with Ephraim? Like generations of women before her, she chose to leave her home for that of her husband, to bear her babies among his people. Only, for her, leaving home meant something quite extraordinary—like changing her skin, like a butterfly in reverse. She had crawled out of the new to put on the old. Yes, Hannah still lived. He felt it.

Even the image of marriage and babies, however, could not ease the ache of loneliness. One thing alone sustained him: he had seen her face, and she was happy. He would not begrudge her that.

With leaves from overhanging birches raining down gold, he pondered the change in Mike that Ardyth had found so objectionable. In his opinion, it was a decided improvement, but then, his opinion had never counted for much.

What does that matter, Peter? Opinion has never held much importance in the courts of life and death. Your business is here in the wilderness, searching through layers of detritus for that different dimension of reality. Gold doubloons are piling up, and they will bury you, too, just as they bury Hannah. But wilderness is a double-edged sword, Peter; walk carefully lest you be cut down with the trees.

"Stand at the crossroads and look; ask for the ancient paths, ask where the good way is, and walk in it, and you will find rest for your soul."

Stand at the crossroad, Peter. Look down the corridor of the years, the ancient path of the Catechism. Gather your tears and bottle up the wine of their warm love to sip during the long winter ahead. Vushondio, Peter! Peace! Be comforted now; be comforted.

Wild Harvest was typeset by
the Photocomposition Department
of Zondervan Publishing House,
Grand Rapids, Michigan
Compositor: Nancy Wilson
Equipment: Mergenthaler Linotron 202/N
Text type: Granjon
Titles and Folios: Garamond
Editor: Joyce Ellis
Designer: Bob Hudson
Decorations: Heda Majlessi
Cover Painting: Bill Greg
Printer: Color House Graphics, Grand Rapids, Michigan